Mother-Daughter Book Camp

THE MOTHER-DAUGHTER BOOK CLUB

Mother-Daughter Book Camp

Heather Vogel Frederick

Simon & Schuster Books for Young Readers
New York   London   Toronto   Sydney   New Delhi

SIMON & SCHUSTER BOOKS FOR YOUNG READERS
An imprint of Simon & Schuster Children's Publishing Division
1230 Avenue of the Americas, New York, New York 10020

SIMON & SCHUSTER BOOKS FOR YOUNG READERS is a trademark of Simon & Schuster, Inc.
For information about special discounts for bulk purchases, please contact
Simon & Schuster Special Sales at 1-866-506-1949 or business@simonandschuster.com.
The Simon & Schuster Speakers Bureau can bring authors to your live event. For more
information or to book an event, contact the Simon & Schuster Speakers Bureau
at 1-866-248-3049 or visit our website at www.simonspeakers.com.
Book design by Lucy Ruth Cummins
The text for this book is set in Chaparral Pro.
Manufactured in the United States of America
0416 FFG
First Edition
2 4 6 8 10 9 7 5 3 1
Library of Congress Cataloging-in-Publication Data
Names: Frederick, Heather Vogel, author.
Title: Mother-daughter book camp / Heather Vogel Frederick.
Description: First edition. | New York : Simon & Schuster Books for Young
Readers, [2016] | Series: Mother-daughter book club | Summary: Emma, Jess,
Megan, Becca, and Cassidy go to Camp Lovejoy in New Hampshire to serve as
counselors and when some of the young campers are stricken with
homesickness, the friends decide to start a summer camp book club.
Identifiers: LCCN 2015021613| ISBN 9781442471832 (hardcover : alk. paper) |
ISBN 9781442471849 (pbk. : alk. paper) | ISBN 9781442471856 (eBook)
Subjects: | CYAC: Interpersonal relations—Fiction. | Camps—Fiction. |
Clubs—Fiction. | Books and reading—Fiction. | New Hampshire—Fiction.
Classification: LCC PZ7.F87217 Mom 2016 |
DDC [Fic]—dc23 LC record available at http://lccn.loc.gov/2015021613

To my #1 fan—you know who you are!

Mother-Daughter
Book Camp

JUNE

> "*Oh, it will be like having a little sister!*"
> —*Understood Betsy*

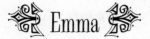 Emma

"And then something happened which changed Elizabeth Ann's life forever and ever!"
—*Understood Betsy*

"I can't believe I gave up my internship for this," moans Megan, staring glumly out the rain-streaked window.

Cassidy turns the windshield wipers on the minivan to the highest setting. "Whose idea was it, anyway?" she asks, scowling at the road ahead.

"C'mon, you guys!" Jess protests. "It's not that bad."

My friends have been needling Jess ever since we left Concord. Not that I blame them—I haven't seen this much rain since that soggy year I lived in England. It drizzled all week back at home, but Mother Nature really turned on the faucets when we crossed the border from Massachusetts into New Hampshire a couple of hours ago.

"Things won't seem so bad once it clears up," says Becca, who is calmly filing her nails.

I give her a sidelong glance. Becca's not usually this cheerful. I'm guessing her good mood is the result of the care package she got from Theo Rochester, her long-distance crush. He sent it care of Pies & Prejudice, Megan's grandmother's tea shop, where Becca has been working part-time after school. It's kind of our hangout—and by "our" I mean the mother-daughter book club that we started back in middle school and that's been going strong ever since.

We all happened to be at the tea shop when the package arrived yesterday afternoon.

"Box of snakes?" Cassidy had asked, smirking.

Snakes are Theo Rochester's passion in life.

Becca had refused to take the bait. She'd just laughed and opened the box eagerly, pulling out a University of Minnesota T-shirt—the one she's now proudly wearing—some fudge, and a small stuffed gopher with an *M* on the front. Goldy Gopher is the university's mascot, as Becca has told us about a zillion times since she got her acceptance letter. A gopher isn't exactly the most inspiring mascot—it's not like a tiger or a bear or something—but Becca is so ridiculously happy about the fact that she's heading to Minneapolis for college this fall that no one wants to burst her bubble.

"Where are all the other cars?" asks Megan. "I haven't seen one for ages. It feels like we're in the middle of nowhere."

"That's because we *are* in the middle of nowhere," Cassidy replies, scanning the road ahead from under her baseball cap—her favorite Red Sox one, of course.

Jess suddenly lets out a screech. "There's the sign! On the left!"

"Sheesh, Jess, way to give me a heart attack!" Cassidy slows,

Heather Vogel Frederick

flipping on the blinker, and a moment later we turn off onto a gravel road marked CAMP LOVEJOY.

She pulls into a parking area in front of a small log cabin. There's a sign over the front door that says OFFICE, but no lights are on inside, and as far as I can tell, no people, either.

Cassidy frowns. "Are you sure this is the right place? It seems kind of deserted."

"I thought for sure we were supposed to check in at the office," Jess replies. Pulling the hood of her rain jacket over her head, she opens the minivan door and hops out. "You guys wait here, I'll go check."

We watch as she picks her way gingerly across the puddle-pocked gravel, knocks on the door, peers through the window, knocks again, then looks over at us and shrugs.

"Nobody's there," she reports, climbing back in beside me again and shaking raindrops from the end of her long blond braid.

"Oh good, we can go home," chirps Megan. "Maybe Wolfgang will still let me be an intern."

"Shut *up*, Megan," Jess snaps.

Megan was offered an internship at *Flash* magazine this summer, and even though the editors assured her that it wasn't her only chance, and that she could take them up on the offer any time she wanted, and even though she signed up of her own free will to be a counselor here along with the rest of us, she's been lamenting her choice ever since we started our road trip this morning.

"I guess we should head down to the Dining Hall," Jess says, pointing Cassidy to where the road disappears into a forest. "We're kind of late, so maybe everyone else is here already."

The minivan lurches and swerves as Cassidy tries to avoid the potholes in the unpaved road. A moment later, we plunge into darkness. The sky is completely obscured by tall trees overhead. Tall, wet trees, their branches dripping nearly as much rain as the clouds above.

"They should call it Camp Sleepy Hollow instead of Camp Lovejoy," says Megan. "It feels like the set of a horror movie."

"*Megan!*" Jess protests again. Her face is flushed. "Will you knock it off!"

I reach over and pat her knee. She's my best friend in the whole world, and because I know her inside and out, I can tell she's just about had it.

The thing is, though, Megan's got a point. It's only 4:30 in the afternoon and it's the middle of summer, but this road is as dark and gloomy as something out of one of Grimms' fairy tales.

I stare glumly out the window. This was supposed to be a fun adventure—what could be better than spending our last summer before college together, working as camp counselors?—but so far the adventure hasn't been off to a good start. I'd been so looking forward to getting away from Concord. Too many memories in our hometown right now, and too much heartache.

Stewart and I were done. He'd gone off to Middlebury College and gotten himself a shiny new girlfriend, and even though we're technically still "friends," it's been really hard seeing him around town all the time these last few weeks. Which is pretty much inevitable, since he's

Heather Vogel Frederick

Becca's brother and the Chadwick family and my family live on the same street. Plus, Stewart got a summer job at Vanderhof's Hardware, just a few doors down from Pies & Prejudice, and we'd been crossing paths almost daily ever since he got home from Vermont. So when the opportunity came to get out of town and head to a camp in the New Hampshire woods, I'd jumped at the chance.

Jess's mom and aunt were the ones who suggested it. I guess they went here when they were kids, and Jess was a camper for a couple of summers too. Her aunt and uncle own an inn not too far from Lake Lovejoy, and when her aunt saw an ad in the local paper that said the camp was hiring, she told Mrs. Delaney and Mrs. Delaney told Jess.

Technically, Camp Lovejoy prefers that their counselors spend a summer as CITs first—that's short for "counselor-in-training"—but we were all too old for that program. Jess's aunt Bridget is good friends with the camp director, though, and she vouched for us, so here we are.

Cassidy swerves to avoid another pothole, and Jess and I bump shoulders. She glances over at me. "Everything's going to be fine, I promise," she whispers.

She's not just talking about the weather. Jess is my best friend in the whole world too, and she knows me inside and out. She knows how hard these past few months have been. "I hope so," I whisper back.

She leans forward as the minivan rounds a sharp curve in the road. "We should be able to see the lake soon."

"Good," Cassidy mutters. "I'm beginning to think you made it up."

As we emerge from under the protective canopy of trees, water drums against the roof. The rain isn't letting up a bit. If anything, it's coming down harder.

"There's the Dining Hall," Jess tells us, pointing through the water-streaked windshield to a large, rambling log building ahead. Lights gleam from the windows—that's a promising sign—and there are a dozen or so cars in the parking area near the flagpole. "See?" she says triumphantly. "We aren't the only ones here after all." Then she shrieks, and the minivan swerves again.

"Jess!" Cassidy hollers.

"Sorry," Jess replies meekly. "But check it out—there's the lake!"

Sure enough, in the distance beyond the Dining Hall, shrouded in mist, I can just make out the expanse of gray that is Lake Lovejoy. Right now though, it doesn't look the least bit inviting. Just big and cold and wet.

Cassidy pulls into a parking spot and we all climb out, trying to avoid the mud puddles as we huddle together in our rain jackets, peering at what we'll be calling home for the next seven weeks. My heart sinks. It's not exactly the picture-perfect postcard setting I'd been expecting.

A gust of wind sends the rope on the nearby flagpole slapping soggily against the metal pole and drives a rivulet of cold water under my hood and down my neck. I jump, letting out a yelp of displeasure.

Jess turns around. Spotting the expression on my face, she shoots me a look that clearly says, *Not you, too?*

Heather Vogel Frederick

"I'm fine," I mutter, flinching as another gust rattles the big wooden WELCOME TO CAMP LOVEJOY! sign.

I'm feeling anything but welcome right now.

The door to the Dining Hall flies open, and someone emerges carrying a giant umbrella.

"Jessica Delaney!" the someone cries, splashing over to join us. She enfolds Jess in a one-armed hug while raising the umbrella high in an attempt to shelter the rest of us. We crowd under it like chicks under the wings of a mother hen.

"It's so wonderful to have you back, Jess!" says our greeter, a woman who looks to be about the same age as my mother. "And these must be your friends?"

Jess nods. Under the hood of the woman's rain poncho I catch sight of close-cropped Afro-style hair flecked with gray. Beneath it, a pair of bright brown eyes regard me cheerfully. When the woman smiles, I can't help smiling back.

"I'm Guinevere Olsen," she tells us. "The camp director. You can call me Gwen. I was beginning to worry you'd gotten lost. We tried to call, but cell service can be spotty around these parts."

Behind me, I hear Cassidy give a quiet snort. "Spotty?" she whispers, "How about nonexistent."

"Leave your gear in the car, girls," Gwen continues, pretending not to hear her. She tucks her arm through Jess's. "We'll help you take everything to your cabins after dinner. First things first—come inside where it's warm and dry!"

We follow her across the parking lot to the Dining Hall's wide front porch. I make a mental note to revisit it on a sunny day, as the row of rocking chairs looks like a promising spot to sit and read. Inside, we hang up our rain jackets on wooden pegs in the coatroom, then continue into the main dining area.

"If Camp Lovejoy has a beating heart, this is it," Gwen tells us, raising her voice to be heard above the hubbub. The other counselors are clustered around a crackling fire in the big stone hearth at the far end of the room, talking and laughing. For a moment, I feel that familiar flutter of anxiety in my stomach that comes from being with a bunch of people I don't know, but I tell myself to quit being an idiot. I'm not in middle school anymore. I'm heading to college in a few months, and the girls all look friendly enough.

Jess glances over at me, her blue eyes glinting with sly merriment. "Not gonna barf, are you?"

I give her a rueful smile. Sometimes it's a pain to have a best friend who knows you so well. Jess loves to remind me about the day we met. It was the first day of school, and I was so nervous I threw up on our kindergarten teacher's shoes.

"Help yourselves to hot cider or cocoa," Gwen instructs us, waving a hand toward a long table under one of the banks of windows. "I'll be back to introduce you in just a moment—the cooks want to speak with me."

She heads to the kitchen, and my friends and I make a beeline

Heather Vogel Frederick

for the hot drinks. As I take a sip of cocoa, I feel myself start to relax. Jess is right. Everything is going to be just fine. The rain will stop, the sun will come out, and we'll all have an idyllic summer by the lake with a bunch of adorable girls to mother.

The best part? Jess and I are going to be co-counselors. We'd been assigned to Nest, the cabin for the youngest girls at camp. Becca and Megan will be right next door in Balsam, with the eight-year-olds, and Cassidy gamely volunteered to share a cabin with a stranger. She'd been assigned to Twin Pines, along with a seasoned counselor named Amanda Dixon. They'll be in charge of the nine-year-olds.

"Ladies! Listen up!" says Gwen, clapping her hands as she returns to join us. "I know you're all excited to see each other and I know you've got a lot of catching up to do, but there'll be plenty of time for that in a moment over dinner. We have a lot to accomplish this week to get everything ready for our campers. First of all, some good news: The rain is supposed to let up by morning."

This announcement prompts a hearty cheer.

"Next, I'd like to introduce our new staff members." The camp director gestures toward my friends and me. "With the exception of Jessica Delaney, who was a camper here many moons ago and whom some of you may remember, they're all first-timers. Let's give them a big Camp Lovejoy welcome!"

The girls by the fireplace start clapping rhythmically, then burst into song:

Welcome to Camp Lovejoy,
Welcome one and all!
Welcome to Camp Lovejoy,
Welcome short and tall!
Summer is our favorite time
We wait for it all year—
It's gonna be the best time
Now that all of you are here!

The song ends with a chant:

L-O-V-E-J-O-Y, GO CAMP LOVEJOY!

Cassidy elbows me in the ribs. "Stanley would totally love this place," she murmurs, and I have to stifle a laugh. Her stepfather has a cornball sense of humor. We all love him for it, though.

I'm not much for being the center of attention, but I muster a smile and wave gamely when Gwen announces my name. The other counselors smile and wave back, and I feel the flutters in my stomach subside.

Then Gwen drops a bombshell.

"I'm afraid there have been some last-minute changes," she says, glancing at her clipboard. "Amanda Dixon's family is moving unexpectedly, and she's needed to help out at home with that, so she won't be joining us this summer."

The fireplace crowd groans loudly. Amanda is clearly a favorite. I look over at Cassidy to see how she's taking the news about her co-counselor, but it doesn't seem to faze her.

Heather Vogel Frederick

"In thinking about her replacement," Gwen continues, "I've decided to do a little reshuffling. Jess? Would you be willing to move up to Twin Pines?"

Wait, what? Aghast, I turn to Jess. She looks flustered. Flicking me a glance, she replies, "Um, okay, I guess."

Panic washes over me. We're not going to be together?

"Excellent," says the camp director. "I appreciate your flexibility."

And then the bombshell explodes.

"I'll be assigning Felicia to take Jess's place in Nest," Gwen continues.

The crowd by the fireplace parts. A girl steps forward and I stare at her blankly for a moment. There's something familiar about those blond braids coiled around her ears like a pair of cinnamon rolls. For a moment I can't put my finger on it.

And then it hits me.

The Felicia that Gwen is talking about is Felicia *Grunewald!* Jess's know-it-all cousin!

"You didn't tell me she was going to be here!" I whisper frantically to Jess.

"I didn't know!" Jess whispers back, just as frantically. "Mom told me she was sick of camp, and was going to work at the Edelweiss Inn with Aunt Bridget and Uncle Hans this summer!"

I look over at Gwen, hoping beyond hope that she was kidding. She had to be—Felicia nearly ruined my friendship with Jess the last time our paths crossed.

But she wasn't. "Wonderful," the camp director says. "It's all settled, then."

I clutch Jess's arm. This couldn't be happening! Our summer was ruined. With Felicia as my co-counselor, camp wasn't going to be any fun at all.

It was going to be a disaster.

Heather Vogel Frederick

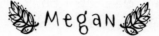

Megan

> *"Poor Elizabeth Ann was being sent straight to the one place in the world where there were no good times at all."*
> —*Understood Betsy*

Plink. Plink. Plink.

I lie in my cabin with my comforter pulled up to my chin, staring into the dark and listening to the sound of rain on the tin roof above. It's dripping steadily into one of the buckets Gwen issued to all of us after dinner. Some of the cabin roofs had sprung leaks, she told us. Better safe than sorry.

Of course ours would have to be one of the leaky ones.

Gwen's husband, Artie, who is the camp handyman, is scheduled to start on repairs in the morning. That doesn't help us much tonight, though.

Becca is oblivious. She was out the minute her head hit the pillow. I can hear her snoring softly across the cabin.

The wooden shutters are closed to keep out the rain, and it's darker than dark in here. Cold, too. I pull the covers over my head, hit by a wave of homesickness. I miss my own comfortable bed in my own comfortable room—leak-free, I might add—and I miss Coco and Truffle, our cats, and I miss my parents, and most of all I miss Gigi. My fun-loving grandmother would find a way to put a positive spin on all this and get me laughing—either that, or rescue me and whisk me off to the nearest luxury hotel and spa.

But Gigi won't be coming to my rescue. Not this time. I'm stuck here for the next seven weeks.

I try to picture what Gigi might be doing right now. Probably relaxing in the screened-in porch of the little house next door to ours that my father built for her and Edouard as a wedding present. Sophie was probably with them too, playing cards—the three of them are mad about gin rummy—or looking at fashion magazines. Sophie's my new cousin, thanks to the fact that her grandfather married my grandmother a couple of summers ago. She flies over from France every school holiday and every summer to hang out with us and help in the tearoom, bewitching the boys of Concord while she's at it. With her dark curls and green eyes, petite Sophie is *très* chic and *très* French.

If I don't stop thinking of home, the roof won't be the only thing leaking. I'm feeling perilously close to tears.

I roll over and adjust my pillow, trying to get comfortable in an unfamiliar bed. Why on earth had I turned down that internship at *Flash*? I could be in a plush apartment in New York City right now, instead of in the middle of nowhere. The nearest slice of civilization is a town called Pumpkin Falls. Pumpkin Falls! What kind of a stupid name is that?

At least there's light at the end of the tunnel. Come September, I'll

Heather Vogel Frederick

be in New York, and I'll be staying there for the next four years. My mother's been in mourning ever since I got my college acceptance letter this past spring, but by now she's mostly resigned herself to the fact that I'm not headed for MIT or one of the Ivies like she'd hoped, but rather to Parsons for a BFA in Fashion Design. If there's a silver lining for my mother, it's the fact that Parsons offers a focus in sustainable design. That cheered her up. My mother's all about the environment. She was elected mayor of Concord a couple of years ago, and coming up with green initiatives for our town has kept her busy ever since.

My dad doesn't need a silver lining and neither does my grandmother, but there's one for her anyway: Parsons has a Paris campus! I'm already fantasizing about my junior year abroad.

Gigi loves Paris. She loves everything French, and likes to brag about how she brought Edouard home as a souvenir. The two of them go back to visit as often as they can, as my new grandfather has a little cottage on an estate where he used to work as the chauffeur.

Gigi is the only one in the family who's totally, unreservedly thrilled about my college choice. She understands how I feel about fashion, because she feels the same way. It's our passion in life. Gigi is already talking about how she's going to come and visit me in New York, and take me to all her favorite spots in the city. I can hardly wait.

But first, I have to get through this summer.

Which right now is stretching out ahead of me like an endless bolt of fabric. Blank, boring, colorless fabric.

I bury my head under my pillow, trying to block out the rhythmic drip of rain. I'd better get some sleep. Tomorrow will look a lot worse if I don't.

"Megan! Wake up!"

Becca is shaking my foot. I crack open an eye, peer at my alarm clock, and groan. I can't believe it's morning already.

"You can't be serious," I tell her. "Go away!"

"Look!" she insists. "The lake is so beautiful!"

Groggily, I raise myself up on one elbow. Becca has opened the heavy wooden shutters, and a cool, pine-scented breeze is wafting in through the screened windows. Our cabin is perched right on the edge of the lake, and I can hear it lapping against the shore. The rain has stopped, the sun is out, and mist is rising from the surface of the water.

Becca's right. It is pretty.

But it's also way too early to be admiring the view.

I flop back down and burrow under the covers again. It's no use. Becca sits on the edge of my mattress and jiggles it a little. I sigh. She's wide awake and clearly wants me to be too.

Grumbling, I sit up and reach for my hoodie. The rain may have stopped, but it hasn't warmed up a speck since last night. "I thought Gwen said we don't have to get up until we hear the morning bell."

"She did," says Becca, smiling.

"What are you so happy about?"

She shrugs a shoulder. "Do I need a reason?"

I stare at her. Is this the same Becca I know? Night-owl Becca, who

Heather Vogel Frederick

doesn't do mornings? Then it dawns on me. "You heard from Theo, didn't you?"

Her smile widens.

"Did he text you?"

She shakes her head. "How could he? We gave our cell phones to Gwen last night, remember? 'Camp Lovejoy is a tech-free zone' and all that?"

I make a face. When I saw that rule in the brochure, I thought it meant the campers, not the counselors, too. Gwen had to practically pry my cell phone from my hand. Just one more reason for me to wish I was in New York City.

Becca waves an envelope at me. "He wrote me a real letter! Someone left it here in our cabin for me, but I didn't see it last night in the dark."

"Sweet! What did he have to say? No, wait—let me guess. Instructions for collecting rare New Hampshire snakes, right?"

"Megan!"

"He mentioned snakes, though, didn't he?"

She flushes. "Just twice," she admits, then laughs. "That's pretty good for Theo, actually."

Shivering, I throw back my comforter and wiggle my feet into the pair of flip-flops I left on the floor last night. My feet recoil and I give a little yelp. The flip-flops are freezing too. "Do you remember where the bathroom is?"

Becca shakes her head. "Somewhere near the flagpole, I think. I've been waiting for you to wake up."

"We might as well take our showers, while we're at it." I grab my towel and shower caddy and we head outside, the cabin's screen door slapping shut loudly behind us. I shoot a glance over at Nest, hoping I didn't wake Emma. Poor thing—she looked so stricken last night when she got the news about the switcheroo with Felicia. None of the rest of us have met Jess's cousin, but we've heard all the stories. Especially the ones about that disastrous Christmas trip back in tenth grade, when Felicia almost torpedoed Jess and Emma's friendship.

As Becca and I scuff down the pine-needle-carpeted path toward the flagpole, the door to Twin Pines creaks open.

"Wait for me!" whispers Jess. No surprise there. She's always up early. Her family lives on a farm, and they all get up at the crack of dawn. She disappears back inside, then reappears carrying her stuff.

"Where's the bathroom?" Becca asks her. "Are we headed in the right direction?"

Jess nods. "Keep going past Primporium."

We give her a blank look.

"You know, the cubie house?" She jerks her thumb toward the long building on our right.

"Oh, yeah," says Becca.

Cubies are another Camp Lovejoy tradition. I guess whoever founded the camp a zillion years ago decided that every girl deserved a space of her own for the summer, so they designed these two buildings full of cubicles that serve as private dressing rooms. Ours is called Cubbyhole, and we'll be sharing it with Nest and Twin Pines.

Heather Vogel Frederick

Primporium is shared by the other three cabins in Lower Camp: Blue Jay, Meadow, and Shady Grove.

"What's this cute little place?" I ask as we pass a tiny cottage with flowers spilling from its window boxes.

"Shhhhh!" Jess whispers. "People are sleeping! That's Cabbage. It's the head counselor's cabin."

We tiptoe past it and past the flagpole in the middle of the grove, then head toward the Dining Hall.

"The Biffy's over there," says Jess, pointing to another building beyond it.

"Biffy?" Becca looks puzzled.

Jess smiles. "'*Bathroom in the Forest for You*,' remember?"

"Oh yeah. Dorky."

"But kind of funny," I add.

It's primitive inside, just bare wood walls and floors, but there are flush toilets at least, and the showers are spotless. There's plenty of hot water, too. I feel myself start to relax a bit as I shampoo my hair. Maybe camp won't be so bad.

I change my mind a few minutes later when a huge daddy longlegs crawls across my foot as I'm brushing my teeth.

"Shhhhhhh!" Jess warns me again as I let out a bloodcurdling shriek. "You'll wake up the entire camp!"

"I don't care!" I reply, flapping frantically at my toes with a towel. Becca starts to laugh, and I give her the stink eye. "It's not funny!"

"Yes it is," she replies. "Too bad I don't have my cell phone—that video clip would be hitting the Internet by now."

Spider vanquished, we head back to our cabins. The morning bell clangs as Becca and I are getting dressed. Gwen told us we don't have to wear our uniforms until the campers arrive, so I opt for jeans and a T-shirt. Camp Lovejoy's uniforms aren't all that bad—navy blue shorts and white polo shirts that sport the camp emblem (the letters *CL* interlocked inside a large circle, with the silhouette of a pine tree underneath)—but ever since the fiasco with the hideous ones we had to wear in middle school, I haven't been a big fan of uniforms.

I trade my flipflops for running shoes, since I don't want to take any more chances with toe-loving spiders, and on my way out the door I grab my navy Camp Lovejoy hoodie. Becca grabs hers, too. It hasn't warmed up much yet.

"Navy is not really my color," I complain, then tilt my head as I consider my friend. "You can rock it, though."

It's a good shade for Becca's peaches-and-cream complexion and blond hair. Which is currently ahead in our little summer competition. The two of us decided to let our hair grow out this summer, just to see whose is longest by the time we head off to college. Mine just barely brushes my shoulders at the moment, and hers is about an inch longer. She's got it pulled up in a high ponytail this morning; I just tucked mine behind my ears. I figure I'd better get used to a low-maintenance beauty routine.

The two of us stop in next door at Twin Pines to get Jess, but she waves us on. "You guys go ahead. I'm going to wait for Emma."

"Where's Cassidy?" asks Becca, shading her eyes as she peers through the screen door.

Jess smirks. "You mean Ms. I'm-Always-First-in-Line-for-the-Breakfast-Buffet? Three guesses."

Sure enough, Cassidy is already seated at one of the long tables by the time we reach the Dining Hall.

"Hey, guys!" she calls, waving us over. I stare at her plate, which is piled high with food. Typical Cassidy. My father says she has a hollow leg. She eats like a horse but never gains an ounce. I know it's because she's an athlete and all, but still, it's really annoying.

"Don't miss the cinnamon rolls," she mumbles, taking a bite. "They're phenomenal."

Becca and I get in line. I'm suddenly starving. Skipping the cold and hot cereals, I pile my plate with fruit, yogurt, scrambled eggs, and a cinnamon roll, which must be homemade because Cassidy is right, it is amazing.

Jess joins us a few minutes later, sliding into the last seat at our table.

"Where's Emma?" I ask.

"Still sleeping." She frowns. "I told her to hurry up or she'd miss breakfast."

The other counselors at our table introduce themselves, and as Cassidy starts grilling them about camp stuff, I glance around the Dining Hall and do a little math. In addition to the six cabins in Lower Camp, there are three on the Hill, as Upper Camp is called: Far, Farther, and Outback. With two counselors per cabin, that makes eighteen of us, plus Gwen; her husband, Artie; the extra staffers in charge of stuff like the waterfront and the trips programs; and the kitchen help. Altogether, I count about thirty-five people.

"Hey, isn't that Sergeant Marge?" asks someone at our table, a tall girl named Brianna Peterson. She's from L.A. and she's already sporting a tan.

Brianna points toward the door and a dozen heads all swivel around to look. A short, stocky woman with no-nonsense gray hair is standing there. She's wearing the regulation Camp Lovejoy uniform, accessorized with navy blue knee socks, navy running shoes, and a navy lanyard around her neck. A whistle dangles from it, and in one hand she carries a clipboard.

Uh-oh, I think. This is not a good sign. My mother and Mrs. Chadwick love clipboards too.

"What's she doing here?" whispers Melissa Yee, Brianna's co-counselor in Meadow. "I thought she was retiring after last summer. Remember all that hoopla in her honor at the final banquet?"

"Summer wouldn't be summer at Camp Lovejoy without Marge the Barge," quips someone at the far end of the table, and the other counselors all snicker quietly at this.

Jess takes a bite of cinnamon roll. "What the heck is taking Emma so long? She should have been here by now."

Cassidy turns to her. "So what's the deal with your cousin, anyway?" she asks, swatting at a stray bit of food dangling from a strand of her red hair. Her hair bounces between short and longish, and this

Heather Vogel Frederick

summer it's nearly the same length as mine. She's wearing it tucked behind her ears this morning too, I notice, and for some reason this pleases me. Maybe there's hope that I'll get the hang of camp after all. "Emma looked like death eating a cracker last night when she heard that she and Felicia were going to be in Nest together."

Jess puffs out her breath, sending her blond bangs fluttering upward. "Felicia's okay, but she can be a real know-it-all, and now that she's in college, it's only gotten worse."

Jess's cousin is even more of a brainiac than Jess is, apparently, which is pretty hard to believe.

"Plus, she's, well, kind of awkward," Jess continues, slanting a glance in her cousin's direction. Felicia has attached some sort of a cape to her T-shirt, and her hair, which was coiled around her ears like Princess Leia's from *Star Wars* last night, is now piled on top of her head in a tangle of complicated braids. "She's really into medieval history, and sometimes she talks like she's from the Middle Ages or something. She's just a little, you know . . ." Her voice trails off.

"Got it," says Cassidy. "O-D-D."

My friends and I all grin. "O-D-D" is mother-daughter book club code for "odd." People always think we're referring to the abbreviation for some affliction.

Jess pushes back from the table. "I'm going to go check on Emma again."

Before she can, though, Emma droops through the door. She looks like she hasn't slept a wink. I can tell she hasn't showered yet, either, because her short, curly brown hair is mushed down on one side and sticking up in the back, plus she's wearing glasses instead of her contacts, which is a dead giveaway. Emma hardly ever wears her glasses anymore. Only when she's super tired.

She grabs a banana and some yogurt from the buffet and shuffles over to our table. "Shove over," she demands, and Jess and I immediately oblige. Emma squeezes in on the bench, then shakes her banana at us. "I'm going home."

We all gape at her.

"Don't be an idiot," says Cassidy.

"I am not spending the summer trapped in a cabin with Felicia."

"C'mon, Emma," says Jess. "Felicia's kind of goofy, but she's not that bad. I actually thought you guys hit it off that Christmas we spent at the inn. I mean, before the other stuff happened. Don't you remember all those conversations about Charlotte Brontë and Jane Austen?"

Cassidy grins. "Sounds like your soulmate, Hawthorne."

Emma gives her a withering look. "It's no use trying to talk me out of it," she says, ripping open her yogurt container. "I'm calling my mother after breakfast and asking her to come get me."

Jess frowns. "Ems, you can't just quit. You're helping run the waterfront, remember? Plus, aren't you going to do the *Birch Bark*?"

The *Birch Bark* is Camp Lovejoy's newspaper. Emma was the editor of our high school paper back in Concord, and when Gwen found out, she signed her up to be in charge.

"And what about that creative writing workshop you volunteered

Heather Vogel Frederick

to lead during free period?" Jess continues. "The campers will love that."

Emma lifts a shoulder.

"I know you're disappointed with the way things turned out, but once your campers get here, I'll bet you'll be having so much fun that you'll hardly notice Felicia," adds Becca.

"Fat chance," mutters Emma, but she doesn't sound quite so belligerent.

"The mother-daughter book club has your back," Cassidy assures her. "You just let us know if you need us to run interference. We'll do anything it takes—anything at all. You know, short-sheet Felicia's bed, hide her shoes, put a chipmunk in her underwear drawer. . . ."

Emma gives her a grudging half smile.

"You'll feel better once you've had a shower," I tell her. "Trust me, I did." I decide not to mention anything about spiders.

Jess passes her half of her cinnamon roll. "Eat this, you'll feel better."

Emma takes a bite. "Maybe I'm overreacting a little. But it's not fair! We had the summer all planned out."

"I know." Jess puts her arm around Emma's shoulders. "We'll still be spending plenty of time together, though. The other counselors told me that the youngest cabins team up for a lot of stuff."

Before she can continue, Gwen, who is seated at the head table with her husband and Sergeant Marge, taps a spoon against her orange juice glass. "Attention, please!" she says, rising to her feet. "Good morning, everyone! I trust you all slept well, and I know you've eaten well. How about a round of applause for those bodacious cinnamon rolls?"

The Dining Hall erupts in thunderous cheers.

"I'm sure many of you have noticed a familiar face here in the Dining Hall this morning," Gwen continues. "Dorothea Buckman had a family emergency and won't be able to join us as head counselor this summer, so Marge Gearhart, our intrepid former head counselor of many years standing, has very kindly agreed to step in as a last-minute replacement. Our heartiest thanks to you, Marge, for your devotion to Camp Lovejoy."

"Marge the Barge," whispers Brianna, igniting another ripple of giggles at our table.

There's a spattering of polite applause for the head counselor, but no cheers. The cinnamon rolls are the winners in this morning's popularity contest, apparently.

"We have a busy day ahead," Gwen tells us. "A busy week, in fact. Our campers will be arriving Saturday afternoon, and there's a great deal to do before then to get everything ready. As always, you and your campers have been divided into four teams for the summer. This is a Camp Lovejoy tradition that gives everyone a chance to bond with others besides just their cabinmates." She looks over at the head counselor, who waves her clipboard. "Please see Marge on the way out for your team assignment," Gwen continues. "Today, each team will be responsible for cleaning and readying one part of camp. We'll continue this routine daily until everything is shipshape and squared away."

There's a clatter of dishes and scraping of benches as we all stand up and start clearing away breakfast things. Gwen taps her orange juice glass and the room grows quiet again. "We'll meet at the flagpole at 10:30 a.m. sharp. Listen for the bell, and be prompt. You don't want to keep your team members waiting. Between now and then, I'd like you to spend some time cleaning out your cabins and cubies and settling in."

Following the other counselors' lead, we help clear the tables, then go to line up in front of Sergeant Marge.

Brianna turns to me. "I really hope I don't get stuck with the team that has Trip Shack duty," she whispers with a shudder. "Last year during pre-camp cleanup they found a family of possums nesting in the backpacks."

I stare at her, horrified. And I thought a spider was bad! Possums would be a deal-breaker. I'd have no choice but to call my parents and beg them to take me home. My father would totally understand—he likes the great outdoors, but only from a safe distance. His idea of camping is a hotel without room service.

"Name?" Marge barks as I reach the head of the line.

"Megan Wong."

"Wong . . . Wong . . . Wong," she says, tracing a stubby forefinger down the clipboard. No manicures for no-nonsense Marge. *No manicures for me this summer either,* I suddenly realize. I doubt there's a nail salon in teeny-tiny Pumpkin Falls, and the camp packing list specifically requested that we leave makeup and beauty products at home.

"Camp Lovejoy is a place where girls can be girls—naturally," the brochure stated breezily, but the reality of this sets in as I contemplate

Marge's polish-free fingernail. Which finally comes to a halt at the bottom of the clipboard. "Here we are: Wong, Megan. You'll be on the Ruby Team this summer. Rubies will be cleaning and resupplying the Art Studio."

I whoosh out a breath of relief. I dodged the possum bullet.

So did Becca, who is also Team Ruby.

Cassidy's a Sapphire. "We're setting up the waterfront," she tells us happily. "I might just have to accidentally fall in the lake if it gets hot this afternoon."

"How about you, Emma?" I ask.

"Emerald," she says. "Boathouse."

"I'm an Amethyst," Jess tells us. "We're cleaning out the Trip Shack."

"Possum duty!" I blurt out. My friends look over at me in surprise, and I explain what happened last summer.

"Eew." Becca wrinkles her nose.

Jess just smiles. "Bring 'em on," she says. "There's nothing I like better than wrangling animals."

This is true. Not only does Jess live on a farm, but she's also a certified wildlife rehabilitator. It started out as a school science project a couple of years ago, when she took care of an injured baby fox with the help of a local expert back in Concord. Jess has been his apprentice ever since, and earlier this year, after she turned eighteen, she applied for her rehabilitator's license.

"Not that I'll be able to use it in New York City," she told us when the certificate arrived in the mail. Jess is going to be in New York this fall too. She's got an amazing voice, and none of us were at all surprised when she got accepted at Juilliard to study music. "But you never know. Central Park is pretty wild in some parts."

We head off to our cabins, and after sweeping ours out and arranging the furniture the way we want it, Becca and I head over to Cubbyhole.

"This is kind of cool," Becca says, flipping on the light to reveal the cubie house's long central hallway.

Wooden doors on either side lead to individual dressing room cubicles, or "cubies," as they call them here at camp. Becca's and mine are directly across from each other, in the middle of the cubie house. Felicia and Emma are at the end closest to our cabins, since they have the youngest campers, and Cassidy and Jess are at the opposite end, by the door leading to the waterfront.

I open my cubie's swinging door cautiously, on high alert for spiders. The coast is clear from what I can tell. Just some stray cobwebs. There's a window, a small closet area with a shelf above it, and a tiny dressing table with a built-in stool. Basic, but I can definitely do something with it.

"Okay, everyone, let's start at one end and work our way to the other!" calls Felicia, who's been put in charge. She's been coming to Camp Lovejoy since she was practically in diapers, according to Jess. "Mind if I put on some music?" Felicia adds as she hands out brooms and cleaning supplies.

"Great idea," I tell her, hoping she picks something upbeat.

No such luck. A moment later, Cubbyhole is echoing to the sounds of some string quartet. I look over at Jess, who has a pained expression on her face.

"Sorry, guys."

Cassidy grins and picks up her broom. She's getting a kick out of Jess's cousin already, I can tell. I pick my broom up too, and putting my earbuds in, fire up a dance party playlist as I set to work.

An hour later, the floors are swept, the ceilings de-cobwebbed, the windows washed, and Cubbyhole fairly gleams. Sergeant Marge gives us a thumbs-up when she comes to inspect.

"Very nice, ladies. Go ahead and settle in."

The packing list told us to bring along six yards of fabric for decorating our cubies. Cassidy thought the whole idea was stupid until I suggested scarlet-and-white striped ticking. Scarlet and white are her new college colors. She's going to Boston University on a full ride this fall, thanks to her hockey skills.

Back in Concord a few weeks ago, my friends and I took a field trip to the fabric store and I helped everybody pick something out. Becca was easy. I found her a pale lavender cotton with brightly colored shoes scattered all over it. Becca adores shoes. For Jess, it was a toss-up between a musical note pattern and horses. She went with horses.

"More kid-friendly," she decided.

I tried to find a book motif for Emma, but we had to settle on red-and-white gingham decorated with strawberries. Strawberry is her favorite ice cream flavor. For myself, I chose a crisp

Heather Vogel Frederick

black-and-white polka dot, with hot pink grosgrain ribbon for trim.

I pull my fabric out of my trunk and get busy pleating and tacking skirts around the edges of my dressing table and the little built-in stool in front of it. When I'm finished, I step back and survey my handiwork. The cozy room already looks cheerier. I have enough left over to add a short ruffle around the closet shelf, and I even tack faux curtains up at the windows, using more pink ribbon as tiebacks.

Becca pokes her head in as I'm admiring the results. "Hey, this looks fabulous!"

"Thanks."

"Come look at mine," she says, beckoning me across the hall.

"Nice!" I tell her, looking around. "The shoe fabric is perfect." Suddenly, I'm not feeling so gloomy about camp. I go back to my cubie and start hanging up my clothes, humming to myself. I loop my bath-robe over the hook beside the door, set out my shower caddy, and line up my shoes. Then it's time for the fun stuff, all the knickknacks and pictures and posters I brought along to personalize the space.

I'm beginning to see why Brianna and Melissa were so enthusias-tic at breakfast about the cubies. They're a tiny piece of home. I perch on the stool in front of my dressing table, gazing at the walls, where generations of previous campers have signed their names. I grab a marker and sign mine, too: MEGAN WONG WAS HERE.

Next up is hanging my bulletin board. It's covered with pictures— my cats when they were kittens; Becca and me on a Christmas cruise a couple of years ago; Pies & Prejudice on opening day; my grandmother and me at Paris Fashion Week; celebrating with my mother at her election party; all of my friends and family on Gigi and Edouard's wedding day.

I take one last picture out of my trunk. It's in a silver frame that Becca gave me for Christmas this year. It's my favorite picture of Simon, my long-distance British boyfriend. Cassidy took it the year he lived in Concord with his family. Amazingly, we've stayed together, even though we're thousands of miles apart. Not that we haven't had rocky moments, but videoconferencing and e-mail help. It also helps that I get over to France a couple of times a year, now that Gigi is married to Edouard. I always manage to squeeze in a visit with Simon, since England is only a hop and a skip away. I've been to visit him at his house, and he's been to visit me at Gigi and Edouard's cottage, too.

Simon is going to Oxford University next year, which is England's version of an Ivy League school. His parents are bursting with pride, especially since his older brother Tristan, one of the planets orbiting the sun that is Cassidy Sloane, has deferred college to pursue his ice dancing career. We all think Tristan is headed for the next Olympics.

I set the picture on my dressing table and pause for a moment, smiling at it. Then my smile fades. Simon had originally planned to come see me in New York this summer, while I was interning at *Flash*. Now, though, with me here at camp, we won't see each other for at least another six months.

Will our relationship survive? Or will we end up like Emma

Heather Vogel Frederick

and Stewart, slowly drifting apart? What if Simon finds a new girl-friend when he gets to Oxford? And will I feel differently too, living in New York?

The fabric of summer that's stretching out in front of me suddenly isn't blank anymore. It's covered with question marks.

CASSIDY

"She had, of course, little idea how she herself looked because the mirrors at Putney Farm were all small and high up, and anyway they were so old and greenish that they made everybody look very queer-colored. You looked in them to see if your hair was smooth, and that was about all you could stand."
—*Understood Betsy*

I flop onto my stomach in my bunk, totally exhausted.

"Are you as tired as I am?" groans Jess from across the cabin. She's collapsed in a heap on her bed too.

"More," I reply. "I swam a mile this morning, remember?" Since we've been here, I've been superdisciplined about getting up early every day to run or swim. I promised the BU hockey coach I'd arrive at September's preseason training camp in peak condition.

"Show-off," says Jess. She rolls over and pulls the pillow over her head.

We've been working like crazy all week. In addition to cleaning and prepping camp—scouring cabins and cubies, washing down boats and life vests, spreading mulch, pulling all the athletic and waterfront and other equipment out of storage, checking and sorting and arranging it, and replacing whatever needs to be replaced—we've also had team-building exercises and staff training every day. Jess and I both took a wilderness first aid class, and I led a hike up Lovejoy Mountain, which is really more of a big hill. I passed the sailing instructor certification course with flying colors, but Sergeant Marge wasn't as impressed with my kayaking and canoeing skills.

"Barely adequate," she'd told me with a sniff, marking my grade on her clipboard.

That made me mad. My skills are plenty adequate.

Somehow, I've managed to get off on the wrong foot with Sergeant Marge. This is not a good thing, because the two of us will be working closely this summer. I'll be splitting my time between the boat dock, where I'm going to teach sailing, canoeing, and kayaking, and the Trip Shack, which is the head counselor's domain, and where I'll help her plan hiking trips.

It started that first day, when I showed up at the waterfront with the other Sapphires to help put the docks in the lake. I was wearing my whistle around my neck. She'd spotted it and frowned. "Kind of fancy for camp, sport."

I hate it when people call me "sport."

Plus, my silver whistle is one of my most treasured possessions. Eva Bergson, an older lady who used to be in our mother-daughter book club back in Concord, and who was a former Olympic skater and my mentor, left it to me. It's my good luck charm. No way was I going to leave it at home. Besides, I figured it would be useful. You never know when you're going to need a whistle, especially with a bunch of campers running around, right?

Sergeant Marge made me put it back in my cubie, and she's been keeping a close eye on me ever since.

Even with her wet-blanket attitude, though, I still love it here.

The only camps I've ever been to before were sports camps. Which are fine, don't get me wrong. I eat, sleep, and breathe sports, especially ice hockey, and I'm happy for any opportunity I get to play. But those camps were usually on some boring school or college campus, and I barely ever poked my head outside the rink.

Camp Lovejoy is different.

It's about as far from boring as you can possibly get. The lake is huge, and gorgeous, and Lovejoy Mountain looms over the far end, its reflection mirrored in the water whenever it's still.

The peninsula that the camp is on is shaped sort of like a fat hockey stick, if you count Hairbrush Island as the blade. Running along the top of the shaft are the tennis courts, the Dining Hall, the Grove, the Biffy, and the cabins on the Hill. In the middle, Lower Camp's cabins are spaced out on a quiet cove along the east side, where they get the early morning sun. On the west side is the waterfront—the H dock and the big float, the kayak shed, and the water ski beach. Between them are Primporium and Cubbyhole, Lower Camp's cubie houses, along with Lower Lodge. Way down at the end of the stick is the Point—a spit of land marking

Heather Vogel Frederick

camp's farthest boundary. The Director's Cottage is on the Point, and past it, at the very tip, right about where the hockey stick's shaft joins the blade, is the Gazebo, with its fabulous view of the sandbar that leads over to Hairbrush Island.

The Gazebo is my favorite spot at camp. For some reason it reminds me of the turret in my family's Victorian house. I guess because it's round like a turret, and a bit private. For whatever reason, I'm drawn to it like a magnet. We haven't had much free time this week, but during what little we've had, I've made a dash for it with my camera. I've taken pictures of the early morning mist on the water, and of some amazing sunsets, and of the loons, of course. Lake Lovejoy is known for its loons, these cool birds that are kind of like ducks, except their heads are black as hockey pucks and the feathers on their backs are kind of a black-and-white check pattern. They're really beautiful. Plus, they have the most awesome, haunting cry. It gives me the shivers, and I can't get enough of it. Jess calls them by their Latin name, *Gavia immer*, but then she would.

I drift off to sleep thinking about loons.

My nap is rudely interrupted forty-five minutes later by the clanging of the bell. I was dreaming I was playing hockey, and for a minute I think it's the buzzer signaling the end of the period. Then I remember where I am.

"I can tell I'm going to be really sick of that bell by the end of the summer," I tell Jess as I sit up, yawning. Camp Lovejoy's entire day runs by it.

"Yeah," Jess agrees. "Hey, we're supposed to report to the flagpole now, right?"

I nod. "In our swimsuits."

There's one last team-bonding exercise planned for the staff this afternoon. They haven't told us what it is yet, just that it involves water. I suspect it has something to do with kayaks, though, because I spotted Sergeant Marge prowling around the kayak racks earlier today.

Jess and I head over to the cubie house to change, grabbing our swimsuits off the clothesline that's stretched alongside it. I thought cubies were a stupid idea at first—it seemed like it would be way simpler just to keep all our stuff in the cabins—but over the past few days I've changed my mind. With so many other people around, it's actually kind of nice to have a space I can retreat to that's all my own. And I'm sure once the campers arrive, I'll appreciate it even more.

Closing the door behind me, I step out of my shorts and wriggle into my swimsuit—still slightly clammy from my early-morning laps—and blow a kiss to my sisters. Well, to their picture, which is sitting on my dressing table.

I don't really have a best friend. I'm not like Emma and Jess, or Megan and Becca, who seem to have been best friends forever. I consider them all close friends—my dearest ones, actually—but my *best* friends are my sisters. Especially Courtney. I see so little of her these days, though, it's kind of pathetic. She just graduated from UCLA this spring, and she and her fiancé, Grant, are getting married at Thanksgiving. My mom's in a dither helping plan the wedding. I'm

Heather Vogel Frederick

going to be maid of honor, and our little sister, Chloe, will be the flower girl.

I took the picture of them earlier this summer, when we got back from Courtney's graduation. The three of us were up in the turret, where I've taken some of my best shots. The light is always so perfect up there.

Anyway, Chloe was perched on Courtney's lap, and the two of them were looking at a bridal magazine. Chloe looked so serious that it struck me as funny. She's four! What does a four-year-old care about weddings? I ran downstairs for my camera and took a bunch of pictures of the two of them, some serious and some goofy. At one point they both looked up at me at the same time, laughing. That's when I snapped this one. I love it, and them.

In fact, I love my little sister so much that I chose my college because of her. I was heavily recruited by about half a dozen Division One schools, and ultimately it came down to a choice between Boston University or the University of Wisconsin. It was a tough decision—Patriot League vs. Big Ten, for one thing—but at the end of the day, the deciding factor was Chloe.

Madison, Wisconsin, is just too far away from Concord, Massachusetts. I figured if I went to school there, I'd hardly see Chloe at all for four years. She'd be practically grown up by the time I graduated! Boston, on the other hand, is just next door to Concord. My family will be able to come to all of my home games, and I can jump on a train and be at our house on Hubbard Street in nothing flat, anytime I want. So I signed with BU, and I'm a Terrier instead of a Badger, which suits me just fine.

"Cassidy!" calls Jess. "Hurry up!"

"Coming!" I holler back. I hesitate, wondering if I should bring my whistle. It could come in handy if we're doing kayak relays, which is what I suspect they have planned for us this afternoon. I don't want to risk the wrath of Sergeant Marge, though, so I leave the whistle where it is, hanging over a corner of my minuscule mirror.

There are hardly any mirrors at Camp Lovejoy. It's another one of their traditions.

"This is one place where girls can just be themselves all summer, without having to worry about what they look like," Gwen explained to us that first night in the Dining Hall during orientation.

Only counselors are allowed to have them in their cubies, and there aren't any in the cabins or over the bathroom sinks. Becca and Megan squawked at this—they're both totally into fashion—but I'm fine with it. I spend as little time as possible looking in the mirror anyway, even at home. As long as I'm reasonably clean and my hair is brushed, I figure I'm good to go. It's not that I don't like what I see. I may not be a stunning beauty like my mother, who used to be a supermodel, or my sister Courtney, who looks just like my mother, but I'm happy with myself just the way I am: red hair and gray eyes like my dad, tall like my mother, plus I'm strong. I rarely have time to fuss over how I look. I've got more important things to do. Like play hockey.

I pull my hair back in a ponytail and thread it through the back

Heather Vogel Frederick

of my baseball cap, then head outside. My friends and the rest of the counselors are already gathered in the grove by the flagpole, and I hustle on up the path to join them.

Out of the corner of my eye, I notice Emma inching away from Felicia. The two of them aren't getting along very well so far. Emma hasn't tried to hide the fact that she's disappointed with the cabin assignments, which couldn't help but hurt Felicia's feelings. Felicia, on the other hand, isn't helping matters much. She's not exactly trying to fit in. She has this wardrobe of short capes, for instance, that she pins to her T-shirts, and today she's crisscrossed her braids on top of her head in preparation for whatever it is we're about to do. She looks like an advertisement for Swiss cocoa or something. Felicia has a thing for complicated hairstyles. Emma jokes that she probably studies medieval tapestries the way Megan and Becca study fashion magazines.

"This better be fun," Emma grumbles. "I was right in the middle of a chapter."

So far, her favorite part of camp is rest hour. It's the only time she gets to read during the day, she tells us, because at night she's too tired. And reading is at the top of Emma Hawthorne's to-do list. She loves books the way I love sports. I've seen her cubie, and I seriously think she brought along more books this summer than clothes. I guess she was worried she might run out.

"Listen up, ladies!" bellows Sergeant Marge. The woman is a human megaphone. They can probably hear her all the way across the lake.

Felicia suddenly springs to life, rushing across the grove to join her.

"Teacher's pet," I whisper. Emma dissolves in giggles. Jess glares at me. She gets irritated when we make fun of her cousin, but I'm right—Felicia sticks to Marge like tape on a hockey stick.

"Hustle on down to the water ski beach, grab a life vest, and line up with your teams," the head counselor instructs us. "It's Dreamboat Relay Day!"

Judging from the enthusiasm that greets this announcement, I'm guessing this is a popular activity. I have no idea what a dreamboat is.

My friends and I follow the surge of counselors down the pine-needle-carpeted path to the water's edge. I frown as I spot a quartet of kayaks lined up on the beach. Are kayaks called dreamboats at Camp Lovejoy? Did I miss something? Maybe there was a song about it at dinner last night—there's a song for everything at Camp Lovejoy.

Jess heads over to join the Amethysts, who are gathered around the purple kayak, naturally. I line up with the other Sapphires by the blue boat. Becca and Megan trot over to the Rubies, who are clustered by the red one, and Emma makes a face and trudges reluctantly over to the green kayak, and the Emeralds.

Emma is not exactly a bundle of enthusiasm when it comes to sports. She tries, though, she really does. She's light years ahead of where she was when I first met her back in sixth grade. So much so that she was my first choice to help me with Chicks with Sticks. That's the after-school hockey club for girls I coach back in Concord. I started it to help promote the sport, and it's taken off big-time. It's had exactly the ripple effect I was hoping for, too. Because of the demand from my skaters,

Heather Vogel Frederick

there's a middle school girl's hockey team now—there wasn't one when we first moved to Concord, and I had to play with the boys—and the high school program has never been stronger.

Thanks to our work with the Chicks, Emma and I are probably the most prepared of all our book club friends for this particular summer job. Jess is a close second, since she's used to dealing with two younger twin brothers. None of the campers will be able to get anything past her. Becca and Megan, though? Becca babysits now and then and Megan's always talked about wanting a sibling, but I have a feeling their heads are going to be spinning twenty-four hours from now once the campers arrive.

"Sapphires? Got your lineup ready?"

Sergeant Marge is standing in front of me with her clipboard. I look over at my teammates, who are all looking back at me expectantly.

"Uh, I guess I'll anchor if nobody else wants to," I volunteer.

Sergeant Marge jots this down on her clipboard. "Good luck, sport," she says. I can't tell if she means it or not.

"There it is!" cries someone farther down the beach, and I turn to see *The Lady of the Lake*, Camp Lovejoy's water ski boat, heading our way. It's towing something large behind it.

The other counselors all go nuts, screaming *"Dreamboat!"* at the top of their lungs.

My eyebrows shoot up. *That's* the dreamboat? It doesn't look like any kind of boat I've ever seen before. In fact, it looks like a cabin. A floating cabin.

"What the heck is that?" I ask Melissa Yee, the counselor from Meadow.

"A floating cabin," she says. "It's, like, the best thing ever here at camp. Each cabin gets to take a turn having a sleepover in it."

The ski boat draws closer. *Dreamboat* is painted bright blue, with white trim around the doors and windows. There's a white picket fence around the front "porch"—sort of an extended deck in front—and red geraniums spilling from a pair of window boxes to match the red door. A sign above the door says DREAMBOAT.

"Cool, right?" says Melissa.

I nod. I definitely need to take a picture of it to send to my mother. She'll love it. In fact, she'll probably want to put it on her TV show, *Cooking with Clementine*. Which isn't just about cooking anymore, but has evolved into what she calls a "lifestyle" show. The producers are thinking about changing its name to *At Home with Clementine*, and there's even talk of a magazine.

"Okay, girls!" Sergeant Marge has moved out to the end of the H dock, and her bullhorn voice floats back to us across the water. "You know the drill. For the relay, each team member will paddle around *Dreamboat*, take a tennis ball from the bucket on the porch, paddle here to the H dock and drop the tennis ball in the bucket at my feet, then head back to shore. The kayak must touch the beach before the next person can climb in. First team to complete the relay wins coupons for ice cream cones at the Pumpkin Falls General Store."

Gwen is standing on the beach behind us with her husband, Artie,

Heather Vogel Frederick

a grandfatherly type whose cheerful attitude reminds me a little bit of Eva Bergson. Well, if Mrs. Bergson had been an African-American retiree who looked like a former football linebacker. Artie waves a fistful of coupons in the air.

"Got it?" hollers Sergeant Marge.

"Got it!" everyone hollers back.

"Good. On your marks!"

Brianna scrambles into the blue kayak, and we quickly surround her, poised to launch her from shore.

"Get set!"

"C'mon, Sapphires!" I shout, and Sergeant Marge frowns at me. Hey, what does she expect? There's ice cream at stake.

"Go!"

Four kayaks, one from each team, rocket out onto the lake. The rest of us all scramble back onto the beach, screaming encouragement to our teammates. Grabbing a tennis ball from a bucket isn't as easy as it sounds, and the first few kayaks to circle around *Dreamboat* promptly flip over as their occupants reach for the prize. While they're scrambling to right themselves, Brianna zips into place and, using her paddle as a counterbalance, neatly scoops up a tennis ball.

"Go, Sapphires!" I shout again. No frown from the head counselor this time—everybody's shouting by now.

By the time Brianna drops the ball in Marge's bucket and returns to the beach, we're in first place. We hold on to it for four more circuits, then lose ground in the fifth and sixth after double dunkings by the porch. Finally, it's my turn. We've dropped to third place by now, which is a tough but hardly hopeless position. I'm pretty sure I can make up the time.

"Let's go, let's go!" I holler, leaping forward as the blue kayak crunches up onto the sand. I practically yank its occupant out of the seat, snatching the paddle from her as I'm simultaneously climbing in. My teammates give me a mighty shove, and I'm off.

I dig into the water, grateful for all the weights I lift and the push-ups I do day in, day out as part of my hockey conditioning. There's nothing like upper body strength when it comes to canoeing and kayaking. I've almost caught up with the red kayak by the time I circle *Dreamboat*. Team Ruby's anchor is only inches ahead of me, and by paddling furiously I manage to close in. I reach right over her as I snap up a tennis ball. Sometimes it pays to be six feet tall.

I'm in the homestretch now, and I pour it on as I head for the H dock. I pass the green kayak and am gaining quickly on the purple one.

"Sapphires! Sapphires!" scream my teammates. Music to my ears. I can practically taste the ice cream.

I'm neck and neck with Team Amethyst on the final approach to the H dock. Two quick power strokes and I pull forward, passing my competitor, but in my eagerness to do so I come in too fast. I shoot past the purple kayak without enough room to angle up horizontally next to the dock. Instead, I ram it nearly head-on.

The dock gives a mighty lurch. Sergeant Marge rocks back on her heels, teeters for a moment, then topples backward into the lake.

Heather Vogel Frederick

She comes up spluttering. "Sloane!" she hollers.

"Sorry," I reply weakly, dropping my tennis ball in the bucket.

Felicia rushes down the dock and reaches into the water to help haul Marge out. The head counselor shoots me a look I've seen all too often in my eighteen years—the evil-witch-mother eye of death. "I'll see you back onshore," she snaps.

As I start to paddle away, a tennis ball comes flying over my shoulder and lands in the bucket. There's a flash of purple as the anchor for Team Amethyst sweeps past me and sprints triumphantly for the finish line at the beach.

Great.

Not only did I just dunk Sergeant Marge, I also just lost the Sapphires the relay race.

Final score? Sergeant Marge, one. Cassidy? That would be a big fat zero, sport.

 Becca

"Elizabeth Ann sat on the wooden chair . . . looking about her with miserable, homesick eyes."
—*Understood Betsy*

"Hi, I'm Becca! Welcome to Camp Lovejoy!" I crank up the enthusiasm as I step forward to greet the family climbing out of a large green SUV.

"I'm Priyanka Osborne, and this is my daughter, Amy," announces a woman in a long orange sari.

A small, slender girl with dark hair and large dark eyes like her mother's peeks out from behind the bright swirl of fabric. As Mrs. Osborne steps forward to shake my hand, the sari's intricate pattern of gold leaves and vines shimmers in the sunlight. Out of the corner of my eye, I can see Megan, who's chatting with another camper's parents, glancing over at it. She's probably itching to sketch it. A beautiful piece of clothing always does that to Megan.

Mr. Osborne, who is tall and thin and dressed in shorts and a T-shirt, greets me and shakes my hand too.

"My daughter needs to practice an hour a day," Amy's mother continues, holding out a violin case.

"Um, okay." I take it from her and set it carefully in the wheelbarrow where we'll be piling the rest of Amy's luggage.

"The camp director assured me that there would be competent staff supervising the music program." Mrs. Osborne's voice is soft but steely. It kind of reminds me of Cassidy's mother when she's in full Queen Clementine mode. We call her that behind her back. She used to be a supermodel, the kind with just one name, and she can get kind of icy and regal when she means business.

"Yes, ma'am, that's correct." I glance across the grove at Jess, who's holding hands with one of her new campers and chatting with her parents. I can't think of anyone more competent than Jess. "See that girl over there with the long blond braid? She's helping out with the music program, and she's going to Juilliard this fall."

Mrs. Osborne's dark eyebrows wing upward. "Impressive."

"Jess has an amazing voice," I continue. I wink at Amy, who's still hanging back shyly behind her mother. "And she's really nice."

"Amy enjoys singing—"

"Great!" I gush. "We do a lot of that here at camp." This is the understatement of the century. Camp Lovejoy has a song for just about everything.

"—however, it's really her instrumental progress I'm most concerned about," her mother finishes.

I chew my lip, contemplating a red-faced, sweaty Felicia trundling past us with an overloaded wheelbarrow. "We, uh, have just the counselor to help with that, too."

"Is she nice like Jess?" Amy's head pops out again from behind the sari. Her whisper is barely audible.

I hesitate for just a fraction of a second before nodding. Felicia's nice enough, but it's not the first word that comes to mind when I think of her.

"Sackbut" is.

I still can't believe there's an actual instrument called a *sackbut*. There is, though, and Felicia brought hers along to camp. Which pretty much sums up Jess's cousin.

"Felicia plays multiple instruments," I assure Mrs. Osborne. I don't tell her that most of them are these weird medieval things nobody's ever heard of, like the sackbut. I know tough customers from my waitressing experience, and I can tell that Mrs. Osborne is a tough customer.

She nods, satisfied for the moment. "Good."

I help load Amy's trunk and the rest of her gear into the wheelbarrow, then steer it down the sloped path leading from the grove to the cubie houses and our cabin.

"Lovely setting," says Mr. Osborne, who's barely said a word so far. "Amy, I think you'll be very happy here."

Amy, who has finally fully emerged from behind her mother, doesn't look convinced. In fact, she looks terrified. I'm beginning to recognize this look. I've been up close and personal with it several times today. There are a lot of first-time campers at Camp Lovejoy this summer.

Heather Vogel Frederick

"We're going to have so much fun!" I tell the little girl with more confidence than I feel. "Just wait and see."

We stop by Balsam first, where I let Amy pick out a bunk—not that she has much choice, really, as there are only two left: a bottom one toward the front of the cabin, near my bed, and a top one in the rear corner.

Not surprisingly, she goes for the one nearest to me.

"I'll help you make it up later, okay?" I tell her, placing her bedding on it. "You should set up your cubie while your mom is still here."

She trails along behind me as I lead the way across the path to Cubbyhole. Inside, we carry her trunk and other things to the little dressing room with her name on the door.

Mrs. Osborne looks around the cubie's bare wooden walls with distaste. "Rather more primitive than I thought it would be."

"Simple," says Mr. Osborne. "Uncluttered. I like it."

Amy's mother frowns. "Where's the mirror?"

I hear Gwen's words pop out of my mouth. "Camp Lovejoy is a place where girls can be themselves all summer, without having to worry about what they look like."

"Ridiculous," Mrs. Osborne retorts. "Everyone needs a mirror."

Secretly, I agree. But I don't say so.

"I think it's a wonderful policy," says Mr. Osborne, giving his daughter a reassuring squeeze. I'm beginning to like Amy's father.

Mrs. Osborne scrutinizes the daily schedule that's thumbtacked to the bulletin board on the back of the door. I've already got it memorized.

Reveille is at 7:00 (courtesy of Felicia and her sackbut), followed by a quick staff meeting in the grove. Flag raising is at 7:30; breakfast starts at 7:35. Cabin cleanup is after that, along with the morning meeting, when the day's activities are announced. First period kicks off at 9:30, second period follows, lunch starts at 12:15. Rest hour is from 1:00 to 2:00; then comes third and fourth period, and free period. Dinner's at 5:45, followed by a flag lowering. Then comes evening activity at 7:00, showers, and finally "Taps" (Felicia again) at 9:00. It's a full schedule.

"What kinds of stuff do you like to do?" I ask Amy.

She shrugs, staring down at her sandals.

"Do you like to swim?"

Another shrug.

"I'll bet you get really good at it this summer," I tell her. "One of my best friends is going to be teaching swimming lessons."

She looks up at this. "Jess?"

I shake my head. "Another friend. Emma. You'll like her, too."

I was kind of surprised when Emma volunteered to work at the waterfront. I know she likes to swim, but it's not like she's ever been on the swim team or anything back in Concord. She figure-skates a bit, just for fun, and she's been helping Cassidy out with her after-school hockey program, too. The minute we all decided to apply to be counselors, though, she zeroed in on swimming, and spent this spring getting her Lifeguard and Water Safety Instructor certifications.

"It's better than having to trudge around in the woods on hikes," she explained to us.

Heather Vogel Frederick

"What's wrong with hikes?" Cassidy had protested.

Emma made a face. "Nothing, if you like mosquitoes. I just figure if we're going to be at a camp on a lake, I want to spend as much time as possible in the water. Plus, just imagine the tan I'll get."

Megan and I are pretty sure that Emma is in full reinvention mode, what with college on the horizon and all the awkwardness with my brother Stewart. We haven't exactly discussed it with her, but we can put two and two together. For one thing, there's the college she chose. When Stewart first went off to Amherst a couple of years ago, Emma was all hot to go to a school near him in Western Massachusetts. She applied to Mount Holyoke and Smith, and got accepted at both of them. Emma's pretty smart. But in the end, after the breakup, she did a complete 180 and decided on the University of British Columbia, which is so far away she needs a passport.

"It's closer to my grandparents who live in Seattle," she told us. "I'll be able to visit them over my breaks," she told us. "The creative writing program is fantastic," she told us. Yeah, right. I'm pretty sure the real reason she chose it is because she's rebounding from Stewart—all the way to Canada.

I feel like I'm caught in the middle. I love my brother, and I actually like his new girlfriend, Sarah, a lot. But I know how hard this whole thing has been for Emma.

Anyway, she'll be working on the waterfront all day except for free period, when she's going to teach creative writing and oversee the camp newspaper, the *Birch Bark*. That's a lot for one person, but then we've all got a lot on our plates. Cassidy's dividing her time between the boat dock and working with Sergeant Marge on hiking trips, and she'll be piloting *The Lady of the Lake* during free period for wake tubing. Jess is teaching music, of course—under Felicia's supervision, poor thing—and heading up the Junior Naturalists during free period. She loves science, so while dragging campers around looking at birds and bugs and stuff would be torture for me, it's a perfect fit for her.

Megan and I will be in the Art Studio all day, teaching arts and crafts. For free period, Megan's doing a mini fashion design workshop, and I'm teaching quilting. Somehow I caught the bug last time I went to Minnesota to visit my grandmother. She's a mad quilter too.

Megan and I have had a blast this week, getting everything ready up at the Art Studio. This included a couple of shopping trips—always a favorite activity for both of us—to buy supplies. The only thing we didn't need to get was fabric, because Megan brought a ton of it with her. She cleaned out her sewing room back at home before we left Concord.

"I have to do it anyway before I leave for college," she'd said. "Camp is the perfect place to make good use of my extra stuff."

The Art Studio is up on the Hill, way out at the end of a narrow path on the far edge of camp property. Even though there are a couple other counselors working there with us—Michele from Seattle is teaching pottery and jewelry-making, and a girl named Susie from Maine is teaching painting—it still feels like our own private domain. There's a trio of large studio spaces inside with big windows overlooking the lake, and outside there's a deck with picnic tables, where our campers can work when the weather is nice. I can't wait to get started.

"Would you like to see my cubie?" I ask Amy. "It might give you some ideas for decorating your own."

She nods, and I take her by the hand and lead her down the narrow central hall. Her parents are right behind us.

"University of Minnesota!" exclaims Mr. Osborne, spying the maroon-and-gold pennant that Theo sent me tacked to the wall by the window. "Are you a Gopher?"

"Almost," I tell him proudly. "I'll be a freshman this fall."

"My sister is an alum."

We beam at each other. Mrs. Osborne examines the fabric that I pleated around my dressing table and sniffs, clearly not impressed.

"Dinner's in a little over an hour, but we're all meeting in Balsam beforehand so we can go together as a cabin," I tell Amy. "Come on over after you unpack, and I'll help you make up your bed and introduce you to everybody before you say good-bye to your parents."

Amy looks panicked when she hears the word "good-bye." I give her a reassuring smile, then head outside, the screen door to the cubie house slapping shut behind me.

Sergeant Marge is patrolling the path with a clipboard. "How many left to check in?"

"Um, just one, I think," I tell her. "Amy Osborne arrived a few minutes ago."

"Osborne," she says, scanning the list on her clipboard. She makes a checkmark next to Amy's name. "A newbie, I see."

"I'm a little worried she's going to be homesick."

Sergeant Marge frowns and makes a note of this on her clipboard, too. "Another trembling leaf, eh? Well, it happens. She'll get over it."

Sergeant Marge isn't exactly the warm and fuzzy type.

By the time the dinner bell rings, the last of our campers has checked in. Three of them—Grace Friedman, an athletic-looking girl with a tangle of blond hair stuffed under a Yankees baseball cap; Mia Jackson, a sprite with a mischievous smile and short dark curls; and Kate Kwan, the tallest of our campers—were in Nest together last year, and are already a tight little unit. I can tell we're going to have to keep an eye on that. Amy, meanwhile, is looking paler by the minute, and I suspect that Harper Kennedy, who came up by herself from Boston, is on the verge of a homesickness meltdown too. *Who sends an eight-year-old to camp on the bus all alone?* I wonder, looking down at the freckled redhead with the white-knuckled grip on her backpack.

The thing is, I totally sympathize. Six weeks is a long time to be away from home, especially for the first time. I'm not sure I could have done it when I was their age.

"All right, Balsam!" says Megan, clapping her hands to get everyone's attention. "Anybody hungry besides me?"

We lead the girls up the path to the Dining Hall. Tonight is First Night dinner, another Camp Lovejoy tradition, which means spaghetti, garlic bread, salad, and cupcakes for dessert. Inside, things are already rocking and rolling. A rowdy chorus of "Blue Socks" has broken

Heather Vogel Frederick

out at one of the tables of teens from the Hill, and Grace, Mia, and Kate join in gustily as we take our seats. Amy and Harper watch them, bewildered.

Blue socks, they never get dirty
The longer you wear them, the stiffer they get.
Sometimes I think of the laundry
But something inside me says don't send them yet!

"I didn't know any of the songs at first either," I tell the baffled girls, shouting to be heard above the din. "You'll be surprised how fast you'll learn them!"

After we finish eating, Gwen stands up and gives a brief welcome speech followed by a few announcements. "We'll be gathering in Lower Lodge shortly after dinner for our First Night ceremony," she concludes. "Don't be late, and don't forget, swim tests are scheduled for first thing tomorrow morning!"

Hearing this, Amy and Harper's faces glaze over with panic again. I glance over at Megan and grimace. We're going to need to add "pep talk" to our to-do list.

"Anybody who needs to visit the Biffy, come with me," Megan tells our campers as we're leaving the Dining Hall a few minutes later. All the girls except Amy go with her.

"We'll meet you at Lower Lodge!" I call after them.

Amy grips my hand tightly as we head down the path. She was

fighting back tears during dinner, and now that we're alone, they spill over.

"It's okay, honey," I tell her, handing her a tissue. Thank goodness Gwen suggested we keep some extras in our pockets these first few days. "You're going to be fine, I promise."

I lead her to one of the big wooden swinging chairs that dot the waterfront and sit down, patting the seat beside me. Amy obeys, sitting ramrod straight until I put my arm around her. Then she melts against me, dissolving in tears again. The two of us swing for a bit in silence.

I look out over the water. The lake is calm this evening, the colors of the sunset mirrored brilliantly in its still surface. It doesn't take long for the view to work its magic. I feel Amy start to relax a little, and I hand her another tissue and encourage her to blow her nose. She does, vigorously, then gives me a tremulous smile.

"Better?"

She nods.

"Let's go have some fun, then," I tell her as I spot our cabinmates coming down the path with all the other campers.

Lower Lodge is an impressive place, with an enormous stone fireplace and a vaulted ceiling hung with rustic chandeliers made out of antlers. Large windows overlook the lake. It's noisy inside, as campers and counselors alike mill around greeting old friends.

Sergeant Marge holds up two fingers, and the room starts to quiet down.

Heather Vogel Frederick

"Cabin circles, please, ladies!" she calls, and we all join hands with our campers, just as we were instructed to earlier today at our morning meeting, then form circles and sit down on the floor.

The girls in Outback, the cabin for the oldest teens, lead us in a couple more songs, and then Gwen stands for some introductory remarks.

"'Broadening Horizons for Over a Century,'" she says. "That's our camp motto, as you all know. You girls who have been here before know how true it is, and those of you who are new will soon discover it for yourselves. We accept no limitations at Camp Lovejoy. We expect you to challenge yourselves as well as enjoy yourselves this summer, and return home with a wider view of the world, and of what you can do when you set your mind to it."

She talks for a while longer, outlining some of the special activities that are in store, including my own quilting class. Finally, it's time for the ceremony.

One by one, each cabin is called up by Sergeant Marge, joining her in front of the fireplace to receive their nameplates and be introduced to the rest of the camp.

Megan and I slaved over those nameplates. Two days ago, Artie came to the Art Studio and presented us with a wheelbarrow full of what looked like slices of bread. On closer inspection, they turned out to be fragrant pine branches that had been cut into slim rounds of wood.

We drilled holes in the top of each one, threading leather shoelaces through them to make necklaces. Using a wood-burning tool, we wrote the name of each camper on one side, along with their cabin name, the year, and Camp Lovejoy's emblem.

"As Lovejoy girls have done for over a century now, you will each wear your nameplate for the first week," the head counselor explains. "That will help us all to learn one another's names. After that, you'll only wear it to Sunday night council fires. The beads you earn for your activities will be strung on the necklace, too, and at the end of the summer"—Sergeant Marge flips one of the nameplates over and taps its blank side—"you'll receive a special camp nickname from your counselors."

Amy looks over at me and smiles.

I smile back.

"Hers should be 'crybaby,'" I hear Grace whisper behind me to one of her friends.

Amy hears it as well. Her face falls. I cringe inside as I flash back to myself at her age. I was a Grace back then too, quick to find a person's weak spot and expose it.

But I'm not that girl anymore. And I haven't been for a long time.

As Sergeant Marge calls Twin Pines forward, I turn around. "Grace? May I talk to you?"

Without waiting for a reply, I grip her firmly by the arm and tow her outside. "I don't ever want to hear you call Amy that again. Or anybody else. Do you understand?"

Grace blinks up at me, her face the picture of innocence under her

Heather Vogel Frederick

baseball cap. She's not fooling me one bit, though. It takes a former queen bee to know a queen bee.

"Don't pretend you don't know what I'm talking about," I tell her sternly, sounding scarily like my mother. "I heard you! You've been to camp before; Amy hasn't. You know people already; she doesn't. If I catch you picking on her, or teasing her, or making fun of her or any other camper again, I will march you over to the Director's Cottage so fast it will make your head spin! We'll have a talk with Gwen, and then we'll call your parents."

By now Grace is looking close to tears.

Worried that I may have overdone it, I relent a little. "Look, you and Mia and Kate have an advantage over the new girls in our cabin. You know the ropes. You have a lot to teach Amy and Harper. I can tell you're a natural leader, Grace, and I'm counting on you to take on that role in our cabin. Kind of like a counselor's helper."

She perks up a little at this.

"Think you can do that for me?"

She nods.

"Great! I had a feeling I could count on you."

As we take our seats in the cabin circle again, Megan leans over to me and whispers, "Did I just witness you officially scaring the socks off one of our campers?"

I grin. "Just call me Big Bad Becca."

Things unravel again by bedtime, though.

As our campers trail in from one last visit to the Biffy and climb into their beds, accompanied by the mournful notes of "Taps" on Felicia's sackbut, I hear sniffles. Amy is crying again, and so is Harper. Grace and Mia and Kate are having a hard time stifling their giggles.

"That's enough," I tell them sternly.

To make matters worse, there's an explosion of laughter from next door, where Cassidy is showing off for Twin Pines by burping the alphabet.

Great, I think sourly. They're the fun cabin already, and we're the duds, stuck with a cabin full of queen bees and—what did Sergeant Marge call them?—trembling leaves.

The truth is, I'm starting to feel like a trembling leaf myself. Getting things ready up at the Art Studio this week, it was easy to imagine myself surrounded by happy little girls, teaching them to make things out of Popsicle sticks and glitter. But now, sitting here on my bed, listening to the chorus of sniffles, I'm struck with self-doubt.

Being a counselor is a lot harder than being a waitress. At least when you work in a café, the customers leave at the end of the meal. Here, I'm on duty pretty much 24/7, completely responsible for five little girls.

Including Amy Osborne, whose sniffles are threatening to escalate into full-blown wails. I slip out of bed and pad over to her as Megan goes to tend to Harper.

"Hey, Amy," I whisper.

"Hey," she manages to gulp in reply.

"You okay?"

Heather Vogel Frederick

She shakes her head. "I want to go home."

"But just think of all the fun you'd miss out on if you do!" I hand her Goldy, the stuffed gopher that Theo sent me. "I brought a friend to keep you company. He's the mascot for the college I'm going to this fall."

She gulps and takes the stuffed animal in one hand, wiping her nose with the back of the other. I kneel down beside her bunk. "Goldy was homesick when we first got here too," I tell her. "But then he made friends with a chipmunk—"

This earns me a sniffly giggle.

"—and he learned how to water-ski—"

Another giggle.

"—and now he's having a blast. And so will you, I promise." I hand her a tissue and smooth her hair back from her forehead, the way my mother used to do when I was little. "You two go to sleep now, okay?"

"Okay," she whispers, clutching Goldy tightly to her and obediently closing her eyes.

Megan is waiting at the foot of my bed when I return.

"Uh-oh," I say, spotting the tin she's holding. I recognize it from a zillion mother-daughter book club meetings. It's the one her mother brings whenever she's in charge of snacks. Which is practically never. Mrs. Wong is the mayor of Concord and an extremely capable woman, but she's a *terrible* cook. Plus, she has this phobia about sugar. She's seriously trying to get a referendum on the ballot for the next election banning soft drinks from our town's schools. She's convinced that sugar is the root of all evil, and she's always sneaking "healthy" ingredients like tofu and kale into perfectly normal recipes for things like chocolate chip cookies and cheesecake. We try to discourage her from volunteering for snack duty at our book club meetings.

Megan grins. "Don't worry," she whispers. "It's from Gigi and Sophie. French chocolates. They told me to save it for an emergency."

"I think this qualifies," I whisper back.

"Definitely." She pries open the tin quietly and hands me a piece of candy. "We'd better find a cure for homesickness, or this is going to be a long summer."

Heather Vogel Frederick

Jess

> *"Do you know, I am sorry for Elizabeth Ann, and, what's more, I have been ever since this story began."*
> —*Understood Betsy*

"Everybody got a buddy?" I glance back to check. A double file of campers are lined up along the Point behind me, each younger girl clutching an older girl's hand. "Okay, then—Hairbrush Island, here we come!"

Shouldering my backpack, I step gingerly from the shore into the water and head for the sandbar a few yards out. I try to avoid the sharp rocks and pebbles in the shallows, but it's nearly impossible, and more than once I flinch, sucking in my breath when I step on one. Finally, I reach the sandbar, and my bare toes unclench as the rocks give way to soft sand.

Relaxing, I look around. It's another gorgeous afternoon. After the torrential rains earlier in June, which reached a peak during the downpour on the day we arrived, we've had nothing but blue skies and sunshine. Which is a good thing, considering the epidemic of homesickness sweeping through Lower Camp. Gloomy weather would not have been helpful.

I pause halfway across the sandbar, lifting my face to the sun as I wait for the others to catch up. It's such a treat to be outside! I spend most of my days cooped up in Lower Lodge with Felicia, teaching music. Not that I mind, really. Despite my cousin's bossiness, I'm having a lot of fun. The campers are great, and they're really enthusiastic about the Camp Chorale I've formed. Still, I have to admit that my favorite part of the day is free period, when I get to work with the Junior Naturalists.

Junior Naturalists are another camp tradition, and one of the electives the campers get to choose for free period. It's just basic outdoor science stuff—bird-watching, exploring habitats, that kind of thing—but it's right up my alley. The main thing is, it takes advantage of all the natural beauty at Lake Lovejoy.

The water is shallow here on the sandbar, and warm, and it laps against my calves as I watch the girls splashing toward me. Hearing a series of low, tuneless toots coming from the deck of Lower Lodge, I smother a grin. My cousin decided to offer sackbut lessons during free period this week. One lone camper signed up. I'm guessing she's sorry she did.

There are other sounds drifting over from camp too—the rhythmic clatter of tap shoes from the dance platform on the Hill; the roar of the water ski boat and shrieks of glee as Cassidy and Brianna take a group of girls out wake tubing; and the welcome clash of pots and pans from the kitchen, signaling that dinner isn't far away.

Camp Lovejoy has a rhythm to its days as distinct as music and

Heather Vogel Frederick

as predictable as a math equation. This suits me just fine, and over the course of the last week I've slipped effortlessly into the routine. Unfortunately, that has not been the case with a number of the younger campers—especially the ones in Nest and Balsam.

Emma and Felicia's cabin has been struck the hardest, since their little seven-year-olds have never been to sleepaway camp before. Emma says she's gone through four entire boxes of tissues already. Bedtime is the most difficult, as that's when missing home seems to hit the girls the hardest.

Becca and Megan are struggling too, especially with the utterly adorable Amy Osborne, who is quite an accomplished violinist for someone so tiny, and Harper Kennedy, who's here with me this afternoon. I glance back, hoping that Harper remembered to put on extra sunscreen. Like so many redheads, she has pale skin, and it's already blooming with a new crop of freckles.

So far, Cassidy and I have been pretty lucky on the homesickness front. We have the nine-year-olds, and two of them are gung ho seasoned campers: Brooklyn Alvarez, a boisterous charmer who actually is from Brooklyn, and Carter Stevens, whose mane of loose Afro curls gives her a distinctive flair, and who's almost as devoted to fashion as Megan. The first couple of days with our other two— newbies Frederica and Monica Simpson, sandy-haired twins from St. Louis—were a little rocky, but Cassidy is really experienced dealing with kids, thanks to her work with Chicks with Sticks, plus she's so funny that she manages to get the twins, who go by the nicknames Freddie and Nica, laughing whenever they start to droop.

I'm keeping an eagle eye out to make sure that the other two girls in our cabin don't shut them out. The whole clique thing drives me nuts. I'm supersensitive to it, because I remember only too well how miserable my life was for a few years back in middle school, thanks to the Fab Four, as we used to call Becca Chadwick and her posse. That was a long time ago, of course, and Becca is a completely different person now—she's one of my closest friends, in fact—but still, those memories resurface now and then, and they can still sting.

"Almost there, girls!" I call to the flock following me, and we all wade on toward the island's shore.

Jennie Norris, a cheerful counselor-in-training who's been assigned to help me with the Junior Naturalists, brings up the rear with little Tara Lindgren. Tara is one of Emma's campers, a timid girl with a pixie haircut who has to be coaxed into having fun. She lives in Manhattan and doesn't spend much time outside. According to Emma, Tara's idea of the great outdoors is sitting at a sidewalk table at a coffee shop.

"The stuff she comes up with!" Emma exclaimed this morning as we were heading to our early staff meeting in the Grove. "I try so hard to keep a straight face, but I can't help laughing."

"Like what?"

"Well, the first night she was here, she heard a loon and thought it was a moose, and she cried because she was scared. Then, last night

Heather Vogel Frederick

at bedtime, she had a total meltdown. 'I miss New York!' she kept sobbing. 'I miss skyscrapers and smog and . . . and *pretzels!*' "

I had to laugh at that. "Well, those pretzels are pretty good."

Emma grinned. "Yeah."

"You've got to write that stuff down and use it in a story."

"Already in my notebook," she told me smugly.

Emma is going to be a writer someday. She already is one, in fact—she had a picture book published a couple of years ago, and she sold a poem to a literary magazine right before graduation last spring.

"Okay, everybody, put your shoes back on and we'll get started," I tell my group as we clamber onto the rocky beach. I rummage through my backpack for my sandals. It's amazing how much stuff I have to haul around with me on these little excursions, even though we never leave camp property. First aid kit, emergency whistle, extra snacks—not to mention a counselor-in-training.

So far this week, Jennie, the CIT, and I have taken our Junior Naturalists on bird walks, spent time identifying trees and leaves and flowers, searched for crawfish with nets along the shore by the boathouse, and hunted for newts and salamanders in the bog at the top of the hill. For our grand finale this afternoon, I promised them a scavenger hunt.

Yesterday was my day off—counselors get one night and one day off every week—and I spent most of it scouting the island, planting a few surprises for the girls to find. It's going to be fun.

"Same two teams as before," I tell them. "Chipmunks, you line up over by Jennie, and Squirrels, you all come join me. If you have questions, remember that Jennie and I both have guidebooks to all the New Hampshire flora and fauna. Who remembers what those words mean?"

A hand shoots up. It's Holly Andrews, the oldest girl on my team. She's in Farther, one of the cabins up on the Hill. "*Flora* is Latin for all the plants that grow in a particular area, and *fauna* are the animals."

"Way to go, Holly!" I've been sneaking in as many Latin names for things as I can this week, hoping some of them will stick. "Flora was the Roman goddess of flowers—isn't that perfect? And Fauna was the sister of Faunus, the Roman god of the forest." I love making these connections. It's part of why I think science is so cool.

I hand out the checklist of things they need to look for, along with a paper bag for each team to carry what they find back to Jennie and me. "First group to gather all the items on the list gets a prize. Ready? Let's go!"

Jennie and the Chipmunks trot off on the path that hugs the shoreline, while the Squirrels follow me into the woods. My girls find the first few items easily—a pinecone, a fern, some moss—and then it gets harder. It takes a while for them to spot anything edible (I discovered several stands of wild blueberry bushes on my scouting trip yesterday, so I steer them discreetly toward one), and they're stumped briefly at lichen, and have to consult a guidebook.

Heather Vogel Frederick

"There's some!" says Harper, squatting down and pointing to a patch of it on a boulder, after carefully examining the picture.

"Good job!" I tell her.

Brooklyn Alvarez frowns at the checklist. "I haven't seen a single feather."

"We'll have more luck with those closer to shore," I promise.

She nods, consulting the list again. "Hairbrush plant? What's that?"

"It's the plant the island is named for," I tell her, somehow managing to keep a straight face.

"Really? What does it look like?"

"Kind of like that plant over there," I reply, pointing across the clearing.

The girls all turn around, then burst out laughing when they spot a pair of pink hairbrushes sticking out of the ground.

"What?" I ask, feigning innocence. "It's Hairbrush Island, right? They grow in the wild here."

"You're teathing uth, Jeth!" cries Pippa Lovejoy. Pippa is the youngest girl at camp this summer. She's in Nest with Emma and Felicia, and along with her cabinmates Tara Lindgren and Meriwether—Meri to her friends—Milligan, has quickly become one of the camp pets. It's pretty hard to resist Pippa's pink sparkly glasses and strawberry-blond curls, plus she's missing her two front teeth, which gives her the most appealing gap-toothed smile. Despite being not quite seven, Pippa hasn't suffered the slightest pang of homesickness. Probably because she's from nearby Pumpkin Falls, which her ancestors settled—they named a bunch of stuff around here, including Lovejoy Mountain and Lake Lovejoy. Plus, Pippa's older sister Lauren is here for the summer too.

I put my arm around her shoulders and give her a squeeze. "You think so?"

We're all still laughing when it happens. A counselor's worst nightmare—screams from the other side of the island.

I grab Holly. "You're in charge! Stay here and don't let anyone move a muscle. I'll be back as soon as I can."

Heart racing, I dive into the underbrush, bushwhacking my way toward what has now escalated into full-blown wailing.

"I'm coming!" I holler, fumbling for my emergency whistle. My imagination kicks into overdrive, churning out vivid pictures of all the horrible scenarios that might be awaiting me. I trip over a root and fall, dropping my whistle and skinning my knee. As I scramble to my feet, a branch slaps me in the face and another one grabs at my hair.

I finally reach the shore path, where I spot Jennie and her charges. "What?" I shout. "What is it? Who's hurt?"

"I don't want to look for bears!" shrieks Tara. She's cowering behind the CIT, who is trying in vain to comfort her. "I want to go home!"

"We tried to tell her it's just a joke," Jennie says helplessly.

"No bears!" Tara shrieks again.

My surprise has backfired, big-time.

Heather Vogel Frederick

I kneel in front of the wailing camper. "Tara, listen to me," I tell her, using the same quiet voice I use when comforting an injured animal. "We're not looking for *real* bears."

"I want to go home!" Tara wails again, gulping back sobs.

I fish a tissue out of my backpack and hand it to her. "Sweetie, I was just kidding—it's *teddy* bears we're looking for, see?" I point to a nearby tree that's leaning out over the water. Nestled in its branches is one of the stuffed bears I planted on the island yesterday. He's posed with his arm in the air, as if he's waving at the campers.

Tara regards it suspiciously. She wipes her nose on her sleeve, and her sobs begin to subside.

I retrieve the bear, hand it to Tara, and then—sticking to the path this time—lead the Chipmunks back to where I left my group.

Which now contains not one but two crying campers: Harper and Pippa, who may not be homesick but who still has her limits, apparently, especially when it comes to wilderness adventures.

"We were thcared you wouldn't come back for uth!" she sobs.

"I thought I heard wolves!" wails Harper.

I take a deep breath. "The scavenger hunt is over for today," I say as brightly as I can. "How about a cookie break instead?"

Things calm down a bit after everyone has had a snack, but it's a subdued group that I lead back across the sandbar.

"More tears?" mutters Felicia as I deliver Pippa and Tara, who is still clutching my teddy bear, to the doorstep of Nest. "I swear, it's like the plague around here this summer."

Trust my cousin to find an appropriate medieval metaphor.

"What happened over on the island?" demands Sergeant Marge, intercepting me a few minute later as Cassidy and I lead our campers into the Dining Hall for dinner.

She shakes her head when I finish explaining. "First of all, you should never, never, *never*, under any circumstances, leave campers on their own," she tells me sternly. "Do you realize what a risk you took?"

"But I put Holly——" I start to protest.

"And second of all," the head counselor continues, barging ahead, "well, second of all, Gwen should have taken my advice about not hiring inexperienced counselors." She spins on her heel and stalks off.

Now I'm the one who feels like crying. Hairbrush Island is so small it barely qualifies as an island, and the girls were with a perfectly capable teenager and out of my sight for what, five minutes, tops?

"You look like you swallowed a lemon," says Cassidy as I join her at our table. "What happened?"

"I'll tell you later," I mutter.

Fortunately, our campers are too busy rehashing their afternoon activities to notice how quiet I am. While our cabin may not be suffering from the homesickness plague, we're not without our own drama, which today centers on swim lesson placement. I had no idea nine-year-old girls could be so competitive.

"I'm going to be a Shark by the end of the summer," boasts Brooklyn.

Heather Vogel Frederick

"You're all gonna be Sharks by the end of the summer," Cassidy promises.

Cassidy is the queen of competition, and she's been fanning those flames like crazy ever since our campers arrived. She put up charts on the walls of Twin Pines to track our cabin's progress. There's one for inspection—the cabin and cubie house with the highest tidiness score at the end of the summer win banana splits from the General Store in Pumpkin Falls, and after the fiasco with the *Dreamboat* relay, Cassidy is determined to win that—and another for each of the sports our girls are involved in, to help record everyone's athletic progress.

"I don't think Nica and I will be Sharks," says Frederica sadly. "We're only Minnows."

Her sister nods in agreement.

Freddie does most of the talking for her twin, who's on the shy side. I know all about that. I used to be so shy I was practically mute.

Last Monday's swim test determined each camper's swim level: Guppy, Minnow, Sunfish, Dolphin, and Shark. There's also Junior Lifeguard, Senior Lifeguard, and Water Safety Instructor, but those are mostly for the older campers in the cabins on the Hill.

"You guys just keep practicing, and you'll see," Cassidy assures her. "All my girls are winners."

A CIT comes by just then with a basket of breadsticks, and Cassidy grabs one in each hand. "Let the carbo-loading begin!"

I poke at my lasagna, which I'm guessing is on the menu for everyone planning to run in this weekend's Four on the Fourth road race over in Pumpkin Falls. A lot of campers and counselors have signed up for the traditional Fourth of July race.

Dessert is brownies and mint chip ice cream, one of my favorites. I still have no appetite, so I shove my plate over to Cassidy, who happily scarfs it down.

"Attention, girls!" says Gwen. "Tonight is our first Cabin Night, and your counselors will tell you shortly what they have in store. First, though, I'd like to ask all cabin counselors to join me at the Director's Cottage for a brief staff meeting."

My stomach lurches. A staff meeting? I don't think I can stand it if Gwen scolds me in front of everyone. It's bad enough that Sergeant Marge bawled me out.

"Campers, you'll remain here in the Dining Hall, where the CITs will lead you in a sing-along until your counselors come back for you," Gwen continues, and we leave the Dining Hall to the strains of "Make New Friends, but Keep the Old." Emma tucks her arm through mine, humming along as we follow Gwen down the path toward the Director's Cottage. I tell her about the disastrous afternoon and my run-in with the head counselor.

"One is silver and the other gold," Emma sings softly. "That's you, Jess—you're gold. Don't pay any attention to Marge the Barge."

"I don't feel very golden at the moment," I retort. To be honest, I'm worried that maybe I'm going to get fired. I need the money from this summer job—even with the scholarship and grants that I was awarded, Juilliard is expensive.

Heather Vogel Frederick

Emma gives my arm a squeeze. "It'll blow over. And hey, tomorrow is our night off, remember?"

I give her a half smile. "Yeah." We're both really looking forward to that. Not that there's much to do around here, but still, it will be nice to spend some time together.

The breeze has picked up, and Emma and I dart inside Cubbyhole to grab sweatshirts from our cubies. Approaching the Point, we jog the last stretch to the Director's Cottage.

Inside, a fire is snapping in the living room's stone fireplace. Emma and I make a beeline for the last empty armchair beside it, squeezing into it together.

"I could totally live here," I announce, looking around. The cabin is rustic, with plain, unpainted wood paneling, and windows on three sides that look out over the Point and the gazebo and the lake beyond. Red-cushioned window seats flank the fireplace, and cozy red sofas and armchairs are bathed in the warm glow of a scattering of lamps.

Emma nods. "It's like the keeping room at Half Moon Farm," she says, referring to the snug family room off the kitchen that's my favorite spot at my house back in Concord. Well, besides my own bedroom, that is.

Ironically, I'm suddenly struck by a pang of homesickness myself. My parents are probably out in the barn right now, getting the animals settled for the night. I can picture Led and Zep, our big Belgian horses, quietly munching their hay, and all the goats bedding down for the night, and even the quiet burbling of the chickens as they head sleepily to their roosts.

"I want to go over the plans for our busy weekend ahead," says Gwen once everyone has arrived and taken a seat. If Sergeant Marge gave the camp director an earful about what happened on Hairbrush Island this afternoon, Gwen doesn't show any sign of it. She doesn't single me out at all, in fact, although she does bring up the subject of homesickness.

"I know some of you have girls struggling with it—especially in the younger cabins," Gwen acknowledges. "This is part of the challenge that goes along with being a camp counselor. I've weathered nearly twenty summers here at Camp Lovejoy, and believe me when I say that there's a cure for what ails your girls. But it's different every summer, because the girls are always different. Be creative; be persistent. I know you'll find just the right way to deal with this."

She gives me a sympathetic smile as we file out. "Don't worry about Marge," she tells me quietly. "She's more bark than bite, and trust me, there's no one you'd rather have in your corner when the chips are down."

"She said what?" Cassidy asks, incredulous, when I repeat Gwen's words to her and Emma on the way back to the Dining Hall. "That's hard to imagine."

We collect our campers, and Cassidy, who is all perky and full of energy, thanks to the sugar rush from double desserts, prances ahead as we lead them away.

Heather Vogel Frederick

"We are going to have so much fun tonight!" she tells our girls.

Cabin Nights are a once-a-week bonding activity planned by each set of cabin counselors. For Twin Pines, Cassidy and I decided to take our campers to Upper Meadow for a game of flashlight tag. Nest is trying to turn this afternoon's lemons into lemonade with a teddy bear's picnic in Lower Lodge, and for Balsam, Megan and Becca have arranged a canoe bubble bath. Artie helped them set everything up on Boathouse Beach with the big war canoe, which is large enough to fit all of them inside, and he's supervising as they ferry buckets of warm water to fill it up.

"Only Megan and Becca would dream up something like that," I tell Cassidy, waving to our friends and their campers as we pass them on our way up the hill.

"Can we do that for our next Cabin Night?" begs Freddie. "Please?"

"Aren't you guys a little old for bubble baths?" I ask her.

"What are you talking about?" scoffs Cassidy. "No one's ever too old for bubble baths."

I look at her in astonishment. "Seriously?"

"Seriously what?"

"Seriously, you are so not the bubble bath type."

"I take baths!" she protests.

This strikes our campers as funny, and they start to laugh. Cassidy plays it up, sniffing her armpits for effect, which makes them laugh even harder.

Our game of flashlight tag is a big hit, and my day ends on a much-needed high note. We corral our girls into the showers afterward, and they're asleep before their heads hit the pillows.

Not me.

I lie awake listening to the loons out on the water and thinking about what Gwen said earlier about finding a way to deal with the homesickness. As I drift off to sleep, it occurs to me that I might be able to kill two birds with one stone. If I can find a cure for the plague, as Felicia calls it, maybe I can redeem myself in Sergeant Marge's eyes too.

Morning arrives not to the sound of reveille from Felicia's sackbut, but rather to the insistent banging of metal spoons against pots.

"SCUM!" hollers someone right outside our cabin. "SCUM! SCUM! SCUM!"

"What's going on?" I ask, sitting up and rubbing my eyes. I peer through the screened window at the pack of CITs thundering through Lower Camp.

"Saturday Clean Up Morning, remember?" Cassidy tells me, yawning.

"Oh yeah. I forgot."

Surprisingly, SCUM is a popular activity at camp. Probably because it always starts off with French toast. There's real maple syrup, too. Breakfast is so good it earns the cooks, or "Cookies," as they're affectionately nicknamed, a song:

Skinnamarink-a-dink-a-dink,
Skinnamarink-a-do,
Cookies, we love you!

The song ends with everyone drumming their feet under the tables until Ethel and Thelma Farnsworth, two older ladies from Pumpkin Falls who cook for camp every summer, come out from the kitchen and take a bow.

Afterward, the four teams get their marching orders. In addition to a thorough sweeping of Cubbyhole and Primporium, the Sapphires are put in charge of weeding Lower Camp, while the Rubies do the same for the Hill. Emeralds spread mulch and rake the beaches, and the Amethysts wash all the windows in the Dining Hall and lodges. The CITs, meanwhile, have a special assignment: decorating for the upcoming Fourth of July beach party and BBQ.

There's an extra air of anticipation surrounding this, because the beach party means one thing: boys. Boys from Camp Pinewood, to be exact. The party is an annual event, which Camp Lovejoy always hosts because we have the best spot for watching the fireworks over the lake. The boys return the favor in August at their camp with a luau and dance for the older campers.

Sergeant Marge blasts the *William Tell* Overture over the loud-speakers—a SCUM tradition—and we're off and running. By lunchtime, everything is sparkling clean, and the Dining Hall has been transformed.

Red, white, and blue bunting hangs from the railings of the porch and the big fireplace mantel inside, and a giant American flag waves from the rafters. Bouquets of smaller flags in beribboned mason jars serve as centerpieces on the tables, and crepe paper streamers flutter overhead. I spot a helium canister in the corner, along with a big pile of red, white, and blue balloons waiting to be inflated.

"Nice," says Cassidy.

The girls in our cabin don't really have the bandwidth yet for boy stuff, but they know there's a party coming in a few days, and they're excited about seeing fireworks.

After lunch, it's time for mail call. It's my turn to retrieve it for our cabin, and while our campers line up outside along with everyone else, I wait by the small office in the Dining Hall's lobby until Sergeant Marge calls out "Twin Pines!" When I step forward, she hands me a small stack of letters. Just four today for our cabin—one each for Frederica and Monica, one for Cassidy (which is probably from Tristan because it has a British stamp on it), and one for me. It's from my boyfriend, Emma's brother Darcy, which is unexpected. This summer Darcy is interning at the Smithsonian down in Washington, DC, and he's been so busy he hasn't had much time to write.

I glance over to where Felicia is handing out the mail for Nest. I can tell by the droop in Emma's shoulders that there's nothing for her.

"Sorry, Ems," I tell her as we head back to our cabins for rest hour.

"It's no big deal," she replies, but I know Emma almost as well as I know myself, and I can tell from the tone of her voice that it is a

Heather Vogel Frederick

big deal. She hasn't gotten any mail at all since we've been here. Her parents are away in England, visiting the Berkeley family and doing research for Mr. Hawthorne's new book, and of course Stewart isn't writing to her. I remind myself to put a bug in Darcy's ear to at least send her a postcard.

Maybe she'll meet somebody new this summer, I think, giving her a sidelong glance. Maybe someone from Camp Pinewood, at the Fourth of July barbecue. There has to be life after Stewart, right?

As the bell rings for the beginning of rest hour, I stretch out on my bed and open my letter. I'm really grateful for this little oasis during the day—being a counselor is tiring, and it's nice to have a whole hour to myself, with nobody asking me questions and nothing I have to do. I glance around the cabin at our girls. Freddie and Nica are reading their letters. Brooklyn is playing solitaire, and Carter, who's been inspired by Megan's example, is drawing in her sketchbook. Cassidy, as usual, is already asleep. She naps during every rest hour, thanks to her early-morning training sessions.

I start to read:

> Dear Jess,
> Washington is incredible! My internship is going well—the Smithsonian is huge, and I keep getting lost, but there are so many cool things to see, I actually look forward to when that happens. Maybe I'll think about working for a museum someday. It's hot hot hot here—a lot hotter than

Concord—and ridiculously humid, but the dorm I'm living in for the summer is air-conditioned, of course, and so are the museums.

I got your letter. Camp sounds really great. Are your campers there yet? What's your favorite thing you've done so far with them?

I miss you!

Love,
Darcy

I read it again, then fold it up and put it back in its envelope, smiling.

The rest of the day passes quickly. Saturday is laundry day for Lower Camp, so we collect all our dirty clothes and make sure they get into the right laundry bags, then drop them off on the Dining Hall's porch.

There's a free swim this afternoon, and Cassidy takes our girls down to the waterfront for some extra coaching. She's serious about making Sharks out of all of them. I help out with group games for the youngest campers, playing freeze tag while starting the count-down to my night off, which begins right after dinner.

I'm actually kind of sorry to be missing tonight's activity, which is an all-camp float-in movie. Artie's busy inflating inner tubes and rafts over by the kayak shed, and earlier he took *The Lady of the*

Lake, the camp's water ski boat, and hauled *Dreamboat* around in front of the H dock. A big screen is now set up on the floating cabin's front porch, ready for the movie to be projected. Tonight's feature is *The Parent Trap*, which is a perfect movie for camp and one of my all-time favorites.

As sorry as I am to miss it, I'm not sorry enough to skip my night off. I could really use a little time away, especially since Sergeant Marge is still giving me the cold shoulder. Plus, I need some Emma time.

Since we didn't get to be co-counselors the way we planned, Emma and I asked Gwen if she could try to schedule our days and nights off together. She said she'd do her best, but couldn't promise anything. In the end, we weren't able to have the same day off this week, but Gwen came through for our night off.

We mean to enjoy every minute of it. After dinner we change into our civvies—camp-speak for regular clothes instead of uniforms—sign out at the office, then grab the keys to Cassidy's minivan, which she's lending us so that we can drive over to Pumpkin Falls.

"Ooh, a covered bridge," says Emma a little while later, as we descend the hill toward town.

We stop and take pictures, then turn down Main Street.

"Cute," says Emma, looking at the buildings and shops, and I nod in agreement. Everything is decorated with red, white, and blue in anticipation of the coming holiday. I park in front of the General Store, which is still open, and we go inside to do some shopping.

"Don't let me forget to get extra mosquito repellent," I tell her. "My poor Junior Naturalists were nearly eaten alive up at the bog this week."

"Too bad they don't sell homesickness repellent," Emma replies.

I grin at her. "Plague-B-Gone. We could make a fortune."

We buy ice cream cones and drop our purchases in the car, then wander down Main Street through the town center. Most of the shops are closed, except for Lou's Diner, which we decide to visit on our next day off. Emma spots a bookstore she wants to come back to browse through as well.

"I think that's the one Pippa's family owns," she tells me.

"Lovejoy's Books? Cool."

There's no movie theater, and really nothing much to do, so we end up sitting on a bench on the village green while we're finishing our ice cream. After that, we still have a couple of hours until curfew, so we head back to camp to hang out in the Counselors' Cabin. It's the only place at Camp Lovejoy with a TV, plus there's a computer terminal. A bunch of other counselors who have the night off are waiting in line to check their e-mail, though, so I head for the big sectional sofa where another group is watching a movie.

Emma wanders over to a bookshelf and scans the titles, then pulls one down and settles into an armchair to read.

Halfway through the movie, I glance over at Emma. She's oblivious, of course, a half smile on her face. The Counselors' Cabin could

Heather Vogel Frederick

be in flames and she wouldn't notice. It's always that way when she's immersed in a book.

And then it hits me.

The perfect solution.

I jump up off the sofa and tiptoe across the room. "Emma!" I whisper.

She drags her gaze from the page. "Yeah?"

"I have an idea!"

"What?" She sounds irritated. Emma hates being interrupted when she's reading.

"A cure for the plague!" My voice rises in excitement. The counselors watching the movie shush me, and I lower it to a whisper again. "We need to round up Cassidy and Megan and Becca. It's time to work a little mother-daughter book club magic."

"It is possible that what stirred inside her head
at that moment was her brain, waking up. She was nine
years old, and she was in the third-A grade at school,
but that was the first time she had ever had
a whole thought of her very own."
—*Understood Betsy*

CASSIDY

"Your Uncle Henry is just daft on being read aloud to . . ."
—*Understood Betsy*

When I was a little kid, the Fourth of July ranked right up there with Christmas and Halloween as one of my favorite holidays.

We lived in California back then. My dad loved boats, and we had a small ketch that we'd sail over to the Old Glory Boat Parade in Newport Beach. Afterward, we'd hang out with friends until it was time for fireworks.

It was magical.

And then my father died, and we left California and moved across the country, and things were pretty bleak for a while. But life has a way of surprising you, and some of my surprises have included a stepfather I've grown to love and a baby sister I adore. Not to mention the mother-daughter book club, which I hated at first, but which I can't imagine not being a part of now.

A person could get kind of choked up thinking about this kind of stuff, if a person was the type to get choked up.

Which I'm not.

I finish stretching and turn to face the nearly two dozen campers and counselors milling around behind me. "ARE YOU READY, CAMP LOVEJOY?" I holler at them.

"READY!" they all holler back, and I punch my fist into the air and let out a whoop. We're at the starting line of the Pumpkin Falls Four on the Fourth road race with what feels like half of New Hampshire. The excitement in the air is electric.

I scoped out the route yesterday on my early-morning run. It's a 4K loop that heads out of town through the covered bridge, follows the river for half a mile or so, crosses another bridge and doubles back through the tiny downtown, then goes straight up Hill Street. That's the toughest part, especially toward the top, where it gets really steep. From there, though, it's all downhill—literally—as the route cuts over to the main road and back through the covered bridge again to the finish line.

Even though it's mostly a "just for fun" kind of race (the prizes are gift certificates for ice cream cones at the General Store, and everyone who finishes gets one), I can still feel the adrenaline kicking in as we approach the start time.

"Hey, Camp Lovejoy!" someone calls. I look over to see a group of guys nearby, watching us. The tallest one, who looks to be about my age, is wearing a neon green T-shirt. He turns his back to us and points to the words CAMP PINEWOOD STAFF printed across it. "Hope you like the view, because that's what you're going to see all the way to the finish line!"

Heather Vogel Frederick

"In your dreams!" I shout back at him.

Now my adrenaline is *really* pumping. I can't help it; I was born competitive.

Scanning the crowd, I spot my friends and the rest of the campers gathered at the edge of the village green, near the church with the big steeple. They came on the buses from camp and will be waiting for us there at the finish line. They've all tied red bandannas around their necks, and together with camp's regulation white polos and navy shorts, they're a patriotic-looking bunch. Jess spots me, and there's a flutter of American flags as she and the rest of our cabin wave them at me. I wave back.

A moment later, a voice over the loudspeaker tells us to take our places.

The other counselors and I coordinated ahead of time as to who would be placed where, and I'm on tap to keep pace with the three fastest campers. Melissa Yee volunteered to run sweep with the slowest ones, and Brianna is keeping an eye on the middle of the pack. No campers from Nest or Balsam are running, but Brooklyn Alvarez runs regularly with her mother back home, so we gave her permission to sign up. She may only be nine, but she's strong and she's fast.

At the crack of the starting pistol, we're off.

It's a gorgeous morning, sunny and clear with a bit of a breeze. Our thundering herd makes a racket pounding across the wooden floor of the covered bridge. I look over at Brooklyn and cover my ears, grinning. She grins back.

Once we reach the other side of the bridge, the herd starts to thin out. The group from Camp Pinewood, including neon T-shirt guy, are ahead of us. For now, anyway. If it's up to me, things won't stay that way.

"Wanna see if we can catch them?" I ask Brooklyn and the other two campers in my care. They nod enthusiastically. "Let's kick it up a notch then, ladies!"

Our group closes in on the Pinewood runners as we approach Main Street. The sidewalks are packed with cheering onlookers, and we wave and smile at them. I haven't run a road race in a while, and I've forgotten how much fun they are. The four of us fall back a bit as we begin heading up the big hill. I wasn't planning on being in it to win it this morning—not with campers to keep an eye on—but when neon T-shirt guy looks back over his shoulder at us and smirks, something inside me uncorks and the competitive genie pops out.

Like I said, I can't help it.

I start to speed up, then hesitate as I realize that my campers aren't speeding up with me.

"Go for it!" calls Brooklyn. "We'll be right behind you."

"Are you sure?"

She and the other two campers nod.

I'm not a particularly fast runner, but I am an athlete, and my training pays off. As we reach the top of the hill and make the turn onto the downhill stretch, I dig deep and am rewarded with a burst of energy. I can practically reach out and touch the neon-green T-shirt

Heather Vogel Frederick

now. I pour it on, legs and arms pumping as I fly down the road. As we enter the covered bridge, I pull up even with the Pinewood pack, then whoosh past them and on across the finish line.

Neon T-shirt guy and one of his friends come over to me, panting. "Nice race," he says. "I knew if I gave you a hard time it would light a fire under you."

"As if," I retort.

He grins and extends his hand. "I'm Jake."

I shake it. "Cassidy."

"This is Chase," he says, pointing to his friend. "We're working at Pinewood this summer."

"So I gathered." I'm not giving either of them any encouragement.

"I guess we'll see you at the beach party later?"

I nod politely, and they head off toward the Pinewood buses.

Sergeant Marge marches over, brandishing her clipboard. "Where are your campers?" she demands. "You're supposed to be with them at all times."

Over her shoulder, I see my trio trot across the finish line together. "Do you mean these ones?" I ask innocently, slapping them each a high five. "Way to go, ladies!"

Sergeant Marge shoots me a look as she checks off their names. "Nobody likes a smart aleck, sport."

After the rest of our teammates cross the finish line, we all head over to the General Store to collect our hard-earned ice cream cones. The bus ride back to camp nearly deafens me, thanks to the boisterous, nonstop songs. What is it with Camp Lovejoy and singing?

Back at camp, I hit the showers, then head to the Dining Hall.

"I'm starving," I tell Jess, who's on the porch steps handing out bag lunches. I grab one and peer inside. Ethel and Thelma must have their hands full getting ready for the big barbecue later today, because the contents are pretty low-tech: PB&J, an apple, and an oatmeal cookie.

"You're always starving," Jess replies, sneaking me a second bag. "Bug juice is down at the water ski beach."

"Bug juice" is camp's all-purpose term for drinks: fruit juice, punch, soda, and lemonade.

I saunter down to the lake, where I find Jess and our campers sitting on beach towels with Megan and Becca and the girls from Balsam.

"Nice race," says Becca.

"Thanks! It was fun."

There's a burst of hilarity from the towels over near the kayaks. We all look over to see a group of older campers laughing hysterically about something. With Camp Pinewood due here shortly, the giggles and whispers that started a few days ago have reached a crescendo. I suspect that some contraband mirrors are floating around too, because the girls on the Hill are looking a lot spiffier than usual, and there have been some lip gloss and mascara sightings.

Boys can do that to you.

It even happens to me now and then. Not very often, though, because in my opinion there are very few guys worth busting out the

Heather Vogel Frederick

lip gloss for. Neon T-shirt guy, for example, is not lip gloss–worthy.

"So do you still think you'll be able to stop by the bookstore tomorrow on your day off?" asks Jess, handing Freddie a wet wipe. Freddie is our messy camper. She ends up with food on her somewhere after every meal. Today it's peanut butter on her nose.

"Yep," I reply. "No problem."

When Jess rounded us up the other night, all excited about a homesickness cure, it didn't take long for the mother-daughter book club to get on board. We know a great plan when we hear one.

The only fly in the ointment is Felicia, who's dead set against the whole thing.

"A camper-counselor book club? That's a stupid idea," she'd said when we invited her to join us.

Jess thinks it's because Felicia was never in a book club herself, and she's always been a little jealous of ours and how close we are because of it. Emma says it's because Felicia thinks the books we read are beneath her mighty intellect. "If we were reading Dostoevsky or something," she told us afterward, "she'd be all over it."

Whatever Felicia's reasons, we decided we're going to go ahead with our plan anyway.

"Do you think we should invite some of the other cabins?" Emma wanted to know.

Jess shook her head vigorously. "Nope. Let's just keep it to Nest, Balsam, and Twin Pines. It's more special that way, plus our cabins are the ones most in need of a homesickness cure."

This made sense, and we all agreed to keep the book club a secret from our campers until the first meeting. Our next step was picking something to read. Emma said she knew the perfect book, of course—she's read just about every book on the planet—and the next day she called the local bookstore to place our order. We're all chipping in to pay for them, as a gift to our campers.

"Attention please!" It's Sergeant Marge, marching up and down the beach, armed with her bullhorn once again. "Finish up and clean up, ladies! The buses from Pinewood will be arriving here approximately one hour from now."

Judging by the squeals from the older campers, you'd think she just announced that we'd be eating nothing but dessert for the rest of the summer. Of course, the youngest campers start to squeal too, even though they don't quite get the whole boy thing yet. They worship the girls on the Hill, though, and follow them around camp like puppies.

Rest hour is impossible. Jess and I try to get our girls to settle down, but they're way too excited. Not that I don't feel a little excited myself—not about the soon-to-be arriving boys, but about the fireworks. Who doesn't like a good old-fashioned Fourth of July?

Which starts with a song, of course:

> *You're a grand old flag, you're a high-flying flag*
> *And forever in peace may you wave.*
> *You're the emblem of the land I love.*
> *The home of the free and the brave.*

Heather Vogel Frederick

Jess's Camp Chorale greets the Pinewood buses as they arrive, bursting into song on cue as the boys clamber off. I sidle up next to Becca as they reach the finale:

Ev'ry heart beats true 'neath the Red, White and Blue,
Where there's never a boast or brag.
Should auld acquaintance be forgot,
Keep your eye on the grand old flag.

"Hey, Old Glory!" I whisper slyly, slipping my arm around her shoulders.

She shrugs it off. "Don't start with me!" she warns, but she's smiling.

I love to push Becca's buttons. Years ago, way back when we were in seventh grade, the mother-daughter book club put on a fashion show to help raise money for the taxes on Jess's family farm. Becca was in her snotty stage back then, and we teased her mercilessly about this one red, white, and blue outfit she had to model. Just to give her a taste of her own medicine, of course.

As soon as the boys are off the buses, Sergeant Marge and the head counselor from Pinewood hustle us all up the road to Upper Meadow, where they have a whole lineup of games planned. We cheer our campers on for the sack race, and the egg-on-a-spoon race, and the tug-of-war. The best one is the cracker whistling contest, which is hilarious because the littlest campers are so serious, stuffing their mouths full of salty crackers and then puckering up all determined to win, and of course they can't keep their faces straight because we're all hooting and hollering, trying to distract them and make them laugh. Tara Lindgren, who cries at the drop of a hat, is so frustrated she bursts into tears right on cue. Emma is ready with a tissue, though. She's gone through a lot of tissues since camp started, comforting her campers.

Finally, it's time for the three-legged race, which is a free-for-all for everyone in both camps, including the cabin counselors, who are teamed up in pairs.

"On your marks!" calls the head counselor, and Jess and I hop over to join the other counselors at the starting line. The two of us are so poorly matched it's ridiculous—Jess is just a whisker over five feet tall, and I tower over her at six feet—and we get to laughing so hard as the race starts that we fall down after just a couple of ungainly steps.

"Nice form, Cassidy!" calls a male voice, and I turn to see neon T-shirt guy—what was his name? Jack? Jake?—trot by in perfect sync with another Pinewood counselor. He's not wearing his neon T-shirt anymore, of course. He's in a regulation gray Pinewood polo. He gives me a brisk salute as he passes us.

Pretty much everybody else passes us too as I struggle to scramble to my feet and drag a still-laughing Jess across the finish line.

After the games are finished, we all head back down the hill to the lake for open swim, and then it's time for the barbecue.

"One of each, please," I tell Artie, who's manning the grill, and he obligingly serves me up a hamburger and a hot dog.

Heather Vogel Frederick

"Growing girls need food to grow on," he replies with a wink.

I really like Gwen's husband.

I pile a huge helping of Ethel and Thelma's homemade potato salad onto my plate, add an ear of corn, a piece of watermelon, some baked beans, and top it all off with a bag of chips. Grabbing some bug juice, I go to look for a seat.

"Over here!"

It's neon T-shirt guy again.

I ignore him, and shading my eyes I search for Jess and our girls. They're crammed in around one of the picnic tables, and Jess waves me away with an I've got it covered gesture. I shrug, heading reluctantly to the Pinewood table instead.

"Hey, guys," I say, taking a seat on the bench.

"Hey, Cassidy," Jake—or is it Jack?—replies. I feel kind of bad for forgetting his name, since he clearly remembers mine. "Chase and I would like to introduce you to our campers."

Like Emma and Felicia, the two of them have the youngest cabin.

"You took a lot of food," pipes up one little boy in glasses at the far end. He's staring at my heaped-up plate.

"Yes I did," I reply, keeping a straight face. "Growing girls need good food to grow on."

He looks at me suspiciously. "You're not still growing."

Across the table, Jack/Jake is grinning at me again.

"You don't think so?" I raise my eyebrows. "I was your height just a couple of months ago."

He stares at me, and so do the rest of the little boys at the table, trying to figure out if I'm teasing them or not. They look so puzzled I finally have to laugh. "You're right, I do eat a lot of food, but then I have to," I explain. "Athletes need to keep their strength up. I'm playing hockey at Boston University this fall."

"You don't want to tangle with a Terrier, Jake," says Chase, nudging his friend as he looks at me with new respect.

Jake. I file his name away for future reference.

"Maybe, maybe not," Jake replies, smiling.

After dinner, I join my cabin again, and we loll around the waterfront, playing horseshoes and sand volleyball with Nest and Balsam and the younger campers from Pinewood while we wait for the fireworks.

Which is when I get even for the three-legged race.

I time it perfectly, too, waiting until everyone's attention is riveted on the bursts of color in the sky. Then I grab the cooler full of slushy leftover ice and sneak up behind Jake and Chase.

"HAPPY FOURTH!" I bellow, sloshing the cooler's contents over their heads.

They both let out gratifyingly high-pitched squeals of rage, and I sprint for cover. I barely manage to get away, and then only because I know the terrain and they don't. I stay hidden behind the boathouse until the fireworks are over and it's time for Pinewood to leave. Once the two of them are safely on one of the buses, I emerge to join the throng of girls waving good-bye.

Heather Vogel Frederick

"You'd better watch your back!" yells Jake, sticking his head out the window when he spots me.

I just laugh.

"We'll even the score when you least expect it!" Chase promises.

I'm still laughing as the buses chug up the hill.

The next morning I'm awake early, excited about my day off. First, though, I swim over to Cherry Island and back with the Polar Bear Club—the campers and counselors who get up at 5:30 a.m. every Tuesday and Thursday to make the one-mile round-trip swim. It's a good way to vary my workouts.

After breakfast, I sign out at the office, where I'm given my cell phone back for the day; then I hop in the minivan and head for Pumpkin Falls. The bookstore isn't open yet, so I grab a couple of doughnuts from Lou's Diner (completely canceling the benefits of my workout, but hey, it's my day off), and wander over to hang out on one of the rocking chairs on the porch of the General Store. I have a zillion text messages waiting for me, and it takes me a while to sort through them. My heart skips a beat when I see that there's one from Tristan.

IN CHICAGO. TIME 2 TALK?

Unfortunately, his message is from three days ago.

SORRY, I text back. JUST GOT THIS NOW. STILL IN U.S.?

I wait a bit, but there's no reply. I try calling, but it goes straight to voice mail. He must either be on the ice or traveling. I can't keep track of his competition schedule.

I think about calling my sister Courtney, but then I remember it's, like, six a.m. in L.A., so I call my mother instead.

"Sweetie!" she cries when she hears my voice.

I smile. "Hey, Mom!"

We talk for a while—she's wrapped up in wedding plans, of course, and fills me in on every little detail—and then I ask to say hi to my little sister.

"Miss me, Monkey Face?" I ask when she gets on the phone.

"I heard that!" says my mother in the background. She hates it when I call Chloe "Monkey Face." Which is why I do it, of course.

"When are you coming home?" Chloe demands.

"Four more weeks," I tell her. "Ask mom to show you on the calendar. But I'll see you soon for Parents' Weekend."

I hear barking in the background, and then heavy panting on the phone, which Chloe is clearly holding up for our dog.

"Murphy wanted to say hi too," my little sister says when she gets back on. "Do you miss him?"

"Not as much as I miss you," I tell her.

"Do you want to talk to Murphy again?"

"I'd rather talk to you." Chloe ignores me, of course. I hear more panting, so I try to coax a bark out of Murphy, which alarms an older gentleman sitting near me. He gets up and moves to a rocking chair farther down the porch. Despite my efforts, Murphy doesn't bark back. He's pretty ancient now, and almost completely deaf.

It's close to ten by the time I get off the phone, so I head down

Heather Vogel Frederick

Main Street to Lovejoy's Books. The bell over the door rings as I enter, and a golden retriever who's napping on a dog bed in front of the sales counter raises its head and glances over at me with idle curiosity.

"Hey, boy," I say, squatting down to give him a pat. Despite what I told my sister, I really do miss Murphy.

"She's a girl, actually," says a voice from the other side of the counter. "Her name is Miss Marple."

"Miss Marple like in the Agatha Christie mysteries?"

"Got it in one," the voice replies, and I straighten up to see a tall woman—as tall as me if not a little taller, in fact—smiling at me.

"My stepfather is a big Agatha Christie fan," I tell her, smiling back.

I try not to stare as she steps out from behind the counter. She's dressed kind of like a cross between Mrs. Wong and Mrs. Chadwick back in her "it's a whole new me" phase. A few years ago, Becca's mother had a midlife crisis and underwent a transformation, egged on by Megan's friend Wolfgang, the fashion editor of *Flash* magazine. Mrs. Chadwick cut her hair in this spiky style and started wearing bizarre clothing in superbright colors and loud animal prints. Becca was mortified, of course, but the rest of us thought it was hilarious.

The bookstore lady is decked out in orange leggings, earthy-crunchy sandals, orange-and-white striped socks, and a loose, flowing white top and beads. Lots of beads.

"How can I help you?" she asks.

"I'm here to pick up an order for Emma Hawthorne," I tell her.

Her eyebrows shoot up. "So you're the one who ordered two dozen copies of *Understood Betsy*?"

"Sort of. Emma's actually the one who ordered them—I'm just her friend. We're counselors together at Camp Lovejoy."

The woman's face lights up. "That's where my nieces are spending the summer! Do you know Lauren and Pippa Lovejoy?"

"Sure. Pippa's in Nest—she's one of Emma's campers."

"Well then, you're practically family! And seeing how that's the case," she continues briskly, going back behind the counter, "I'm prepared to offer you the special family discount." She rings up our order, which ends up being almost twenty dollars less than we'd calculated.

"Hey, thanks," I tell her as she slides a box of books across the counter.

"Why so many copies, may I ask?"

I explain about our mother-daughter book club at home, the plague of homesickness at camp, and Jess's brainstorm about starting a book club with our campers to try to tame it.

"Splendid idea!" says the bookseller when I'm done. "Nothing beats bibliotherapy." Seeing my puzzled expression, she adds, "Book therapy."

"Right."

"I'm sure the girls will love reading *Understood Betsy*—it was one of my favorites when I was growing up. Have you read it?"

I shake my head.

"You're in for a treat. Speaking of which, how would you like to take yesterday's leftover pumpkin whoopie pies back to your campers?"

"I never turn down food."

Heather Vogel Frederick

She laughs. "A girl after my own heart. Hang on a sec while I get them."

She disappears into the back office, reappearing shortly with a second box. "Here you go," she says, stacking it on top of the first one. "They're our signature treat."

"Wow, thanks!"

"You're welcome." She sticks out her hand. "True Lovejoy."

I shake it. "Cassidy Sloane."

"Hope to see you in here again, Cassidy Sloane."

"If you bake whoopie pies every day, you definitely will," I promise her.

The rest of my day off passes swiftly. I meet up with a couple of other Camp Lovejoy counselors for lunch and a hike, and afterward we hang out at one of the lake's public beaches, swimming and lazing in the sun.

"We ran into some guys from Pinewood at the General Store this morning," Brianna tells me. "They have the day off too, and they invited us to meet them at the drive-in tonight. Want to come?"

I feel a pang of nostalgia. We used to have a drive-in theater back in California when I was little, and my dad took me and my sister Courtney to the movies there often. "Wish I could, but I have other plans," I tell them. "Maybe another time."

Jess and Emma are eager to get started with the book club. Plus, it's Felicia's night off tonight, so the timing is perfect.

"You're back early," says Sergeant Marge as I sign in at the office. She holds out her hand for my cell phone.

"Yeah," I tell her, turning it over reluctantly. I still haven't had any luck reaching Tristan. "I'm going to call it a night. I'm still kind of tired from yesterday's run."

I leave quickly, before she can call me "sport" again, and head back to Twin Pines. It's in an uproar.

"I had to let them in on the secret, since we're hosting," Jess explains. "They've been pinging off the walls since dinner."

"Girls!" I say severely, doing my best imitation of my mother in displeased Queen Clementine mode. The cabin instantly quiets down. "The whole camp is going to know something's up if you don't settle down," I continue in a whisper.

"When will everyone be here?" Carter whispers back.

"Soon," I reply. "Now you two get on up there," I tell her and Brooklyn, pointing to Brooklyn's top bunk at the rear of the cabin. "And Freddie and Nica, you two double up on Freddie's bunk underneath. We need to make room for everyone."

Balsam is the first to arrive, scuttling over to join us as soon as the on-duty counselor finishes her first patrol around Lower Camp. I hold the door open as the girls dash inside. Megan brings up the rear, arms piled high with extra blankets and comforters.

"Good idea," I murmur.

She nods. "Gotta keep everyone cozy."

As Jess sorts the campers onto bunks, another tap on the door signals that Nest has arrived. Emma's girls cluster around her like ducklings, staring at the rest of us with round eyes. Tara is clutching Jess's teddy bear. Jess has pretty much given up on trying to get it back.

"Ith it a party?" asks Pippa.

"Kind of," Emma tells her. "You'll see."

Jess leads the little trio over to the last empty bunk, and they take their places on it obediently while Emma tucks some of the extra blankets around them.

"Snug as bugs in a rug," she tells them. Giggling, their feet bounce under the blankets in excitement.

"So," Jess announces, as Megan and Becca sit down on my bed and Emma perches at the foot of Jess's, "we're going to start a book club!"

Meri's dark ponytail swings back and forth as she looks from me to the other counselors. "What's a book club?"

"It means we're all going to read the same book at the same time," Jess explains, holding up a copy of *Understood Betsy*. "This one. And then we'll get together once a week and talk about it."

"I thought this was going to be something fun!" groans Grace Friedman.

"Reading together sounds like school," says her friend Mia, and Kate Kwan nods too. Tara is looking as if she might cry. But then, she always does.

"There will be snacks," I assure them, and the campers perk up at this. All except Amy, whose forehead puckers in concern.

"But we're not allowed to have food in the cabins," she whispers. "It says so in the rule book."

"So don't tell anybody, okay?" I hold my finger to my lips.

"We're all in a book club back home, and we always have snacks," Megan explains. "At our kickoff meetings, we usually go out for ice cream."

"Ice cream!" squeals Meri, and Emma shushes her.

"Okay, enough about the snacks, it's time to talk about the book," says Jess. "Your counselors are going to take turns reading it aloud to you during rest hour, and then, when we have our book club meetings, we'll all talk about it together."

"And have snacks, right?" Meri sounds anxious.

Emma looks over at Megan and Becca and me and bugs her eyes at us in mock exasperation. "Yes, and have snacks."

"During rest hour?" Tara asks.

"No, just at our meetings," Emma tells her.

"Can we have our thnacks now?" asks Pippa.

Emma sighs. Becca and Jess are biting their lips, trying not to laugh. Megan shakes her head in disbelief. I just grin. None of them have little sisters. This is totally the way Chloe thinks. She has a one-track mind, especially when treats are involved.

"Why not?" I say, getting up and pulling the box with the pumpkin whoopie pies out from under my bed. "No time like the present. And speaking of presents, Pippa's aunt sent along our snacks for tonight."

"My aunt True? I love her!" cries Pippa, and Meri clamps a hand over her cabinmate's mouth to shush her.

While I'm passing around the whoopie pies, Emma hands out

pieces of paper. "This is a Fun Fact sheet," she tells the girls. "We do this in our book club back at home, too. It's so you girls can learn a little something about the author."

"Emma is turning into her mother right before our eyes," I whisper to my friends.

FUN FACTS ABOUT DOROTHY

1) Dorothy Canfield Fisher was born Dorothea Frances Canfield on February 17, 1879, in Lawrence, Kansas.

2) She was named for a character in a novel: Dorothea Brooke in George Eliot's *Middlemarch*. Her family called her "Dolly" when she was growing up.

3) Her father was a professor and her mother was an artist and writer.

4) Dorothy spent summers at her grandparents' home in Arlington, Vermont, and would later move there permanently with her husband.

5) When she was ten, she moved to Paris for a year with her mother, who was pursuing her art studies.

6) Dorothy took fencing and boxing in high school, as well as swimming and diving.

"Sounds like a kindred spirit," I say approvingly when I read this.

7) She flatly refused to wear a corset.

"Definitely a kindred spirit," I add.

8) Dorothy once said: "A mother is not a person to lean on, but a person to make leaning unnecessary."

"Great quote," I tell Emma. "It sounds like something my mom would say."

"Yeah," she replies. "Mine too."

"I love it that she was named after a character in a novel," says Jess. "Just like you and Darcy, Emma."

Emma's mother is a Jane Austen nut, and she named Emma and her brother after characters from a couple of Jane Austen's books.

"Everybody ready for me to start the story?" Jess asks, and our campers all nod. "Okay, here we go then: *Understood Betsy*, by Dorothy Canfield Fisher."

"When this story begins, Elizabeth Ann, who is the heroine of it, was a little girl of nine, who lived with

Heather Vogel Frederick

her Great-aunt Harriet in a medium-sized city in a
medium-sized State in the middle of the country;
and that's all you need to know about the place, for
it's not the important thing in the story; and anyhow
you know all about it because it was probably very
much like the place you live in yourself."

I lean back against the cabin wall and close my eyes. I actually really like being read aloud to. I always have. My dad used to read to me when I was little, and sometimes now when my mother is putting Chloe to bed, I go in and sit on the floor and listen while she reads to her. My little sister loves bedtime stories. She's especially crazy about the silly ones that Stanley makes up for her—especially the dorky ongoing adventures of this character he calls "the fastest little weasel in the forest."

All of a sudden our cabin door flies open with a loud bang.

I jump, startled, and our campers all shriek and clutch one another.

Felicia is standing in the doorway. Sergeant Marge is right behind her.

"I came back early from my night off, and I couldn't find you!" Felicia says accusingly to Emma. "I was worried, so I went and got Marge."

"What's going on in here?" the head counselor demands.

"We're, uh, reading," says Jess.

"Doesn't look like that's all you're doing." Sergeant Marge's eyes narrow as she spots the whoopie pie box. "Is that *food*?"

"Um," I say, sliding the evidence under the bed with my big toe. "Maybe?"

She glowers at me, an expression I'm beginning to know all too well. "You know the rules. No food in the cabins, no exceptions."

Tara starts to cry. Amy Osborne quickly follows suit, and one look at Freddie and Nica tells me they're on the verge.

"I want to go home!" Meri whimpers.

So much for the homesickness cure, and so much for getting our counselor-camper book club off to a good start.

Final score? Sergeant Marge and Felicia: one. Cassidy? That would be another big fat zero, sport.

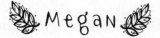

Megan

"Elizabeth Ann had never had anything to do with children younger than herself, and she felt very pleased and important to have anybody look up to her."
—*Understood Betsy*

"This is the life!" says Becca, leaning back in her chair on the Art Studio deck and lifting her face to the sun. We have ten minutes before the next group of campers descends, and we're making the most of it.

"No kidding." I lean back too. Closing my eyes, I listen to the breeze rustling through the branches overhead and the lazy lap of water against the shore a few yards below. I'm more of a city girl than an outdoors girl, but even I have to admit this is a pretty fabulous place. "So," I continue, "what are we going to do about Amy?"

Becca whooshes out her breath.

Little Amy Osborne is still our problem camper. At least she's not crying herself to sleep every night like she did the first week she was here. But she's still scared of everything in sight, and she's still home-sick. Having Sergeant Marge burst in on our first book club meeting didn't help either.

Plus, somehow Amy has convinced herself that her parents are going to move away while she's here in New Hampshire.

"This isn't 'Hansel and Gretel,'" I've assured her over and over. "You haven't been dumped in the forest to fend for yourself. Besides, you just got a letter from your parents, remember? Same return address. And didn't they tell you they're planning to come for Parents' Weekend?"

I sympathize, really I do. Amy is an only child, like me, and she's used to being part of a tight family unit. Plus, she's never been away from home for this long. But anything outside of her comfort zone, which pretty much means anywhere beyond her violin, is intimidating and requires lots of hand-holding and pep talks. The swim test was a huge deal; so was her first hike. Water skiing and wake tubing are out of the question, of course. Even our super-fun Cabin Night canoe bubble bath last week—which was a big hit with all of our other campers—drove Amy to tears, thanks to a run-in with a drowned June bug.

"How do you solve a problem like our Amy?" sings Becca softly, to the familiar tune from *The Sound of Music.* "I don't know what else we can do, Megs. Just continuing doing what we're doing, I guess. Gwen says campers are like plants, remember? We need to give them—"

"Plenty of water and sunshine, I know."

Encouragement and love, Gwen keeps telling us, are the water and sunshine that campers thrive on, and the secret ingredients to being successful counselors.

Gwen totally saved our bacon after the book club fiasco.

Sergeant Marge was breathing fire after she spotted the whoopie

Heather Vogel Frederick

pie leftovers. Leaving Felicia with all of our campers, she hauled the rest of us over to the Director's Cottage for a showdown. I guess she figured Gwen would bawl us out, and maybe even fire us. In fact, I think she was secretly hoping for that. But after Emma and Jess finished explaining what we were doing and why, Gwen had just smiled.

"Brilliant!" she'd said. "We told you girls to be creative, didn't we, Marge? I can't think of a more creative cure for homesickness than this one." She'd looked over at the head counselor, who was still clearly unhappy with us, and lowering her voice to a stage whisper, added, "I think we can stretch the rules this once."

Gwen made the book club official, and told us we could use Hilltop Lodge for our meetings. Hilltop is just down the path from the Art Studio, and it's smaller and cozier than Lower Lodge. Plus, it has a woodstove. One night a week, our three cabins will have it all to ourselves. We've got everything figured out—each of us will take a turn hosting a meeting, and then during the last week of camp we'll have a big end-of-the-summer and end-of-the-book party.

Shrieks of laughter pierce the quiet, signaling that the next group of campers are on their way. Becca and I haul ourselves out of our chairs and go back inside, where two tables are already prepped with supplies for the craft we have planned for second period: Popsicle stick keepsake boxes.

For the next hour, I'm up to my elbows in glue guns and glitter, shells, sequins, tiny pinecones, acorns, beads, fabric rosettes, and paint. Becca and I make our way around the tables, instructing and offering

Mother-Daughter Book Camp

suggestions. It's not as easy as it sounds. There's a wide age spread among the campers, and some of the younger girls are struggling.

"Mine is stupid," grumbles Meri, gazing with envy at the turquoise perfection of a painted box belonging to one of the girls from Outback, the cabin on the Hill for the oldest campers.

"No it isn't." I hand her a small blue jay feather. "Here, why don't you glue this to the lid, right there between the acorns? It matches your pretty eyes."

She gives me a shy smile, and I move along to Carter Stevens from Cassidy and Jess's cabin. Carter is carefully stenciling the outline of a leaf on the lid of her box. "Nice," I tell her, nodding. "Is it for you?"

She shakes her head. "It's a present for my best friend back at home."

"Maybe you could paint a message for her inside," I suggest. "You know, as a surprise for when she opens it."

Carter's face lights up. "Sweet!"

No one is quite finished by the time the lunch bell rings, so the girls place their projects on one of the studio's many shelves.

"You can come back any day this week and finish up," Becca tells them.

The two of us do a quick tidy-up after the campers leave, then head down the path to the Dining Hall.

"I'm having fun so far," says Becca, linking her arm through mine. "How about you?"

I nod.

Heather Vogel Frederick

"Still regretting not going to New York?"

I laugh. "I've hardly had time to even *think* about New York!" It's true—being a counselor is all-consuming.

"*Flash* said they'd let you do the internship next summer, right?"

"Yeah," I reply. "I made Wolfgang promise."

"Fabulous, darling!" Becca's voice swoops dramatically in a Wolfgang impression.

I have to pinch myself sometimes, to think that I'm actually friends with one of the top editors at one of the top fashion magazines in the world. Wolfgang and I have known each other since I was in sixth grade. He took me under his wing, encouraged my interest in fashion, and even hired me to cover Fashion Week in Paris as a teen correspondent for *Flash* a couple of years ago.

He also helped me with my blog. *Fashionista Jane* got me in a lot of trouble for a while there, thanks to an excess of what my mother calls "snark," but I've had a lot of fun with it these past few years. It's temporarily on hold for the summer, since there's not much to blog about anyway, fashion-wise, between sleepy Pumpkin Falls and a camp full of girls in uniforms. I can't wait to fire it up again this fall, though—in New York! I already have the title for my first post: "Fashionista Jane Takes a Bite of the Big Apple." It will be fun to record my first impressions of life in the city through the eyes of my slightly snarky alter ego.

Tuna melts are on the menu for lunch—not my favorite sandwich, but I'm hungry enough to eat just about anything. For some reason, I'm starving almost all the time here at camp. So is Becca. She says it's all the fresh air and exercise we're getting, but I'm not sure about that, because really the only exercise I'm getting is walking back and forth to the Art Studio. And to the Biffy, and the Dining Hall, and the Lower Lodge, and—okay, maybe she's right. That's a lot more walking than I usually do.

As I'm wolfing down my lunch, Cassidy Sloane–style, I notice Amy and Harper toying with their uneaten sandwiches.

"You know the rules, girls," I remind them, watching as Amy pokes at the tuna in disgust. "Two bites."

They both grimace at me. Amy and Harper hate this rule. We're supposed to strictly enforce it, though. It's part of the whole "Broadening Horizons for over a Century" thing.

"Girls." I try to sound firm without being stern. Stern makes Amy cry.

Harper holds her nose and forces herself to take a bite. Amy slowly follows suit, swallowing with painful effort.

"I don't like tuna melts," she whispers, her big dark eyes filling up with tears.

I don't either, I want to tell her, but I don't. "Camp is about broadening your horizons, remember?" I say cheerfully instead, channeling Gwen. "That means trying new things—even tuna melts."

"What's the most fun thing you did this morning?" asks Becca, in an attempt to distract them.

Harper brightens. "I passed my float test in swimming."

I reach across the table and slap her a high five. "Wow, that's great! You can go out to the big float now!"

Heather Vogel Frederick

Becca turns to Amy. "How about you, Amy?"

"I saw a chipmunk," she replies cautiously.

"How cool is that?" says Becca, shooting me an amused look. Chipmunks are about the only thing Amy likes about camp. She's been trying, unsuccessfully, to tame one that lives under Balsam.

Each of our campers chimes in with her accomplishments as I go around the table, asking the campers for an update on their mornings.

"Ladies, I am impressed!" I tell them when they're done. "I'm having lunch with masters of archery, canoeing, and the tennis court! All I've done today is cover myself in glitter." I hold up a forearm to prove it, which gets a laugh.

Amy and Harper perk up as the CITs bring dessert around. It's chocolate-orange tofu pudding today, which my mother would totally flip over. I naturally assumed it was hideous the first time they served it, given my extensive prior experience with tofu, but to my surprise it's actually turned out to be my favorite dessert here at camp so far.

We're just finishing up when Gwen rings the bell for announcements.

"It's Meal Ticket night!" she says as the hubbub in the Dining Hall subsides. "Counselors, I'd like you to devote rest hour today to making sure all your campers complete their assignment."

"Meal tickets" are what they call letters home here at Camp Lovejoy. They're mandatory once a week, I guess to make sure that parents hear from their kids.

"And since it's Thursday," Gwen continues, "you all know what's coming next . . ."

What sounds like thunder erupts in the dining hall, but it's really the drumming of many feet on the floor. All around the room, campers and counselors alike hold up crossed fingers, grinning in anticipation. Tuesdays and Thursdays are when Gwen chooses a cabin to sleep over on *Dreamboat.*

Sergeant Marge parades over to Gwen, holding aloft a big glass fishbowl. The camp director dips a hand inside and pulls out a slip of paper. She holds up her other hand for silence, and the drumming stops.

"And the cabin that will be spending the night aboard *Dreamboat* is . . . Balsam!"

Becca lets out a whoop. I leap to my feet and do a little victory dance as our campers squeal in excitement. Cassidy and Jess give us a big thumbs-up from the other end of the table.

"Marge will give you full instructions after dinner," Gwen tells us. "Meanwhile, girls, whenever your table is finished with lunch, the mail is ready for pickup."

It's Becca's turn to collect ours, so the rest of us clear our dishes, then hustle outside to wait.

"We're going on *Dreamboat!*" sings Grace, linking arms with Kate and Mia. Catching Grace's eye, I nod my head slightly at Harper and Amy, and she turns to them and adds, "You guys are going to love it!"

Harper quickly joins in their excited chatter, but Amy hangs

Heather Vogel Frederick

back, her big dark eyes clouded with concern. I slip an arm around her shoulders.

"I'm sure Grace is right—*Dreamboat's* going to be fun."

Amy doesn't look convinced.

"So, are you still planning to try quilting?" I ask. "Becca is hoping to see you during free period."

She nods.

It's kind of hilarious that Becca of all people is teaching quilting. It's the last thing I ever would have expected her to develop an interest in, but she spent this past spring break in Minnesota with her grandmother again, and came home a full-fledged quilter. I think her grandmother brainwashed her. Grandmothers can do that.

Summer Williams is thrilled, of course. She's one of our friends from the Wyoming book club we're all pen pals with, and that we visited a few years ago. Summer's been a mad quilter ever since we've known her. I have one of her quilts on my bed at home, in fact. It's one of my prized possessions and will definitely be coming with me to the dorm at Parsons in September. Anyway, Becca and Summer chat online all the time now, sharing patterns and tips and mailing fabric squares back and forth.

Becca finally emerges from the office with our mail. There's not much for the girls, just a letter each for Harper and Grace, but I have a care package from Gigi and Sophie, a postcard from Wolfgang, and a letter from my mother.

"Lucky you," sighs Becca. "Not a thing for me today."

"Like you've got anything to complain about!" I retort. "Theo has written to you practically every day since we got here."

I duck into my cubie before rest hour to take a quick peek inside the care package. Score! Gigi and Sophie came through with more goodies. No French candy this time around, but they sent homemade brownies, which is even better. I stick my nose in the tin and breathe in the heavenly smell of chocolaty goodness. If I weren't so full of pudding, I'd have to sample one. I close the tin and put it in my footlocker for later. It's the perfect thing to sneak aboard *Dreamboat* tonight.

Between supervising the writing of meal tickets and keeping a lid on the excitement about our sleepover, rest hour is not very restful. Our girls are practically bouncing off the walls with anticipation. All except Amy, that is. I can hear Becca over by her bunk, trying to comfort her. Amy's convinced that she's going to sleepwalk, which she's never done in her entire life, and fall into the lake in the middle of the night and drown.

"What if *Dreamboat* sinks, like the *Titanic*?" Amy whispers.

Becca and I exchange a quick glance. One of the things we've had to learn as counselors is not to crack up when campers say something unintentionally funny. Which is hard, because they often do. I tuck this one away to share with our friends later.

"First of all, Amy, *Dreamboat* is not going to sink," Becca assures her. "And second, even if it did, it's anchored in the cove, where the water's barely over your head."

Amy's worried look doesn't budge.

Heather Vogel Frederick

"You could always wear a life vest over your pajamas, I guess," Becca jokes, and Amy perks up at this suggestion. Becca looks over at me and rolls her eyes.

Eventually we get everybody settled down and busy writing their letters home, and I finally have a chance to read my mail.

Wolfgang's postcard has a picture of a swanky New York hotel on the front, and a brief message on the back, penned in his trademark spiky handwriting:

> Hope your time in the north woods is FABULOUS,
> darling! Can't wait to have you here in MY neck of the
> woods! Tea at the Palm Court as soon as you're settled in
> the dorm? Kisses!

I grin. It doesn't matter if he's on the phone, sending me an e-mail, or writing me a postcard, Wolfgang always manages to sound like Wolfgang.

Next I open the letter from my mother.

> Dear Megan,
> We're all looking forward to Parents' Weekend so
> much! The house seems too quiet since you've been gone.
> Coco checks your room every day to see if maybe you've
> magically reappeared, and I find her curled up on your bed
> often.

I give my eyes a surreptitious swipe, embarrassed to realize that I've been struck by a sudden pang of homesickness. All I need to do is start crying—that would totally set Amy off.

We can't wait to see you, and meet your campers, and tour the Art Studio and the Gazebo and the Dining Hall and all the other places that you've described to us.

Life here in Concord continues apace. As always, work in general keeps me busy, especially since my referendum about soda in the schools is gathering steam. With any luck, it will pass and we can have it in place before the new school year starts.

Your grandmother and Edouard are looking forward to their trip to France at the end of the summer. They're planning to spend a few weeks at their cottage after they help get Sophie settled at the Sorbonne.

I've talked to Sophie about the possibility of doing my junior year abroad in Paris, and she's excited about it too. She's going to ask and see if I might be able to room with her in her dorm. I would love that.

It's hard to believe that you're all grown up and about to start college. You'll be spreading your wings for the wider world soon. You leave for Parsons in 56 days—can you believe it?

Heather Vogel Frederick

My mother is counting the days? This surprises me. Does that mean she can't wait for me to leave, or that she'll miss me? Is she worried about the whole empty-nest thing everybody talks about? At least she'll still have our cats, Coco and Truffle, to keep her company. And Gigi and Edouard too, most of the year. The nest won't really be empty.

I miss you, Megan Rose! See you soon!

Lots of love,
Mom

P.S. Your father and I have a surprise for you! We're planning to bring it with us for Parents' Weekend.

A surprise? That sounds intriguing. I fold the letter up and put it in the envelope, wondering what it could be. I know it's not a car—I've wanted one forever, but after Gigi and Edouard got married, we added the truck they bought to help out with teashop deliveries to the two cars already in our garage, and there wasn't room. Plus, with three vehicles in the family now there's almost always one around for me to use, so it didn't make sense. And I'm certainly not going to need one in New York. It's not a car kind of city. It's a subway and bus and walk everywhere kind of city.

I ponder the surprise all through third and fourth period—more Popsicle stick boxes—and only manage to put it out of my mind when the bell rings for free period.

I have to admit, this is my favorite time of day. Crafts are fun and everything, and the campers absolutely love doing them, but fashion is my world, and free period is when I get to play in my sandbox.

When we were planning stuff during pre-camp, I decided to divide the six weeks of camp into half a dozen different projects. That way, I figured, some girls who might want just a taste of fashion design could take a class with me for a week, complete a whole project, and then go off and do other things during free period over the rest of the summer. And those who want to do nothing but sew all summer would have a chance to work on multiple projects.

Last week, we kicked things off with easy fabric hobo bags. That was a big hit, and I actually have several girls back this week who are making more, as presents for their moms and sisters and friends back home.

But the main project this week is a sarong-style skirt that can double as a swimsuit cover-up. I brought yards and yards of gauzy fabric in various shades that I thought would be perfect. Everyone picked out their fabric yesterday, and we got started cutting it. Today we'll be pinning it to the pattern that I designed and printed myself, thanks to a computer software program my dad created for me. When I'm sewing at home, I almost never use a pattern. Ideas just come to me, and I transfer them directly to the fabric. But that doesn't work for teaching. I have to be able to give the girls specific instructions.

"Hi, Megan."

I look up from where I'm setting out sewing supplies to see Amy standing shyly in the doorway.

"Hey, Amy! Looking for Becca?"

She nods.

"She's out on the deck with the other quilters," I tell her, and she gives me a fleeting smile and scurries off.

My fashionistas arrive next. They find their projects, which I've spread out on the large tables in the studio, and get to work cutting and pinning.

"That's it, but make sure the pins are all facing the same way," I tell Carter from Twin Pines. "It makes it easier to cut." I demonstrate with a few of the pins, then watch over her shoulder as she tackles the rest. "Perfect."

Circling the room, I pause at each table to answer questions and offer assistance. By the end of free period, the skirts are all cut out and most of them are pinned and ready to go. "Good job, girls!" I tell them. "Tomorrow we sew."

Back at Balsam, it's time to inspect the meal tickets. Gwen warned us that some campers would try to get away with murder, and she was right.

"Grace, you can't just write 'This is a meal ticket' inside!" I protest.

She grins at me. Kate and Mia think it's hilarious, of course.

"C'mon, you can do better than that."

Thanks to the rewrite I force her to do, we're late for dinner.

"What's on the menu?" I ask Becca, sliding into my seat.

"Chicken pot pie," she tells me.

"Mmm." Ethel and Thelma are amazing cooks. The food here is fabulous, as Wolfgang would say.

Our campers can hardly sit still, they're so excited about tonight, and dinner feels like it takes forever. Finally, Sergeant Marge comes by our table with the sleepover checklist.

"It's pretty straightforward," she tells Becca and me. "Artie swept *Dreamboat* out this afternoon and made sure there were fresh batteries in the lanterns. All you need to bring are sleeping bags, pillows, and a flashlight each. There'll be wet sacks for all your things waiting for you in the canoes at Boathouse Beach."

"When should we plan to paddle over?" Becca asks.

"At the start of evening activity," the head counselor replies. "Lights out at the usual time, and just make sure you're back in time for breakfast." She hands us a walkie-talkie. "I'll keep mine on all night in case you need anything."

After dinner, our cabin joins the rest of the campers in a circle around the grove. As a pair of CITs step forward and start to take down the flag, Gwen gives the signal and we all sing softly:

Day is done, gone the sun,
From the lakes, from the hills, from the sky;
All is well, safely rest, God is nigh.

Heather Vogel Frederick

Singing "Taps" is one of my favorite moments in the day. A hush settles over the camp, and I breathe it in, enjoying the sense of peace—for about thirty seconds, that is.

"Dreamboat!" shouts Grace the instant Gwen gives us the nod to go. She and Mia and Kate pelt down the path toward Balsam. Harper jogs along after them, red braids bouncing. Only Amy hangs back, clinging to Becca. She's still worried about the whole sleepover/shipwreck scenario.

I'm feeling nearly as giddy as our campers, to be honest. I duck into my cubie and change into my pajamas, pull a sweatshirt over them, then stuff the care package from Gigi and Sophie into my backpack. When I'm done, I head over to Balsam to get my sleeping bag and pillow and a few other things.

"Let's go, girls!" I call when our campers are ready, and Becca and I lead them down to Boathouse Beach. *Dreamboat* is bobbing peacefully at anchor out in the cove, a battery-powered lantern hanging from a hook by the bright red front door. Artie has a pair of canoes waiting for us on the beach, and after stowing our gear in the wet sacks, we all start to pile in.

"Wait—did everyone visit the Biffy?" Becca asks.

Everyone but Amy nods.

"I'll take her," I tell Becca. "Be right back."

Five minutes later, we're finally ready to go. Sergeant Marge and Artie help shove us off, and we paddle out toward the middle of the shallow cove.

"You go first," I tell Becca as we arrive at *Dreamboat*, reaching over to help steady her canoe. She and Grace, Kate, and Harper climb out. After they grab their gear, it's my turn.

Becca kneels on the front "porch" of *Dreamboat*—actually a narrow deck that juts out from the front of the floating cabin— and holds our boat steady as Mia and I clamber out.

"Come on," I say to Amy, who's still seated in the canoe. I extend my hand but she shakes her head, refusing to release her white-knuckled grip on her seat in the canoe. I sigh. "Amy, it's perfectly safe. You're going to have fun, I promise."

She shakes her head again.

I exchange a glance with Becca. It's time to resort to bribery.

"Amy, you know that package I got in the mail today?"

She peeks out at me from under her veil of dark hair and nods shyly.

"My grandmother sent a surprise for our cabin—brownies! The best homemade brownies in the entire world. If you stay in the canoe all night, you're not going to get any."

That does it. Trembling, she loosens her grip and reaches for my hand. I haul her up onto *Dreamboat*.

The floating cabin is similar to Balsam, just a bit smaller. There are four bunks, and the girls each quickly claim a spot.

"Guess you and I will be sharing a bunk bed, too," I tell Becca.

"I call top!" she says, before I have a chance to. I pretend to be mad at her, which makes our campers laugh. As they unpack their

Heather Vogel Frederick

sleeping bags and pillows, I spread a big blanket on the floor.

"How about a game of cards?" I suggest.

We play old maid and go fish and Becca and I teach them gin rummy, and then we tell them stories about goofy stuff we did when we were younger. They love hearing about how Cassidy and Emma and Jess scared the pants off us one Halloween at Sleepy Hollow Cemetery.

"Cassidy taped a flashlight to a hockey stick and stuck it inside a plastic jack-o'-lantern," I explain. "Then they waited behind one of the tombstones, and stuck it up in the air and wagged it at us when we walked by."

"Megan just about fainted," Becca tells them.

"What? You screamed so loud, all of Concord heard us!"

Mia laughs so hard she gets the hiccups.

"Tell it again," begs Harper, and I do.

As I listen to my campers' laughter, I'm aware of other sounds drifting across the cove—the slapping of screen doors, girls calling to one another in Lower Camp and on the Hill, a loon in the distance, and then Felicia playing the "lights out" "Taps" from the grove.

I also hear the splash of a paddle in the water. Peering through the dusk, I spot Sergeant Marge approaching in a kayak.

"Everything okay out here?" she calls.

"Yes!" Becca and I chorus back.

"See you in the morning, then. Sleep tight." Her paddle resumes its soothing swish as she glides away.

I wait until she's safely out of earshot, then pull out the brownie tin. "Are you guys ready for some more *Understood Betsy*?"

Our campers nod.

"You read, Becca, and I'll pass around the snacks."

Our girls climb into their sleeping bags as I distribute the brownies. Then I climb into mine, too, and we all listen as Becca reads.

> "You can imagine, perhaps, the terror of Elizabeth Ann as the train carried her along toward Vermont and the horrible Putney Farm! It had happened so quickly—her satchel packed, the telegram sent, the train caught—that she had not had time to get her wits together, assert herself, and say that she would *not* go there!"

Becca and I take turns reading the entire chapter. We follow Elizabeth Ann as she arrives at the Putney Farm, discovers that her Vermont cousins aren't as horrible as she'd been led to believe, and learns how to make butter.

"I like Elizabeth Ann," says Harper as Becca finally closes the book.

"Me too," says Kate Kwan, and the other girls all nod too.

"I like the part where she gets a kitten," says Amy softly.

"Have I told you about when my parents surprised me with a kitten for my birthday?" I ask, and they all shake their heads.

I'm in the middle of telling them about Coco's arrival when I hear

Heather Vogel Frederick

another splash outside. With a guilty start, I grab for the brownie tin and close it, then stuff it down inside my sleeping bag. Sergeant Marge must have a nose like a bloodhound. How on earth did she know?

But it isn't Sergeant Marge.

"You might as well surrender," says a low voice.

I look out the window. Cassidy holds a flashlight under her chin, grinning.

"We have you surrounded," says Jess, and their campers all giggle.

"With one canoe?" I scoff. "Liars!"

"Shhhh! What are you guys doing out here?" Becca whispers. "If Sergeant Marge catches you, you're dead!"

"Rumor has it Gigi sent a care package," Jess whispers back.

Becca and I exchange a glance. Our campers have left their beds by now and are crowded around me, jockeying for position at the window.

"She must have spotted the return address when she was picking up Twin Pines's mail today," Becca mutters.

I decide to torture my friends a bit. "Maybe we ate everything that was in it."

"Maybe you want us to dump you in the water," says Cassidy.

Beside me, I feel Amy stiffen.

"Fine," I reply hastily. "We'll share. Hang on a sec."

I wriggle out of my sleeping bag and pad across the cabin. Opening the door, I hold out the tin. Cassidy takes it. "You've gotta give some to Nest too, though," I tell her.

She snorts.

"Fat chance," adds Jess, and their campers all hoot with glee.

Cassidy shushes them. "See you in the morning, suckers!" she says to us as her canoe turns back toward shore.

"We're popular tonight," says Becca as I climb back into my sleeping bag.

"No kidding. Good night, you guys."

"Good night," everyone choruses.

As *Dreamboat* rocks gently at anchor, I lie there listening to our campers' even breathing. I close my eyes and feel myself drifting toward sleep when—

"Megan?"

I open one eye. It's Amy. "Yeah?"

"I have to go to the Biffy again."

"You went before we left!"

"I know, but I have to go again."

I heave a sigh. "Fine. Hang on a sec, honey."

Wriggling out of my sleeping bag, I pull my sweatshirt back on, slip my feet into my flip-flops, and shuffle quietly out the door. Amy is right behind me. Outside, I buckle on a life vest. Amy's already wearing hers. Not surprisingly, she opted to sleep in it.

I lift her into the canoe, then climb in myself and pass her a flashlight.

"Point it toward shore," I tell her as I start paddling.

Camp is deserted and silent. There are no lights visible in the Director's Cottage or in Cabbage or anywhere else. There's nothing but

Heather Vogel Frederick

a sliver of moon overhead and the faint beam from Amy's flashlight to light our way. *Simon would love this place,* I think, and am struck with a sudden pang of guilt.

I've hardly thought of him in days. I haven't had time to. As we approach shore, I remind myself to write him a letter during rest hour tomorrow.

Rolling the legs of my pajamas up, I step out into the shallow water. I pull the canoe quietly up onto Boathouse Beach and lift Amy out, then take her hand and lead her up the path toward the Biffy. *Is this what it's like to have a little sister?* I wonder, glancing down at her. Even though she's kind of annoying sometimes, I can't help but feel protective.

After she's done—I go again too, since we're here anyway—we start back to our canoe. We've almost reached Boathouse Beach when I hear laughter.

Male laughter.

It's coming from somewhere over by the Dining Hall.

"Stay here," I whisper to Amy, setting her in the canoe. "I'll be back in a second."

Following the muffled snickers, I sneak back across camp. I peek around the corner of the kayak shed and spot a pair of dark silhouettes down by the water. The two figures climb into a waiting canoe and push off, laughing softly. I stand there and watch as they paddle away and disappear into the darkness.

Something is clearly up.

I chew my lip, wondering if I should sound the alarm or wake Sergeant Marge. I could go get Cassidy—she'd know what to do. I don't dare leave Amy any longer, though. She's probably already convinced I've been devoured by wolves.

Sure enough, back at the canoe I find Amy clutching her paddle and sniffling. "You left me!" she says, swiping at her eyes. "I was worried I'd float away."

"Amy, the canoe is sitting on the *sand*," I reply in exasperation. "It isn't going anywhere."

Whatever the two mysterious figures were doing can wait until morning, I decide. I've had enough for one night. I paddle back to *Dreamboat*, where I dry Amy's tears and make her blow her nose and tuck her into bed again. Then I crawl into my sleeping bag, where I finally fall asleep, still wondering what the intruders were up to.

No good, that's for sure.

Heather Vogel Frederick

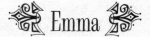 Emma

"*Aunt Harriet never meant to say any of this when Elizabeth Ann could hear, but the little girl's ears were as sharp as little girls' ears always are.* . . ."
—*Understood Betsy*

"Is that my *underwear*?"

I gape at the flagpole in shock. My favorite pair of red-and-white polka-dot underpants are pinned to the rope, fluttering proudly in the early-morning breeze alongside a bunch of other people's lingerie.

"*Forever in peace may you wave,*" sings Jess, coming up beside me. A group of campers and counselors gather behind us, pointing and laughing.

"Someone must have raided the cubies," says Melissa Yee, the counselor from Meadow.

"I heard somebody on camp property last night, but I couldn't tell what they were up to," Megan tells us. "It was two guys, I think. They got away in their canoe before I could get a closer look."

Cassidy shakes her head in disgust. "It's gotta be Pinewood."

Felicia darts across the grove and starts hauling down the parade of underwear. Her face turns as red as my underpants when she gets to a leopard-print pair. She plucks them from the rope and quickly stuffs them into the pocket of her shorts.

Becca slings an arm around my shoulders, grinning broadly. "Didn't know your co-counselor had it in her!"

"Your mother must have sent them to her," Cassidy tells her. "From the 'It's a whole new me' drawer."

"Shut up!" But Becca can't help laughing.

Sergeant Marge joins Felicia at the flagpole. "Go on in to breakfast, girls," she tells the rest of us. "We'll put everything in a laundry basket on the porch, and you can retrieve whatever's yours on the way out."

"Something's different about Sergeant Marge's face," Jess whispers.

We all turn around to look.

Jess is right. There's definitely something different about the head counselor. It takes me a minute to realize that she's *smiling*.

"Marge the Barge has a sense of humor!" Cassidy exclaims, pretending to be in shock.

The Dining Hall is abuzz with speculation as to the identity of the pranksters, and there's a lot of teasing about whose underwear was on display and whose wasn't.

"All right now, girls," says Gwen when it's time for announcements. "Settle down. It's just the boys' camp having a bit of fun. Nothing to get stirred up about. We've had this happen before, right, Marge? In fact, I distinctly recall one time back when we were campers that someone took your—"

Heather Vogel Frederick

"How about we go over the schedule?" Marge says hastily, fumbling with her clipboard. "As you all know, we've got a double-header in store with Parents' Weekend, and then our Council Fire on Sunday night."

She drones on for a while before Gwen circles back to the underwear.

"I just want to emphasize that this was a harmless prank," she tells us. "Let's not get carried away plotting payback, okay?"

My eyes slide over to where Cassidy is sitting. Too late! I can tell by the smirk on her face that she's already got a scheme in mind.

After breakfast, Felicia and I lead our campers back to Cubbyhole to get ready for our morning activities. I swear I'm starting to feel like a mother duck—wherever I go these days, I'm trailing girls.

Meri follows me into my cubie.

"Aren't you going to get ready for first period?" I ask her.

She nods, but continues to stand there.

"Is something the matter?"

Her lower lip starts to tremble. "My parents aren't coming this weekend."

"Oh, sweetie!" I put my arms around her. "It'll be okay, I promise. Tell you what, how about I share my family with you?"

My parents finally called a couple of days ago to let me know they'd arrived home safely from their trip to England. They said they sent me a bunch of postcards, but I haven't gotten any yet. In fact, I haven't gotten a single piece of mail so far this summer. I think it's some kind of a camp record. Everybody feels sorry for me.

My mom and dad are planning to caravan up with the rest of the group from Concord. All of our parents are coming except the Delaneys, who can't get away. Summer is a busy time at Half Moon Farm. My brother's coming too, as a surprise for Jess. She's going to flip when she sees him. I've almost spilled the beans about a zillion times already.

I reach for a picture in a heart-shaped frame that's sitting on my dressing table and hand it to Meri. "This is my dog," I tell her. "His name is Pip and my parents promised they'd bring him along this weekend. You'll love him. And I know he'll love you."

Meri stares at the picture, then nods. "Okay."

I hand her a tissue and help her dry her eyes and blow her nose, then send her off to her cubie to change into her swimsuit. Putting the picture back on my dressing table, I give a rueful sigh. My friends all have pictures of their boyfriends on display; I have one of my dog. How pathetic is that?

What's even more pathetic is that I still have a picture of Stewart. It's in my trunk. I try not to look at it too often, because it just makes me sad.

And mad, too, if I'm honest.

Stewart and I managed to stay together all through his freshman year in college—my junior year in high school—and three-quarters of the way through this past year. And then, at spring break, he came home and asked if we could talk.

"I can't believe you're breaking up with me!" I'd said after he told me he thought we should both date other people. Which meant that *he* wanted to date other people, of course. And probably already was.

He was nice about it—he is Stewart, after all—and in a way, I suppose I was half expecting this to happen. My mother warned me a long time ago that most high school relationships don't last through college. But I guess I thought that Stewart and I would. Afterward, he'd hugged me and told me I'd always have a special place in his heart, which wasn't exactly comforting. If I was so special, why was he breaking up with me?

And then I went and did the dumbest thing I've ever done in my life. I turned down two perfectly good colleges in Massachusetts and chose one in Canada instead. Not just anywhere in Canada either, but in British Columbia, which is practically on the other side of the world. What was I thinking?

My parents have promised that they'll come to visit me at least once a year, and I'll be able to fly home for Christmas and spring break, of course, but it's not like my brother, Darcy, who's just a couple of hours away at Dartmouth and who can come home whenever he wants. And even though I have grandparents in Seattle and will be able to see them more often now, that doesn't make up for the fact that I've stupidly decided to go to college so far away from my best friend.

"Emma, I checked, and you can hop on a bus in South Hadley or Northampton and be in New York City in four hours," Jess had informed me happily after I got accepted at Mount Holyoke and Smith and was trying to choose between them. "Or I can come visit you. Or Megan and I can meet you in Boston for one of Cassidy's games. This is going to be so much fun!"

And even more fun, since my good friend Bailey Jacobs from Wyoming got accepted at Mount Holyoke as well. I'd been leaning toward going there, and we were talking about maybe being roommates. So why did I go and ruin it all?

Now, the closer we get to September, the more terrified I feel. Jess is not just my best friend, she's my security blanket. It's not like the year we were apart when my family lived in England, either. That was different. This is *college*. It's four whole years we're talking about.

Lately, I've started thinking that maybe it's not too late. I'm really hoping that Stewart will come with his parents this weekend, and that we'll have a chance to talk. We haven't really talked since spring break. It was too awkward when he came home earlier this summer, so I just avoided him. Which was stupid and childish, because I'm convinced now that if we could just spend some time together, he'll realize he's made a mistake.

I've got the whole thing planned out in my mind. While his parents are busy with Becca, I'll offer to show him around camp. We'll end up in the Gazebo, and then we'll talk. *Really* talk. And he'll look at me with those serious gray eyes of his, and tell me that he blew it big-time, and that I'm the only one he cares about. And then he'll kiss me and the two of us will be back together again, and I'll withdraw from UBC and see if Mount Holyoke still has room for me.

I smile dreamily, imagining our romantic reunion.

Heather Vogel Frederick

The bell for first period clangs and I jump up with a start, wiggling into my bathing suit—still a bit cold and clammy from yesterday—and throwing a hoodie over it. Stuffing my feet into flip-flops, I grab my whistle and clipboard and dash out of the deserted cubie house.

"Hey, Hawthorne, we were about to send out a search party!"

It's Brianna, who's the Waterfront Head this summer.

"Sorry," I tell her. "I got sidetracked."

She jerks her chin toward a cluster of shivering seven-year-olds. "Your Guppies are all checked in and ready to go."

It's overcast and cool this morning, not exactly the kind of weather that makes a person want to jump in the lake. But that's just what I have to do with my first-period swimmers.

"Okay, everybody!" I chirp, trying to sound as enthusiastic as possible. "Are you ready to have fun?"

They nod, clutching their towels around them. Pippa's and Meri's lips are already turning slightly blue.

"Pippa, did you remember to put your glasses in their case?" They almost got stepped on yesterday, and I recall only too well the trouble I got into when I was her age and broke my glasses. She nods vigorously.

"Take your buddy's hand, then, and let's go!"

We wade out into the shallow, protected water of the inner H dock. It's actually fairly warm, thank goodness, and it doesn't take much coaxing to get everyone in up to their shoulders.

"Today we're going to work on our flutter kick," I tell them. I've spent the past few weeks helping them over the initial hurdles—putting their faces in the water, blowing bubbles, floating on their backs, that sort of thing. Now we're ready to tackle actual strokes.

It's funny, a few years ago I never could have imagined myself teaching swimming. I've always loved the water, but I never wanted to be on a swim team or anything like that. Working at the rink with Cassidy and her Chicks with Sticks, though, gave me the confidence to think about going for it when this summer job came up. I'm really glad I did, because I'm having a blast. At least one thing in my life is going right.

Handing out kickboards, I wade to the far side of the dock and coax the girls to swim to me, one by one.

"Good job, Pippa!" I call, watching her little feet churn the water behind her. When she reaches me, I slap her a high five and she smiles her gap-toothed smile at me.

"My thithter ith on a thwim team," she says. Pippa tells me this every day.

"I know," I reply, just like I always do. "That's so cool. If you keep up the good work, I'll bet you could be on a swim team too."

When second period arrives, I move over into the deep water on the other side of the H dock to work with the Dolphins. Most of Balsam is in this class. They're enthusiastic swimmers, and eager to please. The hour passes quickly, and before I know it, the bell rings to signal the end of class.

"Good job, everyone!" I tell the girls. "Tomorrow we'll work on arm strokes."

Heather Vogel Frederick

Felicia emerges from Lower Lodge as I'm heading back to my cubie to change for lunch.

"Hey, Emma!" she calls, and I pause reluctantly to wait for her. It took a while to resign myself to the fact that the two of us are co-counselors. That first week, I kept hoping for a miracle that would somehow reunite Jess and me. And things were a little awkward at first, especially after the whole book club kickoff fiasco. Felicia and I are getting along a little better now, although she'll never be my favorite person on the planet. "Nest is hosting the book club meeting tonight, right?"

I nod.

"I've been thinking maybe you could have the girls analyze and discuss the theme of transformation."

I stare at her. "Felicia, our campers are in *elementary school*, not college."

"That doesn't mean they can't tackle challenging material," she replies primly. "Camp Lovejoy is supposed to be about broadening horizons, remember? Marge always says we should be willing to push campers out of their comfort zones."

I'd like to push you out of your comfort zone—right into the lake, I think sourly. I swear, if I hear our head counselor's name pass Felicia's lips one more time, I'm going to barf. Felicia totally worships Marge.

"We're talking single-digit birthdays, Felicia!" I remind her. "It's *summer camp*. We're supposed to be having fun, not torturing the poor girls."

I know exactly why she's doing this. She made this huge deal about not wanting to be in the book club, but I spotted her furtively reading *Understood Betsy* after "Taps" a few nights ago. I've been reading it aloud to our campers during rest hour, and the story must have gotten its hooks into her.

Which is what good stories do.

Anyway, now that she's read it, of course she quickly figured out the book's central theme, and she wants to show off. Felicia may be smart, but she's also kind of predictable. She can't resist flaunting her intellectual prowess. I caught her bragging to Tara Lindgren the other day about her IQ. *Tara!* Like a seven-year-old who still sucks her thumb cares! I nearly died laughing when I heard Tara reply in all seriousness, "I think my mom had an IQ once, and it really hurt when they stuck it in her arm."

I don't care if Felicia is a genius and belongs to that stupid Mensa society thing, she's clueless when it comes to people.

"Look, if you want to be in the book club, Felicia, you can be in the book club. But we're not going to make the girls analyze anything," I tell her firmly. "All we're going to do is talk a little about the story, do a project that's related to this chapter, and have snacks."

Felicia rolls her eyes. "Fine," she snaps, and walks away.

I shrug, then continue on to the cubie house. Felicia likes to act as if I'm a hopeless dunce, but I know she's impressed by the colleges I got accepted to. She's intrigued that I chose someplace exotic like the University of British Columbia, too. I don't let on that I'm scared out

Heather Vogel Frederick

of my wits, of course. For Felicia, I put on a brave face and pretend that it's all incredibly exciting.

Lunch is mac and cheese, one of my favorites, which helps cheer me up. And there's a surprise afterward.

"Emma!" shrieks Meri, her dark ponytail bobbing as she runs toward me. Behind her, Felicia is coming out of the Dining Hall with our mail. "You got a letter!"

My heart nearly stops. Could it be from Stewart?

"About time the drought ended," says Jess, but I barely hear her. *Stewart's written to tell me that he's coming up to see me this weekend. No, wait, he sent me a funny apology card. No, wait, he's written to tell me that his new girlfriend broke up with him!*

Felicia hands me the envelope.

It's not from Stewart.

It's from Rupert Loomis.

Jess spots the return address—she'd have to be blind not to see the words "Loomis Hall" in fancy engraved lettering, along with the incriminating British stamp—and cries "Moo!" in delight.

That's what my brother and I used to call Rupert, back when we lived in England. It's because of his deep voice and the way he says his name— *Rooopert Looomis*—with the vowels all drawn out like he's lowing. The minute my friends caught wind of it, they started calling him that too.

Jess waves wildly at Cassidy and Becca and Megan. "You guys!" she shouts. "Rupert wrote to Emma!"

My friends quickly come running. Rupert is prime entertainment.

Cassidy tries to snatch the envelope away, but for once I'm too quick for her.

"C'mon, Emma, you have to read it aloud," she begs. "Do his voice!"

We're gathering a crowd. As our campers cluster around me, Tara pulls her thumb out of her mouth. "Who's Rupert?"

"Moo," Jess says again, and my friends all collapse in giggles.

"Shut up!" Seeing Tara's crestfallen expression, I hasten to add, "Not you, honey. Rupert is a friend of mine from England. He's kind of, um—"

"A nincompoop," says Megan.

"Megan thaid poop! Megan thaid poop!" singsongs Pippa.

"'Nincompoop' is a perfectly acceptable form of vernacular speech," Felicia informs her. "It's of British origin, and was first used in the late seventeenth century. It means a foolish or stupid person."

We stare at her. Felicia has a way of sucking all the oxygen out of a room, even when she's outside.

"He's not a nincompoop!" I retort. "Well, okay, maybe a tiny bit, but he means well. He's just a little, uh, kind of like—" I hesitate. How to describe the indescribable? Last time I saw Rupert Loomis, which was at Gigi's wedding, he had improved a bit. It obviously helped that his great-aunt sent him off to boarding school, where he could be around people his own age, but he could still easily be mistaken for an ancient butler. "He's kind of like—"

Heather Vogel Frederick

"Eeyore?" Cassidy suggests helpfully.

That does it. I start to laugh too. Eeyore is my brother Darcy's other nickname for Rupert, and it totally fits him. Adopting my best mournful donkey voice, I begin to read:

> Dear Emma,
>
> I hope you're enjoying your summer holidays. I've been accompanying Great-Aunt Olivia on a grand tour of Europe, which she felt would be educational. We are currently in St. Petersburg on a river cruise. I am the youngest person aboard.

"Poor Rupert!" says Jess. "Stuck on a boat with a bunch of senior citizens! He must be bored silly."

> Contrary to what you might think, I'm not bored silly. Many of the other guests are acquaintances of my great-aunt's. She felt it would be advantageous for me to meet them, in hopes that their connections might prove valuable in the years ahead. Today at lunch I chatted with a former member of Parliament, a current member of the International Monetary Fund, the head of a media conglomerate, and a renowned barrister. They were all most informative and encouraging.

Shaking my head, I try to picture Rupert breezily "chatting" with anyone. It boggles the mind.

In fact, the barrister told me that after I finish my first year at Cambridge, he'd see about arranging an internship for me at his chambers in London. I would like that very much.

"Rupert! On the loose in London! Perish the thought!" says Jess with glee, her eyes alight.

"What's a barrister?" asks Amy Osborne.

"That's what they call lawyers in England," I explain. "Rupert wants to be a lawyer."

Your parents stopped at Loomis Hall for tea shortly before Great-Aunt Olivia and I left on our voyage. They told us of your plans to study at the University of British Columbia. Isn't that a long way from Concord? Canada was a Dominion of the British Empire for many years, so perhaps you chose it because you are missing your days in England, and some of the friends you made there?

With warmest regards,
Rupert

Heather Vogel Frederick

I sigh. Rupert still writes like he stepped out of the pages of a Jane Austen novel. And it would seem he still nurtures a tendril of affection for me, as Jane herself might put it. Perish the thought, indeed.

> P.S. I'm enclosing a picture taken on the deck of the *Danube Princess*. I'm not the one in the balloon pants. That's a Russian dancer.

I glance at the picture. It takes me a moment to spot Rupert. Last time I saw him was two years ago. He looks—different. He's filled out, for one thing, and for another, he's standing up straight, instead of the way he always used to stand, slumped over like a stalk of wilted celery. *He's grown into himself*, I realize in astonishment. My mother always said that he would.

Becca snatches the photo away from me. "Where's Rupert?" she asks, looking puzzled. "And who's that cute guy next to the man in the balloon pants?"

"Um, I think that's Rupert," I tell her.

She frowns. "He must have changed his hair. His ears don't look nearly as big as they used to."

"Okay, everybody—show's over," I announce, tucking the photograph into the letter and stuffing both back in the envelope. "Time for rest hour."

Felicia heads off toward Nest with our campers. Everyone else scatters too, leaving Jess and me standing alone in the grove. We start up the path toward the Art Studio, where we have permission to spend our rest hour working on beads for Sunday night's Council Fire.

Beads are a big deal at Camp Lovejoy. Campers earn them in many different ways—passing swim tests, getting up on water skis for the first time, climbing a mountain peak, winning a tennis tournament, that sort of thing. Other stuff counts too, like having a perfect score chart for keeping your cubie tidy, or being caught doing something especially kind or helpful.

All of us counselors decorate wooden beads with something that symbolizes each achievement, and the beads are awarded at the weekly Council Fire. Campers string them on the leather thong that holds their nameplates, creating a necklace to take home at the end of the summer.

"It's a tangible reminder of camp, and all that they accomplished," Gwen says.

I think it's a cool tradition. I would have loved it when I was my campers' age.

In the Art Studio, I grab a box of blue beads—blue for watersports—and head for one of the tables on the deck. It's too nice to work inside. Jess grabs a box of white ones (the arts) and green ones (Junior Naturalists) and joins me.

"How many do you have to do?" she asks me.

"Seventeen. You?"

"Fifteen."

We work in silence for a while, accompanied by the distant drone of a motorboat. I carefully paint each camper's name on a bead, then

Heather Vogel Frederick

add her accomplishment on the other side: Big Float for the girls who proved they could swim out to the raft; Cherry Island for those who made the early-morning swim out to the island and back for the first time; and of course Sharks and Dolphins and that sort of thing for those who advanced to a new swim level.

I finish with five minutes to spare. "I'm gonna head over to the kitchen before third period," I tell Jess. "I have to arrange the snacks and other stuff for tonight."

She nods, too absorbed in her task to look up. I set my tray of beads on a high shelf to dry, then jog back down the path toward the Dining Hall, where I knock on the back door to the kitchen.

A round-faced woman with rosy cheeks and a cap of silver hair pops out like a figure in a cuckoo clock. I take a step back, startled.

"Ethel?"

"I'm Thelma," she says. "How can I help you?"

"Um, three of our cabins are meeting in Hilltop Lodge tonight—it's this book club thing we started—"

"Gwen told me! She says you're reading *Understood Betsy*?"

I nod.

"That was a favorite of Ethel's and mine when we were growing up. So glad to know that girls these days are still reading it."

I explain what we need for our meeting tonight, and she nods in response.

"I'll have it ready for you after dinner," she promises. "Stop by when you're ready."

The sun comes out during third period, and I'm finally able to shed my hoodie. I take a short break in the few minutes before fourth period, diving into the water and swimming a couple of quick laps to cool off. Climbing back up on the dock, I notice how brown my forearms are. I've never spent as much time outside during the summer as I have here at camp, and no matter how much sunscreen I use, I'm still getting a real tan for the first time in my life.

Does Stewart like tans? I frown, trying to remember if this is something we ever talked about.

During fourth period, I find myself playing the bargaining game I used to play when I was a kid. *If I spot one of the eagles from Cherry Island in the next five minutes, Stewart will come tomorrow. If Grace doesn't fall while she's water-skiing, Stewart will come tomorrow.*

I know it's stupid, but I can't help it. I have Stewart on the brain.

Free period finally arrives, which is my favorite part of the day. Besides rest hour, that is, when I get to lie in my bunk and read. I never thought that having an hour to myself would feel like such a luxury, but then, I've never been a camp counselor before. After this summer, I'll never take being able to read whenever I want to for granted again.

"So, what have you got for me, girls?" I ask, entering the Director's Cottage. Gwen lets me use her living room for my writing workshops, and for putting together the *Birch Bark*.

The camp newspaper is a low-tech operation. Published a handful of times each summer, it's more of a newsletter, really—just a few pages stapled together and distributed here at camp and mailed home to the

Heather Vogel Frederick

campers' families. Each issue carries brief reports about what's going on in the cabins, along with a summary of our weekly activities, announcements about outstanding achievements, poems and stories written by campers, funny anecdotes, jokes, cartoons, other camp news and information, and even a few ads for local shops and restaurants.

I am proud of a wildly successful new feature that I started called "Overheard." It's a column devoted to funny things that counselors overhear their campers say. I have to edit it carefully, and I keep everything anonymous, because I don't want any of the girls to think we're poking fun at them. We're not—just at the hilarious stuff they come up with. Like mixing up "IQ" and "IV." Or my favorite one this week, when Becca passed by the Director's Cottage, and overheard Harper, who had been given permission to call home, telling her mother that we'd had cat food for dinner. Becca had to grab the phone away for a minute and assure Mrs. Kennedy that it wasn't cat food but tuna noodle casserole her daughter was talking about.

"Okay, girls, let's get busy," I tell them, opening up the laptop Gwen allows us to use. "We have a lot to squeeze into this week's issue."

That's an understatement. It's the special Parents' Weekend edition, complete with a schedule of events here at camp, a list of local restaurants, and things worth seeing in the area, such as the covered bridge in Pumpkin Falls and the church's famous steeple, with its bell made by Paul Revere. I know my father will want to see that—he's a big history buff.

"So are you ready to hand it over yet?" I tease Nica, who's been working on a poem. She reminds me of Jess at that age—incredibly shy. Nica spends a lot of time in her twin sister Freddie's shadow, and she lets Freddie do most of her talking for her. We're all trying to help build up her confidence. "C'mon, Nica, I won't bite."

She reluctantly hands over a piece of paper. I take it from her and read the first verse:

> *The loon sings a tune*
> *By the light of the moon*
> *A sad and lonely loon-y tune.*

"Hey, this is really fun! Great job!"

This earns me a fleeting smile.

"We're going to put this smack-dab on the front page," I tell her. "Right where your parents can read it and be proud of you."

I do just that, and then we start figuring out where everything else is going to go. There's a lot to cram in, including a lengthy account of a trip the girls on the Hill took to the summit of Mount Washington. After we're done, I proofread it carefully, then e-mail the mocked-up newsletter to Gwen. She'll make sure it gets printed out for distribution when the parents arrive.

Friday night is pizza night, and we're shooed out onto the Dining Hall's big deck to eat it. The CITs want to get started on decorations.

"I can't wait to be a CIT," Meri tells me, watching with envy as one of the older girls passes by with a huge roll of crepe paper. "They get to do all the cool stuff."

Heather Vogel Frederick

"You get to do cool stuff too," I remind her. "Stuff like—"

"Book club!" Pippa finishes, and we all nod.

"Exactly. Speaking of which, we'd better get going."

Even the wet blanket that is Felicia, who has deigned to grace us with her presence, can't dampen our cabin's enthusiasm. Our trio of campers has been eagerly anticipating their turn to host the meeting, and a few minutes later, they're scurrying around Hilltop Lodge, setting out candles in jars on the shelves and tables, and pulling the chairs and floor cushions into the middle of the room in a cozy circle.

"Will there be snacks?" asks Tara, sounding worried.

"Of course," I tell her. "Book club wouldn't be book club without snacks."

"They're coming!" squeals Pippa, who's been keeping lookout by the window.

I glance outside and spot a line of flashlights heading toward us. A moment later, the door flies open.

"What's going on in here?" Cassidy growls, in her best Sergeant Marge impression. She chases my campers around the room, and they shriek in delight.

"Let's get this meeting started!" I holler, clapping my hands and herding everyone to the chairs and cushions. I wait for a moment until they're settled. "Who can briefly tell us what happened in these first few chapters?"

Brooklyn Alvarez raises her hand. "So this kid from the city goes to live on a farm in Vermont, right? And she's super homesick and scared of everything."

"Everything meaning what?"

"Her relatives, their dog, school—everything."

"Who else can tell me something that happens?"

Harper's hand shoots up. "They make her do stuff on her own."

"Who does?"

"Her uncle Henry and her aunt Abigail and her cousin Ann."

"What kinds of stuff do they make her do?" I look around for another volunteer. "Amy?"

She blushes. "Um, get dressed, wash dishes, stuff like that."

"Betsy's kind of spoiled," adds Grace. "She's not used to doing chores."

So far, Felicia hasn't said a single word. She's sitting at the far edge of the circle on a beanbag chair, idly fiddling with one of the ends of her bathrobe tie.

"Does she get to do anything fun?" I continue.

"Like making butter?" volunteers Freddie, who still has a smear of pizza sauce on her chin.

"She thought it came from stores, not cows," scoffs Carter.

I hold up the big jar of cream that I got from the camp kitchen. "Guess what? We're going to make butter tonight too! Just like Elizabeth Ann."

Tara's face falls. "Is that going to be our snack?"

Cassidy lets out a whoop of laughter. "Mmm mmm, girls, dig in! Have yourself a nice big spoonful of butter!"

Heather Vogel Frederick

We all crack up at this. "I promise we'll be putting the butter on something yummy," I tell them. "How do some of Ethel and Thelma's apple muffins sound?"

Our campers clap enthusiastically.

"Speaking of apples," says Jess, glancing over at Felicia, who is still silent. She shoots me a "What's up with her?" look, and I shrug. "Who remembers what kind of apple is Aunt Ann's favorite?"

I add a little salt to the jar of cream, screw the lid on tightly, then start to shake it. "There's a prize for the right answer."

A hand by the fireplace goes up timidly. "Yes, Nica?"

"Northern Spy?" she whispers.

"Well done! Your prize is that you get to be our first shaker." I pass her the jar. "We don't have an old-fashioned churn the way Aunt Abigail did, but this will still work. You start, then pass it around so everybody gets a turn."

Nica begins shaking the jar, and as it slowly makes its way around the circle of girls, I hand out this week's Fun Facts.

Fun Facts About Dorothy

1) Dorothy was highly educated for a woman of her time, earning degrees from Ohio State University, the Sorbonne in Paris, and Columbia University. In 1904, she earned her PhD from Columbia. She was the first woman to receive an honorary degree from Dartmouth College.

Jess spots that one right away, just as I knew she would.

"Hey!" she says, sounding pleased. "Dartmouth is where Darcy goes."

Tara's thumb pops out of her mouth. "Who's Darcy?"

"Um, my boyfriend," Jess tells them.

The younger girls make kissing noises, and Jess blushes to the roots of her hair.

"You brought it up," Cassidy tells her, grinning.

2) Dorothy spoke five languages fluently, including German and French.

3) She met John Fisher while they were students at Columbia and married him in 1907. Their daughter, Sally, was born in 1909, followed by a son, Jimmy, in 1913.

4) Instead of pursuing an academic career as she had planned, Dorothy decided to write.

5) On a trip to Rome in 1912, Dorothy met Maria Montessori and became interested in her system of teaching and child-rearing. She would go on to introduce the Montessori Method in the United States.

6) Dorothy wrote over forty books for children and adults,

Heather Vogel Frederick

including novels, short stories, memoirs, and books on education.

7) She was a judge for the Book-of-the-Month Club for twenty-five years, from 1926 until 1951.

8) *Understood Betsy* is the book she's best known for.

"I think the butter's done, Emma," says Jess when the jar reaches her.

Sure enough, there's a pale yellow lump floating inside. Our campers all crowd around to watch as I fish it out and pop it in a bowl.

"Now we have to rinse it," I tell them, grateful for the Internet videos that showed me how this is done. I add water from the pitcher I have ready, swish it around, then pour off the liquid into another bowl. "Harper, do you want to try it?"

She nods, hopping up off her cushion to grab the pitcher. We rinse, pour, and repeat several more times, until I announce, "I think we're done. Felicia?"

My co-counselor gives me a questioning look.

"Would you read aloud from the next chapter while I butter the muffins and pass them around?"

She inclines her head, which tonight is crowned with a coronet of braids. "As you wish."

Cassidy catches my eye and smirks. She gets a huge kick out of Felicia. Probably because she doesn't have to share a cabin with her.

Clearing her throat, Felicia begins:

> "Elizabeth Ann was very much surprised to hear
> Cousin Ann's voice calling, 'Dinner!' down the stairs.
> It did not seem possible that the whole morning had
> gone by."

I've read this book a million times before, and it's as comfortable as my favorite pair of slippers. Jess throws another log in the wood- stove as I'm passing out the last of the muffins. I take a seat on the sofa between Meri and Pippa, who curl up beside me like cats, and let the words wash over me.

Later, when we're all back in our cabins and everyone is finally settled in for the night, I'm not feeling nearly as relaxed. Sleep eludes me as my thoughts circle round and round, like a hamster on a wheel, always coming back to Stewart.

Heaving a sigh, I start bargaining with myself again.

If I hear a loon in the next ten seconds, Stewart will come tomorrow. I lie there in agony, holding my breath and counting.

On seven, I hear a loon and exhale in relief. *The loon sings a tune by the light of the moon.* I smile as Nica's jaunty verse floats into thought. Pulling the comforter up under my chin, I close my eyes, feeling ready at last to go to sleep. My eyes pop open again a second later as an acrid odor drifts in through the screened window. Skunk!

"Gaaah," I sputter. It must be sitting right on our doorstep. No one else seems to notice—there's nothing but the sound of steady

Heather Vogel Frederick

breathing from the four corners of our cabin—and I debate whether I should get up and try to shoo it away. Instead, I stuff my pillow over my head and burrow under the covers, trying not to gag as I seek relief from the eye-watering smell. Finally, I manage to drift off to sleep.

I'm awake before reveille, and dash to the showers while my campers are still sleeping. Back in my cubie, I break out my stash of contraband makeup and contemplate it, wondering what I can apply and still fly under Sergeant Marge's radar. A little mascara and lip gloss should do the trick. As I'm putting it on, my gaze falls on Stewart's picture in my open trunk. With any luck, it will be on my dressing table next to Pip by the end of the day.

Breakfast is a hurried meal, as we need to leave plenty of time for SCUM. The maintenance staff has been busy for days getting things spruced up for Parents' Weekend, but a few finishing touches are still needed. Nest is put in charge of watering all the flower containers around camp, so Felicia and I spend the next forty-five minutes supervising our girls as they scurry around with watering cans.

Promptly at ten, cars begin to trickle down the road to camp. Megan and I are on the greeting committee, along with several other counselors. As I take my place on the Dining Hall porch, armed with the sign-out sheet and other information, my heart is pounding so fast I can barely breathe. *Stewart. Stewart. Stewart.*

I was hoping that the Chadwicks would be among the early birds, but they're not. Pippa's family is the first to arrive, which isn't surprising since the Lovejoys live in Pumpkin Falls and have the shortest distance to travel. I can't believe how many of them there are. They just keep piling out of the minivan.

Pippa's oldest sister is as tall as Cassidy. "Hey, Pipster," she says, giving her a hug. "Having a good summer?"

Pippa nods vigorously, then tugs on my T-shirt. "Truly ith on the thwim team, remember?"

Like I could forget. "Of course. Hi, Truly."

"Hi."

"May we take our daughters out to lunch?" Mrs. Lovejoy asks as Pippa grabs her hand and starts to drag her away.

"Sure," I tell her. "Lauren's in Meadow, right? You just need to check in with Melissa or Brianna, her counselors. I'll sign both girls out for you right now. Oh, and be sure and have them back in time for the afternoon program. Here's the schedule." I hand it to her, along with a copy of the *Birch Bark*.

As Team Lovejoy heads off, I turn and scan the incoming cars. There's still no sign of the Concord group yet. *Come on, Stewart!*

"Our parents are here!" shouts Freddie, who's been waiting on the porch with her twin. She leaps down the steps and across the grove. Nica is right behind her.

"Girls!" cries Mr. Simpson, leaning out the car window as he pulls into a parking spot by the grove.

He gets out of the car and gives his daughters both big hugs. His wife is sitting in the passenger seat, talking on the phone. She waves to the girls, then holds up a finger to let them know she'll be with them in a minute.

Heather Vogel Frederick

Freddie and Nica drag their father over to the porch to meet me.

"This is Emma," says Freddie. "She's not our counselor but she's really nice."

Mr. Simpson laughs. "I'm sure she is." His hair is gray at the temples, and he has what Cassidy's family calls "happiness lines" in the corners of his eyes. He gives me a warm smile. "Hello, Emma."

We shake hands. Mrs. Simpson finally gets out of the car, and the girls sprint off again. She has the same sandy hair as her girls, but not a single happiness line, from what I can tell.

"Nica has a poem in the *Birch Bark*," I tell Mr. Simpson, handing him a copy from the pile on the table behind me.

"Fantastic! She told us in her last letter that she's been doing some writing this summer."

As the twins return to the porch with their mother in tow, Mr. Simpson reaches out and ruffles Nica's hair. "Good work, sweetie." He passes the newsletter to his wife, who glances briefly at the poem.

"Do you want to see our cabin and cubies?" asks Freddie, dancing in excitement.

"Of course," says her father.

Freddie grabs her sister's hand and the two of them lead the way toward Twin Pines. As their parents start to follow, Mrs. Simpson turns to her husband.

"This is what we have to show for all the money we're spending this summer?" she murmurs, flicking a manicured nail at the newsletter. "Some nonsense about loons?"

I freeze. Beside me, Megan sucks in her breath.

Nica glances over her shoulder, a stricken expression on her face. Her parents don't notice; Mr. Simpson has been waylaid by Sergeant Marge, and Mrs. Simpson is on her cell phone again.

"No wonder Nica barely says a word," I whisper to Megan.

"No kidding," she replies. " Even if her mother didn't think she'd be overheard, what a horrible thing to say!"

There's a commotion in the parking lot, and a horn toots long and loud. I whip around, my heart in my throat. *Stewart?*

Nope. Not unless he drives a cherry red pickup truck, towing what looks like a giant silver burrito.

"Uh-oh," says Megan.

"What?"

"I think that's my dad."

Sure enough, the driver's door on the truck opens and Mr. Wong hops out. Mrs. Wong emerges from the passenger side, and Gigi and Edouard and Sophie Fairfax climb out of the backseat. They all wave cheerfully as they head over to join us.

"I told you we had a surprise," says Mrs. Wong, giving Megan a big hug.

"That's it?" Megan stares in disbelief. "A trailer?"

"Not just any trailer," her father replies proudly. "Wait until you see inside."

"*C'est completement fou,*" Sophie whispers, giving me a hug. We smile at each other. I don't know much French, but I know enough to catch her drift. Megan's parents are nuts.

Heather Vogel Frederick

The burrito-shaped trailer quickly draws a crowd.

"He'll be giving tours in a minute, wait and see," mutters Megan as Mr. Wong hurries back to his new toy.

I spot my family pulling into the parking lot. Finally! Leaving Megan with her mother and grandmother, I race over. Could Stewart have come with them?

No, he couldn't. The only ones in the back are my brother and Pip.

"Look how brown you are!" exclaims my mother, giving me a hug. "I don't recall ever seeing you so tan."

"Pretty hard not to be, when you're outside all day," I reply.

My father and my brother both give me hugs too.

"Where's Jess?" Darcy asks.

"On duty down at her cabin," I tell him. "She'll be up in a little while—you should hide."

"You managed to keep it a secret?"

I make a face. "Yes, believe it or not, your little sister can keep her mouth shut when she has to."

My brother laughs. I'm dying to ask about Stewart, but I don't want Darcy or anyone else to suspect that I still have feelings for Becca's brother.

"So," my father asks, slipping his arm around my waist and giving me a squeeze. "Are you having a good summer?"

"Definitely. Wait until you meet my campers. They are so adorable!"

Over his shoulder, I spot the Chadwicks' SUV pulling in.

"Emma?" says my mother.

"Mmm?" I reply, craning my neck to see who's behind the wheel. It's Mrs. Chadwick. *That's okay*, I tell myself. *Stewart's probably in the backseat.*

"Emma, your mother just asked you a question," says my father.

I drag my gaze back, trying to give them my full attention, but out of the corner of my eye I'm still watching as Mrs. Chadwick gets out of the car, followed by Mr. Chadwick.

"Hey, Mrs. H! Hey, Mr. H!" Becca materializes beside me just then.

"Becca! It's so good to see you!" says my mother. My parents both give her a hug.

The Chadwicks are heading across the grove toward us now. Mr. and Mrs. Chadwick, that is. No one else is with them. I struggle to keep a cheerful expression on my face.

"Awww—Stewart didn't come?" Becca is clearly disappointed.

"Sorry, sweetheart," her mom replies lightly, giving her a kiss. "Your brother had, uh, other plans this weekend." She carefully avoids my gaze.

Other plans? That's code for visiting his stupid girlfriend, most likely. Out of the corner of my eye, I can see my mother watching me. She always says my face is an open book to her. I don't even bother trying to hide what's written on its pages right now.

Stewart didn't come.

There'll be no happy reunion, no kiss in the gazebo.

My consolation prize? A letter from Rupert Loomis.

Booby prize is more like it.

Moo.

Heather Vogel Frederick

❀ Jess ❀

"Her heart gave a big jump up. . . ."
—*Understood Betsy*

"This is the coolest thing ever!"

Freddie's face is alight with excitement as she steps inside the Wongs' new trailer. I'm right behind her. It's Twin Pines's turn to take a tour, and Freddie is right, it really is pretty cool. The trailer is shaped like a long, narrow igloo, with an arched ceiling high enough that even Cassidy and her mother can stand up straight. The outside is silver, and the inside is, well, pure Wong.

Which means mostly white, just like their living room.

I'm pretty sure I detect Gigi's touch, though, in a bunch of red accessories. Gigi loves red ("Where I come from, it's the color of good luck," she always tells us), and I suspect she's the one who added the red throw pillows on the sofas, the red area rugs and dish towels and teakettle on the stove, and the red clock on the wall.

"Jess! Cassidy! Come look!" crows Brooklyn from the far end. "There's even a bathroom!"

Of course there is. Biffies are not the Wongs' style.

I head down the hallway behind Cassidy, who's carrying her little sister, Chloe. It's hard to believe that Chloe will be starting kindergarten a year from now. I can remember the day she was born like it was yesterday.

We ooh and aah over the tiny bathroom, then head back to the living area. Mrs. Wong is in full Mrs. Wong mode, earnestly explaining to Brooklyn's mother the trailer's green features, including a solar panel on the roof and the all-natural, environmentally friendly flooring made of sustainable bamboo. Mr. Wong, meanwhile, proudly shows off the fun stuff—hidden storage drawers, awnings outside that retract at the flip of a switch, and a flat-screen TV and killer sound system.

"How many people can sleep in here?" I ask, looking around.

"Six," says Mr. Wong, promptly showing us how the dining table folds down to make a double bed, and how two more people can fit end-to-end on the long sofa. "Including the bedroom, of course."

"It's a little cozy," says Gigi. "But we're having fun, right, Edouard?"

"Mais oui!" he replies, placing a tray of cookies on the table. My campers make a dive for them. "The trailer, she is our little honeymoon cottage on wheels, *n'est-ce pas, chérie?"*

I love the way Megan's grandfather talks like he's still a newlywed, even though he and Gigi have been married for two years already. I hope somebody talks about me that way someday. Maybe even Darcy. I can feel myself blushing at this thought.

"Do you think the Wongs would let our book club borrow this thing sometime?" Cassidy whispers.

"That would be so cool!" I whisper back. "But I don't want to try to drive it."

"I can drive it," Sophie announces smugly. "Megan's father has given me lessons."

I look over at her, trying to picture the oh-so-French and oh-so-petite Sophie at the wheel of the giant red truck. It's a stretch.

"Time's up!" says Gigi as the buzzer on the stove goes off. Our campers all groan.

"Come on, girls," I tell them. "We agreed to take turns, and Nest is waiting."

Edouard hands everyone another cookie on the way out. The last hour has been a busy one. Before the tour, I was stationed at Twin Pines, meeting parents and answering questions about their daughters' progress and activities.

Now everyone's milling around, waiting for the bell to ring so they can leave. It finally does, and as Cassidy and I say good-bye to the Simpsons, I notice that Nica seems a little subdued.

"Have fun at lunch!" I tell her, and she nods but she doesn't look at me.

What's up with that? I wonder. I say good-bye to the Alvarez family, then turn to Cassidy as they head for the parking lot. "I think that's everyone."

"Wait, what about Carter? She's supposed to tag along with my family for a picnic, since her parents couldn't come."

"Didn't she tell you?" I reply. "She got invited to go with the Friedmans. Grace's parents know her parents."

"Really?"

I frown. "I thought that's what they told me the plan was."

"We'd better double-check," says Cassidy.

The two of us head up to the Dining Hall porch, where Sergeant Marge is stationed with her clipboard.

"Yes, Carter went with the Friedmans," Marge confirms, consulting the list. "All of your campers are checked out, so you're free until three o'clock."

Cassidy gives me a fist bump. "Woohoo! Freedom!"

Marge frowns at us. "Make sure you're back in time for the afternoon program."

We hurry away before she can think up a reason for us to stay.

"Later, gator," says Cassidy, who's meeting her family at the top of the hill. She starts to jog up the road, then looks back over her shoulder and gives me a sly smile. "Give, uh, *everybody* a big kiss for me!" Puckering her lips, she makes a smooching sound.

Cassidy can be such a goofball sometimes. Shaking my head, I turn to go and find the Hawthornes. They invited me to come to lunch with them since my parents weren't able to make it. Summer is a really busy time on our farm, and there's no way they could get away. Which is fine; I didn't expect them to. No big deal.

I spot Emma's family's car first, a white minivan parked on the far side of the grove under a pine tree.

Heather Vogel Frederick

Then I stop in my tracks. My heart skips a beat.

"Darcy?" I shout, staring at him in disbelief. So this was what Cassidy was hinting at!

Emma's brother turns and smiles at me. I break out in a run, then slow to a stop just before I get to him, feeling suddenly self-conscious.

"Hey, Jess," he says, reaching out to tug my braid.

"Hey," I reply, my heart doing another somersault. I still get shy around Darcy sometimes, especially when he's looking at me the way he is now.

I smile back at him, noticing that his curly brown hair is longer than usual. I like the way it looks. Of course, I like the way *everything* about him looks.

There are too many people around for anything more than a quick hug, but I'll settle for Darcy Hawthorne tugging my braid any day of the week.

"Jess!" calls Mrs. Hawthorne. I turn to see her coming across the grove from the Biffy. "I see you found the present we brought you." Laughing, she hugs me too. "Sorry your parents couldn't come, honey. But I hope that maybe this"—she nods at Darcy—"will help make up for it."

"Oh yeah," I assure her, keenly aware of the fact that I'm grinning like an idiot.

"How's your summer going?" Mr. Hawthorne comes over to join us. Emma and Meri are with him. Meri, the only camper from Nest whose parents didn't come, is holding tightly to Pip's leash.

"And who is this?" asks Darcy, crouching down.

"Meriwether Milligan," Emma tells him. "Otherwise known as Meri."

"Meri! You're the really good swimmer with the beautiful blue eyes, right? Emma told me all about you."

Meri gives him a shy smile.

While Darcy charms his sister's camper, I turn back to Mr. Hawthorne. "I love it here," I tell him, and it's true. I love everything about being a counselor—I love working with the kids all day, and having a cabin of girls all my own to mother hen, and I especially love being by this incredibly beautiful lake.

"I can imagine you girls must be having the time of your lives," Emma's mother says. "It's a gorgeous spot."

"Anybody hungry?" asks Emma's father.

"Starving," Darcy replies, straightening up.

"What are we waiting for?"

I'm the first one in the minivan, and I head for the back row of seats. Darcy is right behind me. Meri and Pip cram into the middle row alongside Emma, who gives me a wan smile as she climbs in.

I lean forward. "Everything okay?" I whisper.

She shrugs, but doesn't reply. Not a good sign. Emma is hopeless at hiding her feelings.

Meri bounces happily in her seat, her ponytail swinging. "This is Emma's dog!" she tells me.

"I know," I reply, reaching over to give Pip a pat. "He was a puppy when my friends and I gave him to Emma for her birthday."

Heather Vogel Frederick

Meri's eyes grow round. "I wish I'd get a puppy for a birthday present."

Darcy takes my hand as the minivan bumps and jolts its way up the gravel road. He gives it a squeeze, and I squeeze back.

"How does Lou's Diner sound?" asks Mr. Hawthorne. "They're supposed to have the best burgers in these parts."

"We've had them and they're great," I tell him. "Right, Emma?"

No response. I gaze thoughtfully at the back of her head. Something's definitely bothering her.

By the time we arrive at Lou's, a bunch of other campers and their families are already crowded into the booths and tables.

"We might as well have stayed at the Dining Hall," I whisper to Emma, who manages to muster a smile.

After lunch, Mr. and Mrs. Hawthorne suggest a trip to the bookstore. Emma's parents are even bigger bookworms than she is.

"I think Jess and I will take Pip for a walk instead," says Darcy, reaching for the leash. Meri is reluctant to relinquish it.

"Can I go with you?" she begs him.

I hold my breath. *Please say no*, I think.

"Not this time," says Darcy, and Meri's eyes well up with tears.

At this, Emma finally shows signs of life. "You'll like Lovejoy's Books, honey," she tells Meri, detaching her from the leash and handing it to her brother. "Pippa's family runs it, remember? They have a dog too—her name is Miss Marple. And yummy pumpkin whoopie pies. Remember we had some at our first book club meeting?"

"Pumpkin whoopie pies!" exclaims Mr. Hawthorne. "I like this shop already."

"How about we rendezvous at the church in an hour?" Mrs. Hawthorne suggests, giving me a wink. "I hear there's a tour of the famous steeple."

"Sounds good." Darcy is genuinely enthusiastic. Not many people our age would be excited about touring a steeple, but Darcy is a history major and loves old stuff. A historic steeple is right up his alley.

As the others head off down Main Street toward the bookshop, Darcy slips his arm around my waist. "Close call," he whispers.

"No kidding," I whisper back. "I thought we were going to have to babysit."

"Well, we do have Pip," he reminds me.

"Pip doesn't count."

We both laugh, feeling a little giddy now that we're alone together.

Darcy leads me across the village green toward the Lovejoy College campus. "We've played hockey here a few times," he says. "But we were so busy at the rink that I never really got a chance to look around."

We wander around for a while, looking at the white clapboard buildings.

"It kind of reminds me of a smaller version of Dartmouth," I tell Darcy.

"I was just thinking that," he says, nodding. "Hey, do you want to go see the covered bridge?"

Heather Vogel Frederick

I nod, and we trace our steps back to the village green.

"It's that way," I tell him, pointing past the church.

We walk a ways down the road leading out of town until we reach the wooden structure. It's painted red, like most covered bridges in New England, and it's very picturesque. The inside is like an echo chamber. I cup my hands around my mouth. "Hellooooooo!" I call, and my voice bounces back to me.

A car passes us, bumpety-bumping over the bridge's wooden planks. Alarmed, Pip barks. That echoes too. He gets excited, thinking there's another dog, and nearly jerks the leash from Darcy's hand.

"Whoa, boy," Darcy tells him, reeling him back in.

Staying close to the outer wall, we follow the sidewalk toward the middle of the bridge, pausing to lean on the top of the wall and watch the water rush over the falls.

"The famous Pumpkin Falls," I say. "Pretty, isn't it?"

"Mmm-hmm," murmurs Darcy, but he's not looking at the waterfall. I feel my face grow pink under his gaze, and he grins. "This summer needs to hurry up and be over. You are just too far away."

I laugh. "It's not like we'll be any closer this fall. You'll be back at Dartmouth, and I'll be in New York."

He nods. "True. But still, we'll have a week together in Concord before I have to leave for sports camp, and visits now and then in Hanover or Manhattan." We walk a little farther. There's a lull in the traffic, and Darcy suddenly stops. "This looks like a good spot," he says.

I glance around, puzzled. "For what?"

Smiling, he points to the rafters, which are covered with graffiti—hearts and entwined initials, mostly.

"Ohhhhh." I smile back at him, then close my eyes as he leans down toward me.

Darcy's kisses are the best.

"Much better," he says after a few minutes. We move apart as we hear another car approaching. "I figured we might not have time later."

I grin. "Not unless we want an audience."

Our hour is almost up, so we head back to the rendezvous at the church. The tour of the steeple actually turns out to be really interesting—I had no idea that Paul Revere made church bells, and that so many of them are actually still in use, including the one here in Pumpkin Falls.

"I think I just found my capstone project," says Darcy when we're back outside the church again.

"What's a capstone?" asks Meri.

"A really big paper that I have to write," he explains. "It's also called a thesis." He turns to his father. "Wouldn't that be cool? Writing about all the Revere bells?"

"I'd love to help you with the research," says Mr. Hawthorne, sounding excited. He's as crazy about history as Darcy is. "We could drive all over New England to visit them. Maybe the Wongs would let us borrow their trailer."

"Family road trip!" cries Mrs. Hawthorne. "Wouldn't that be fun, Emma?"

Heather Vogel Frederick

Emma bends down to tie her sneaker.

I think I know something that will cheer her up. "Let's go to the General Store," I tell everyone. "My treat. They have the best ice cream ever."

"Better than Kimball Farm?" asks Mrs. Hawthorne, lifting an eyebrow.

I laugh. "Well, okay, maybe it's a tie."

Everyone orders a cone except Emma. For her to pass on ice cream—especially homemade strawberry, which is her favorite—is truly not a good sign.

"So what's going on?" I ask in a low voice as we're walking back to the car.

She shrugs.

With a sudden flash of insight, I continue, "It's Stewart, isn't it?" I can tell from the expression on her face that I've hit the nail on the head. "You were hoping he'd come."

"I just wish I could hurry up and get over him!" she bursts out. "It's so stupid to keep feeling this way."

I put my arm around her shoulders. "Don't be so hard on yourself, Ems. You two were together for a long time. How about you try not to think about it right now, and focus on this beautiful day instead. Focus on being with your family, who loves you; your dog, who loves you; your camper, who thinks you walk on water; and your best friend, who knows you don't but who still loves you anyway."

This finally gets a smile.

"I mean it, Emma," I tell her. "Seriously. Don't let it sour the rest of your summer, okay?"

Back at camp, we check in with Sergeant Marge and then go to get ready for our afternoon assignments. First up is a brief presentation by Gwen in the Lower Lodge.

"Thank you for sharing your daughters with us this summer," she says, beaming at the assembled parents. "It's wonderful to see so many familiar faces here with us today, many of whom were campers themselves—some even when I was a camper many moons ago. The Jurassic era, I think they called it." Everyone laughs. "I am honored to be able to pass along the cherished traditions of Camp Lovejoy to your girls. As you know, our motto here at Camp Lovejoy is 'Broadening Horizons for over a Century!' Your daughters have had an enjoyable and productive summer so far, as I'm sure you've witnessed while visiting with them today, and while reading the new issue of the *Birch Bark*, but they've also been working hard on breaking through self-imposed limitations, trying new things, stretching, and growing."

She outlines the rest of the day's activities—the mini-sessions they're invited to watch and participate in, the open swim, and the special Parents' Weekend dinner, complete with live entertainment.

That's where I come in, along with the Camp Chorale.

"Let's get this party started!" Gwen finishes, dismissing us.

I spend the next hour rotating between my station in Lower Lodge with my music counselor hat on and my station down on the Point at the Gazebo with my Junior Naturalists hat on as I answer questions and give the parents a taste of what their daughters are learning. At Lower Lodge, I lead the parents in a quick song, and at the Gazebo, I pass out binoculars and help them look for loons. It's fun.

Afterward, I head for the boat dock, where I've volunteered to show off the bald eagle family that nests on Cherry Island. Darcy and his parents are among my first customers.

"Looks like it's Parents' Weekend on the island as well," I joke as the boat draws close to the island's shore. I point out the male and female breeding pair hovering by a huge nest high in one of the trees. "And check out that nest! Did you know that a bald eagle's nest can weigh up to a ton and measure up to eight feet across?"

One of the dads gives a low whistle.

"There's the baby!" I cry, pointing to the beach below, and everyone grabs their binoculars and cameras.

"He's a pretty big baby," says Mrs. Hawthorne.

"Yep," I reply. "He's already fledged, and is actually probably about three or four months old, but he'll stick close-by for a while yet. Here's a Fun Fact for you—did you know that baby eaglets can gain up to six ounces a day? That's the fastest growth rate of any North American bird."

I reel through a few more bald eagle Fun Facts as the boat slowly circles the island, pausing frequently for photo ops.

Darcy gives me a big thumbs-up as we head back to the dock. "Since when did you become such an eagle expert?"

"Since I invited the Lake Lovejoy game warden to come and talk to my Junior Naturalists," I tell him.

He laughs and reaches down to help me out of the boat. "Great job."

I smile up at him. "It was fun—I love doing stuff like this."

"You should join those Central Park birders when you get to New York."

"Birders?"

"Yeah—there's a bunch of people who go birding in the park regularly. There's even a movie about them. I think maybe my dad has the DVD. I'll try to find it for you."

"Sweet! Thanks."

I tell him I'll see him at dinner, then head off to find Cassidy and round up our campers.

The Dining Hall is looking festive, with the big Parents' Weekend welcome banner over the fireplace and bright balloon bouquets everywhere.

"We're over here," I tell our campers and their families, leading them to a table by the far bank of windows.

Ethel and Thelma have outdone themselves with a surprise midsummer Thanksgiving dinner—"because we're thankful you're all here," as Gwen puts it—complete with homemade pumpkin pies.

"Is the food always this good?" asks Mr. Simpson, helping himself to a second slice.

I nod. "The cooks are really amazing."

As dessert is being cleared away, I signal to the members of the Camp Chorale and we all file over to the big stone fireplace. I line them up, give them their note, and then we launch into the medley of camp songs that I arranged. It goes over really well, especially at the end when we invite everyone to join in with us on the chorus of "Blue Socks."

We take our seats again to thunderous applause. A series of brief recitals follows—a team of tap dancers, a piano-and-flute duet by a pair of campers from the Hill, and a violin piece by Amy Osborne, who is surprisingly accomplished for someone so tiny.

Amy bows shyly as everyone claps, then rushes back to sit by her mother, who is resplendent tonight in a deep green sari. As Amy takes her seat, my cousin strides out in one of her many robes. "And now it's time for Felicia's Finale," she announces loudly, striking a dramatic pose.

I cringe. I told Felicia not to call it that, but of course she didn't listen to me. I focus on keeping my gaze fixed straight ahead, not daring to look at Cassidy, who I'm sure is grinning from ear to ear.

With a flourish of her cape, Felicia lifts her sackbut to her lips and proceeds to deliver her solo. She's actually pretty good, if you like trombone-type music, but then she has to go and ruin it with one of her little lectures, droning on about the origins of the instrument and its importance in Renaissance- and Baroque-era music. This goes over as expected, which is to say the audience is stunned into silence.

All except for my aunt Bridget and uncle Hans, who managed to slip away from their duties at the Edelweiss Inn in time to catch their daughter's performance. I watch them beaming proudly and clapping like mad. If they think Felicia's O-D-D, the certainly don't let on.

Parents are like that.

Or at least they should be, I think, glancing over at Mr. and Mrs. Simpson. Emma told me what happened earlier today with Nica.

Finally, the celebration is over and it's time to say good-bye. As the Dining Hall empties into the grove, Darcy comes over to join me.

"Today wasn't long enough," he says, putting his arms around me by the car.

"Not at all," I agree.

I stand there for a moment, resting my head on his chest and breathing him in. I wish I were bold enough to kiss him in public. I hug him fiercely instead, then step back as he climbs into the minivan with his parents and Pip. The two of us wave to each other until the minivan is out of sight.

Emma bumps her hip against mine. "You okay?"

I laugh. "So now you're the one worried about me? Yeah, I'm fine." And we head back to our cabins to help get our campers ready for Council Fire.

"We always schedule a Council Fire at the end of Parents' Weekend," Gwen told us at our counselors' meeting in her cottage a few nights ago. "It gets everyone focused back on camp again, and helps avoid relapses of homesickness."

It's a good strategy. Especially since I'm feeling a few pangs myself at the moment. A big piece of my heart just drove away with Darcy Hawthorne.

"Bundle up in hoodies and sweatpants," I tell my girls briskly, trying to shake off the blues. "It's cool up there in the woods."

Heather Vogel Frederick

I duck into my cubie to change, then stop abruptly. A glass jar full of wildflowers is sitting on my dressing table. There's a card propped up in front of it. Darcy must have managed to slip in when I wasn't around.

Smiling, I open the envelope. The card is adorable. On the front, two puppies who look just like Pip are curled up together on a sofa, and inside it says "I Ruff You." He drew a heart underneath and signed it "Love, Darcy." Feeling much better, I tack it happily to the wall above my mirror.

The evening activity bell rings, and Cassidy and I lead our girls to the grove, where we line up by cabins, youngest to oldest. Nest and Balsam are first, of course, then us, then Bluebird and Shady Grove and Meadow, and finally the three cabins on the Hill: Far, Farther, and Outback.

Marge holds up two fingers, and the excited chatter quickly stills. "We tread in silence to the Council Fire," she says solemnly, a pronouncement so corny it makes me stifle a giggle, but at the same time gives me a pleasant prickle of anticipation.

Daylight is fading as we start up the trail through the woods. Nica slips her hand in mine and I give it a squeeze.

"I'm glad you're my counselor, Jess," she whispers.

"Me too." I smile at her, wondering what I can do to make up for a mother who says hurtful stuff that she shouldn't. Emma hinted at dinner about an idea she has for something, but she wasn't sure if she'd have time to pull it off.

Since we're one of the three youngest cabins, we get front-row seats. The logs stacked in the ring of stones are already ablaze, and I stretch my hands in front of me, enjoying the warmth. It's amazing how cold it can get at night here, even in July.

After everyone is seated, Gwen stands up. She has a striped wool blanket draped over her shoulders, and on her head is a sort of tiara with seven stars on it. "Council Fire is a time for gratitude and reflection," she says. "A time to look back at the week behind us and celebrate our accomplishments, and look forward to the week ahead and set new goals."

I glance over at my campers, their smiling faces shining in the reflected light from the fire. It's hard to believe that half the summer has slipped by already.

"I know we're all filled up full of gratitude for wonderful visits with our families today," Gwen continues. "But I'd like you all to close your eyes for a moment and think of at least one more thing you're grateful for this week."

My campers dutifully squeeze their eyes shut. Cassidy and I exchange a smile over the tops of their heads, and then we close our eyes too.

What am I grateful for? What's not to be grateful for? is the real question. I have a wonderful family, of course. And there's college to look forward to—and not just any college, but Juilliard. *Juilliard!* In New York! I still have to pinch myself sometimes when I think about the fact that I'm actually going there.

What else? Emma. I'm grateful for Emma. She's the best friend anyone could ask for. I don't know what I'd do without her, and I can't

Heather Vogel Frederick

believe she's going to be so far away this fall. I am NOT grateful for that. Darcy, of course. I saved the best for last. He's the cherry on top of my gratitude sundae this evening.

"All right, girls," says Gwen, and we open our eyes. "The first thing I want to talk about tonight is Firelighters. As you know, the Firelighter is Camp Lovejoy's highest honor. At our final Council Fire of the summer, two girls—one from Lower Camp and one from the Hill—will be chosen for this award. We have a number of Firelighters from previous summers here with us tonight—girls, would you please stand up?"

About a dozen campers, CITs, counselors, and staff members rise to their feet.

"Whoa, check it out," whispers Cassidy. "Sergeant Marge was a Firelighter!"

Sure enough, the head counselor is standing proudly with the others.

Gwen talks a little more about the qualifications needed for the award—service to camp, kindness to others, willingness to work hard, a cheerful attitude—and encourages everyone to keep those goals uppermost in thought.

After that, it's time for the counselors to hand out beads. When it's my turn, I call out the names of all the girls whose names I painted earlier this week—one each for everyone who sang tonight, plus an extra for the soloists.

Amy's face lights up when she turns the wooden bead over and sees the tiny violin I painted on it.

"Good job," I tell her.

Emma is next. She hands out blue beads to the swimmers in her classes who earned them, white ones to some of the campers in her writing workshop, and finally green ones with "BB" on them (for *Birch Bark*) to all the campers who helped with the newsletter.

"I have one last special bead tonight, for a very special camper," she announces after distributing the others. "Monica Simpson, would you please come up here?"

Nica looks over at Freddie, who nods and gives her a nudge.

"I'm sure you've all read the beautiful poem on the front page of the new *Birch Bark*," Emma continues as Nica shyly joins her. "Since I am a poet myself, I know how hard it can be to share one's work with others. I'm giving this bead to Nica tonight as a thank-you not only for her poem, but also for the courage it took to share it with us all."

Well done, Emma, I think, looking at Nica's beaming face.

"Let me see!" Freddie begs when her twin returns to our bench. She turns the bead over. "Oh cool, look, there's a loon on it!"

I give Emma a big thumbs-up.

Council Fire is winding down when there's a rustling in the bushes behind us. Everyone turns around to see seven figures gliding down the path. They're dressed all in white with pale material draped around their shoulders, and they're wearing beautiful glittery silver eye masks. Each one has a starry crown just like Gwen's, only theirs have just one star each.

"Rise for the Seven Sisters!" Sergeant Marge intones.

A ripple of excitement flows through the gathered campers. The

Heather Vogel Frederick

Sisters only appear once each summer, and nobody knows ahead of time when that will be, or who will be chosen to play the roles.

As we stand up, the masked figures form a semicircle around Gwen. One of them hands her a birch-bark scroll. She unfurls it and begins to read:

> *We are the Pleiades—*
> *We sail the dark skies.*
> *We come to earth each summer*
> *To remind you who you are.*
> *Not born of dust but of starlight—*
> *And, like stars, shining, ever shining.*

When she finishes, the figures step forward one by one.

"I am joy," says the first. "I embrace each day with enthusiasm."

"I am integrity," says the second, whose voice sounds familiar. "I always speak and act honorably."

Cassidy leans over toward me. "I think that's Melissa Yee," she whispers, and I nod.

As they continue around the semicircle, the skin on the back of my neck prickles. Even though I know that these are my fellow staffers in disguise, there's something both eerie and regal about the way they stand by Gwen, their masks glittering in the reflected light of the bonfire.

"I am honesty," says another. "I always tell the truth."

One by one the seven of them step forward, on through

humility, wisdom, and purity. Some of the voices I recognize—including Thelma's, from the kitchen—and some I don't.

The final figure steps forward. "I am courage," she says. "I am never afraid to stand for what is right."

They end by speaking a single sentence in unison. "We come to earth each summer to remind you who you are." And then, just as silently as they came, the seven figures file out, vanishing into the darkness. Without a word, we all reach out and clasp hands, and sing the traditional closing for Council Fire:

> *Peace I ask of thee O river,*
> *Peace, peace, peace.*
> *Ere I learn to live serenely,*
> *Cares will cease.*
> *From the hills I gather courage,*
> *Visions of the day to be.*
> *Strength to lead and strength to follow,*
> *All are given unto me.*
> *Peace I ask of thee O river,*
> *Peace, peace, peace.*

As the last notes fade away, the campers start to file out of the circle, oldest to youngest, walking in silence back to camp.

I'm passing Gwen when I'm suddenly struck by an idea. I pause for a moment and whisper something in her ear. She nods.

Heather Vogel Frederick

Back at Cubbyhole, our campers change into their pajamas and head over to Twin Pines. Before they can climb into bed, I clap my hands quietly. "Put a sweatshirt or fleece on, girls," I instruct them. "Right over your pajamas is fine. Then come with me."

"What's going on?" asks Cassidy.

I smile at her. "You'll see."

We pad down the path to the water ski beach, where I spread a big blanket on the sand. I lie down and motion to everyone to join me. "There's room for all of us," I tell them, then wait for everyone to get comfortable. "Look up, girls," I tell them, pointing to the sky. "Remember the Pleiades, the Seven Sisters who just visited our campfire? Well, the Pleiades are a star cluster, located in the Taurus constellation. You can't quite see it this time of year, but what you *can* see is the Delta Aquarids meteor shower."

"What's a meteor shower?" asks Freddie.

"Shooting stars."

A chorus of oohs and aahs goes up at that.

"The Delta isn't as intense as next month's Perseid meteor shower, but it's still worth staying up late for." I look over at Cassidy and smile. "Gwen thought so too."

"Look!" cries Nica. "I see one!"

"Jess knows what she's talking about," Cassidy says. "If you're all quiet and still, I'll bet you see a lot of them tonight."

"*When you wish upon a star*," I sing softly, thinking back to that night in England a few years ago when Darcy Hawthorne first held my hand.

"Who's got a wish to share?" asks Cassidy. "I'll go first. I wish for the BU hockey team to have its best season ever."

We go around the blanket, each girl sharing her wish. For Freddie, it's to get to be a Shark this summer in swimming. Brooklyn wants a bull's-eye in archery; Carter a baby sister. "One as good as Chloe," she says, and we all laugh.

Finally it's Nica's turn. "I wish I could write better poems," she says wistfully.

I know she's thinking about her mother's curt words earlier today. I reach for her hand and give it a squeeze. "Your poems are brilliant, Nica, and you should never stop writing them."

"She's right," says Cassidy. "Gotta follow your dreams, no matter what anybody says."

"How about you, Jess?" asks Brooklyn, propping herself up on one elbow and looking over at me. "What do you wish for?"

I gaze up at the sky, smiling. I already have everything my heart could possibly desire.

For my girls, though—for my girls I wish the moon and stars.

Heather Vogel Frederick

 Becca

"... it was decided that Betsy should celebrate her birthday by going up to Woodford, where the Fair was held."
—*Understood Betsy*

I hate it when people ask me what I'm going to major in at college.

The truth is, I have absolutely no idea.

I know I have some strengths—I'm an excellent organizer, like my mother, for instance. Maybe it's a Chadwick thing, but we're both really good at taking charge and bossing people around and making sure that stuff gets done. I'm sort of interested in architecture, thanks to my grandmother who suggested it and who keeps sending me books on the subject. But as a future career? I don't know. And I don't know if I have any actual career-type skills. Does waitressing count? Or being a camp counselor?

I really envy people like Theo, who's wanted to be a herpetologist— somebody who studies snakes—since before he could even pronounce the word. Emma's the same way. Megan and Cassidy figured out their goals early too, and Jess has so many things she's good at it's not even fair. Me? I guess I'll just have to make it up as I go along.

"Why don't you take some business classes?" Gigi urged me when I saw her at Parents' Weekend and we had a few minutes to talk. Megan's grandmother is a lot like mine. Well, except for the fact that she's from Hong Kong and my grandmother is from Minnesota. They're both really good listeners and they love giving advice. "A smart, hard-working girl like you," Gigi told me, "should be running her own business."

I've been thinking about that ever since. I really respect Gigi's opinion. She's smart, and she's an amazing businesswoman herself. In addition to the tea shop, she owns rental properties in Hong Kong, and she has a bunch of other investments. Gigi's the one who, when she found out that I was saving for a car, helped me open an account that earned decent interest instead of just keeping my tips in a glass jar on my dresser. It made a big difference over the course of the two years I worked to earn the money, and I finally bought my first car this spring, right before graduation. I'm letting Stewart use it this summer while I'm here at camp, but I'll be taking it to Minneapolis with me when I leave for school this fall.

"Becca!"

I jerk out of my reverie. "Sorry, what?"

"Gwen just asked you a question," says Sergeant Marge.

We're sitting in the living room of the Director's Cottage for our weekly post-lunch cabin counselors' meeting. The CITs are on duty covering for all of us during rest hour. "I was just wondering if you and

Heather Vogel Frederick

Megan have any issues with your campers that you'd like to bring up," Gwen repeats.

Megan and I exchange a glance. I shrug.

"Not really," I tell her. "Harper seems to be over her homesickness, and Amy still struggles with it a bit, but she's starting to come out of her shell."

Gwen nods. "Good work. Anything else?"

"This is probably no big deal," Megan adds, "but last night I overheard Grace and her friends talking about how they think the cubie house is haunted."

Gwen's eyebrows shoot up.

"Yeah, some of our campers have been talking about that too," says Cassidy. "I guess one of the girls heard sounds in there a few nights ago."

Sergeant Marge frowns. "What kinds of sounds? Voices? I'll call over to Pinewood and talk to them, if it's those boys again."

"No, not voices," Cassidy tells her. "More like rustling or scratching."

"It's probably the skunk," says Gwen, making a note of it. "I'll have Artie get the trap out."

"You won't hurt him, will you?" Jess sounds anxious.

"Not at all," the camp director assures her. "We get one wandering through just about every summer, and Artie's become a master at trapping and relocating them." She puts her clipboard down. "Now, girls, tonight is our annual all-camp surprise birthday party."

A few of the other counselors—including Felicia, surprisingly—squeal at this news. I've heard about this tradition. It's one of camp's most popular ones, designed to celebrate everybody's birthday in one fell swoop.

Cassidy looks over at Megan and me. "More songs ahead," she whispers. Cassidy thinks all the singing we do here at Camp Lovejoy is hilarious. I do too, actually, in an annoying sort of way. I've never sung so much in my life, not even in kindergarten.

"As you know, this is all top-secret," Gwen continues. "Ethel and Thelma are working on the cupcakes even as we speak, and the CITs will be decorating the Dining Hall during free period."

Sergeant Marge circles the living room, passing out big paper grocery bags to each pair of cabin counselors.

"What's this?" asks Jess, peering into hers.

"Presents for your campers, wrapping paper, and ribbon. You all get started wrapping while Gwen keeps talking, okay?"

We do, and she does.

"Our evening activity tonight will be traditional birthday games," Gwen continues, "Musical chairs, pin-the-tail-on-the-donkey, that sort of thing. With a Camp Lovejoy twist, of course. The girls love it."

"*Happy birthday to everyone*," sings Cassidy in a whisper, and I stifle a giggle.

"Between the birthday party and our big field trip tomorrow to the state fair, the campers are going to be pretty keyed up this weekend. So if you have any memory-makers up your sleeves, I'd suggest you postpone them for a few days."

Gwen introduced us to memory-makers way back during orientation.

"I want you all to do something special for your campers this summer," she'd told us. "I want you to break a rule—a minor one. Give them the thrill of thinking they'll be caught. Let them go skinny-dipping, raid the kitchen for a midnight snack, do something ever-so-slightly naughty that they can take home with them as a fun and exciting memory."

There's only one condition: We have to tell Gwen first. I guess that way she can make sure we aren't choosing an activity that's lame-brained or unsafe, plus, she'll make sure we don't get into trouble with Sergeant Marge.

Megan and I are pretty well settled on a midnight snack as our memory-maker. Ice cream bars, maybe, or possibly a doughnut run if we can borrow Cassidy's minivan and get permission to take our girls off camp property. Emma's trying to talk Felicia out of her pet plan, which is to have their campers dress up and reenact a medieval joust on the tennis courts. Jess's cousin has this idea to use tiki torches for lights. Cassidy thinks it's kind of cool, but seriously, with seven-year-olds? They'll probably set their costumes on fire.

My eyes slide over to Emma. She's been subdued ever since Parents' Weekend, and I don't think it's because of Felicia. I know she was disappointed that Stewart didn't come. Emma has a hard time hiding her emotions. Plus, knowing her, she's probably been writing all sorts of sad, tortured poetry. I wish I could tell her that my brother isn't worth all the angst. I mean, he's a great guy and I love him to pieces, but at the end of the day he's still, well, just Stewart.

I reach for a present to wrap. Each camper is getting a Camp Lovejoy baseball cap and matching key ring. Wouldn't exactly top my list of coveted birthday presents, but it's the thought that counts, right?

"So, for our state fair trip tomorrow, here are the logistics," says Gwen, consulting her clipboard again. "I want you and your campers to be at the grove, dressed and ready to go, by nine a.m. sharp. That means hustling everyone through breakfast and cabin cleanup. Make sure your campers bring sunscreen and a hoodie, please. Lower Camp will be on Bus Number One; the Hill on Bus Number Two. Camp will cover the entrance fee for everyone, and the kitchen will pack us up bag lunches, but you may want to have your campers bring a little spending money for extras. Got it?"

On the sofa beside me, Megan does a happy little shimmy when she hears the magic words "spending money." Shopping is one of our favorite activities, and even though the state fair is not exactly a prime prospect in the retail arena, still, it's better than the offerings here at camp—which are zilch—or even Pumpkin Falls, which aren't much better unless you really like general stores.

"Becca! You got mail!" whispers Harper as I slip back into our cabin a few minutes later. I give Sarah, the CIT who's been watching over

Heather Vogel Frederick

Balsam for Megan and me, a thumbs-up. She nods and heads out to return to her own cabin.

"Thanks, Harper," I whisper back, my stomach giving a joyful flutter when I see the return address. It's from Theo. Opening the envelope, I settle in to read it in the few minutes we have left of rest hour.

> Dear Becca,
> You'll never guess what happened. Arthur escaped!

Theo has a pet king snake. Of course he named it Arthur.

> I must have left the clamp on the lid of his cage loose.
> Anyway, my mother is not happy in a Very Big Way. Arthur
> got loose once a few years ago, and I ended up finding him
> a week later in my dirty laundry hamper. He'll show up
> eventually. I'm not too concerned, but the rest of the family
> is kind of on edge. I keep telling them they don't have to
> worry—Arthur is harmless.
> Grandma was supposed to come to dinner this
> weekend, but she took us out to a restaurant instead.
> "I'll be back over once Theo's slithery friend
> reappears," she told us, and offered to let my mother come
> stay with her until he does. Isn't that crazy?

I smile. It's so Theo. He can be a little clueless sometimes. If I were his mother, I'd have taken his grandmother up on her offer in a hot second.

The boy definitely has snakes-on-the-brain. Me? Not even a wiggle. But when you're crazy about a guy who's crazy about snakes the way Theo is, you have to at least try to like them a little bit.

And actually, they're way more interesting than I ever would have imagined. Not as interesting as, say, our dog YoYo, or something you'd actually want to play with or cuddle, but still, interesting.

I went to Minnesota again this past spring break and spent a lot of time with Theo. We visited snakes at the zoo, the pet store, and the zoology department at the university, where we'll both be freshmen soon. Theo is already a fixture in the zoology department. He's been hanging around there since he was in middle school. The zoo knows him too—he volunteered there through high school, and this summer they actually started paying him. He's cleaning cages, mostly, but like me, he's got to help pay for college somehow.

Which reminds me, I need to contact the Student Employment office soon and let them know I'll be looking for a part-time job this fall. Between what my parents and grandparents can contribute, my tuition is covered, but I need to help pay for room and board plus any extras, including gas for my car. If the university doesn't have any job possibilities, I'm hoping I can find work waitressing. It pays really well, especially with tips. Theo said he could try to get me a job at the zoo, but cleaning cages is not my style.

The bell rings, signaling the end of rest hour, and as our campers scatter to their afternoon activities, I head up to the Art Studio with Megan.

Heather Vogel Frederick

It's hot this afternoon, with very little breeze, so we move third- and fourth-period crafts outside onto the shady part of the deck. This week we're teaching the girls how to make button bracelets. At Megan's request, Gigi brought us two plastic tubs full of buttons over Parents' Weekend. It's proving to be another popular project, and both sessions are completely full.

I'm making a bracelet for my mother using buttons with an animal theme, since she still has a thing for animal prints, and another one for my grandmother. For her, I've chosen brightly colored buttons with interesting patterns on them. That was as close as I could get to a quilt.

Between working on my own bracelets and helping our campers with theirs, the afternoon passes quickly. Before I know it, it's time for free period, and my quilters.

By now I have a pretty regular following. There are three serious quilters from the Hill, high school girls who are each working on twin-size quilts for their beds at home, plus Pippa Lovejoy's sister Lauren from Meadow and my own Amy Osborne.

It's funny, I'm the last person I ever would have expected to get hooked on quilting, but this last spring break, while Theo was at school—our breaks were different weeks, unfortunately, so he could only hang out after school and in the evenings—my grandmother got me started piecing quilt squares together for one of her projects. Within a day, I was smitten.

"There's something, I don't know, soothing about it," I explained to Theo. "But I feel prematurely elderly. All I've done all week is sit around quilting and talking to my grandmother and her friends."

"What's wrong with that?" he replied, looking perplexed. "It's a cool art form, Becca. Have you see some of the quilts they hang in art galleries? They're phenomenal!"

This is one of the things I really appreciate about Theo. His perspective is so different from most guys I know, who would have just poked fun at quilting. Maybe there's something to be said for spending all your time with snakes.

"Come sit by me, Amy," I say, patting the bench. She's working on a pattern that I got for her from my Wyoming friend Summer Williams. When I e-mailed Summer to tell her I needed something simple and easy, something that an eight-year-old who had never quilted before in her life could do, she wanted to know what Amy's interests were.

"Um, music—she plays the violin—and chipmunks ..." I hesitated, trying to think what else. "Her favorite color is blue."

"Let's go with music," Summer said. "I've got just the thing."

Sure enough, a few days later a package arrived. Inside were all the ingredients for a really cute wall hanging. On the center square, which is white, there's an appliqué of a violin, and surrounding it is a framework of bright blue squares. Around the edge, Summer added a strip of white fabric dotted with a pattern of musical notes. Amy was thrilled.

"It's looking good," I tell her. "Try to keep those stitches as small and even as possible."

"Hey, Amy," says Anna, one of the high school quilters, "I've been

Heather Vogel Frederick

meaning to tell you, your violin solo at Parents' Weekend was awesome."

Amy looks up, her dark eyes shining, clearly thrilled at the teenager's praise. I could hug Anna—this is just the kind of thing my camper needs to hear to boost her confidence.

At dinner, the surprise all-camp birthday party goes off without a hitch. The campers seem really tickled with their presents, and the counselors are surprised with gifts as well. If I'm not all that excited about the special staff baseball cap, at least the fleece blanket with the camp logo on it will be great for my dorm room.

As Cassidy predicted, there are more songs. It's actually really fun, and we end by forming a procession line, all holding up cupcakes lit with single candles as we circle the Dining Hall, singing *Happy birthday to me.*

"Make a wish, girls!" calls Gwen when we're done. "Close your eyes and count to three!"

Can a person wish for a snake to find his way home? I wonder as I blow my candle out.

The games afterward are great, too. There's pin-the-tail-on-the-counselor (with duct tape, thank goodness), a piñata that's supposed to be a giant canoe (Cassidy thinks it's actually a banana turned sideways), and for the grand finale, musical kayaks in the inner H dock, which ends up with most of us getting drenched.

And there's one more surprise in store tonight.

"What are you guys doing?" Jess demands, letting out a yelp as Megan and Cassidy and Emma and I all barge into her cubie while she's getting ready for bed.

"You don't think we'd let your birthday go by unnoticed, do you?" Emma asks her.

"It's not my birthday."

Cassidy grins. "Close enough, right?"

Jess's birthday is tomorrow.

"We figured there'd be too much going on tomorrow, what with the trip to the fair," I explain, and we launch into another rousing chorus of "Happy Birthday."

We're just singing the last line—"*Happy birthday, dear Jessica Joy! Happy birthday to you!*"—when Felicia pokes her head in.

"What's going on?" she asks.

"Uh, nothing," Emma replies sheepishly. "Just a sort of miniparty for Jess."

"Oh." Felicia tries to hide it, but I can tell she's hurt that we didn't invite her.

"Come on in," says Jess, but her cousin shakes her head.

"That's okay. I need to round up our campers anyway."

"Oh dear," whispers Emma after she leaves. "I never even thought to invite her."

"Never mind," says Jess. "I'll make it up to her later."

We pass around a tin of homemade fudge—Gigi and Sophie's contribution to the party—along with a few gifts that Emma collected from friends and family.

"My parents sent me socks? *Socks?*" Jess stares at the contents of their package in disbelief.

"I think there's something inside," I tell her, and sure enough, there's a gift certificate to the mall tucked into one of them. "You're never too old to shop for school clothes" is written on the card that accompanies it.

"Nice!" Jess is pleased. "I need some new stuff for college."

"Maybe we can go on a group shopping trip when we get back to Concord," Megan suggests. "You know, help each other pick out some outfits?"

Cassidy snorts. "As if." She hates to shop.

"You could use a few things," I tell her. "Those jeans of yours are looking pretty ratty."

She lifts a shoulder. "Maybe."

Jess gets another gift certificate from the rest of the book club moms—they must have discussed this and coordinated with Mrs. Delaney—and a really nice messenger bag from all of us.

"A messenger bag is a step up from a backpack," Megan tells her.

"We thought black would look sophisticated," Emma adds. "It'll be helpful for carrying books and music and stuff back and forth to class." She points to the initials "JJD" embroidered on the front. "We even had it monogrammed for you.

"Thanks, you guys," says Jess. "I love it."

The final present is from Darcy. We crowd around as Jess unwraps the tiny box.

"Good things come in small packages," Emma tells her, and Jess turns pink again.

We ooh and aah as she lifts the lid. A small gold heart necklace is nestled inside.

"Is that a *diamond* on it?" I gasp, catching the reflection of a tiny sparkle.

Jess nods, then tries it on. "How does it look?" she asks, angling to see herself in the teeny mirror over her dressing table.

"Beautiful," Emma tells her. "Just like you."

I can't even imagine Theo ever giving me something like that. Unless maybe it had a snake on it.

Jess is so happy, though, that it's impossible to be envious.

"You'll definitely have sweet dreams tonight!" I tell her.

It's been a long day, and I'd give anything to be able to take a leisurely bubble bath, but I have to settle for just falling into bed. I crinkle my nose at the faint smell of skunk outside our cabin, but I'm too tired for it to really bother me. I'm actually kind of hoping it rains tomorrow so we can stick around camp, have an extended rest hour, and maybe just do some quiet stuff. An all-afternoon quilting session would be fantastic.

The next morning, though, there's no sign of rain. Just more hot sun. We lather up our girls and ourselves with sunscreen, make sure everyone has their matching Camp Lovejoy baseball caps, and pile onto the buses.

As we're boarding, I notice Artie unloading a wire cage of some sort from the back of his truck.

"It's probably a trap for the skunk, or whatever's crawling around under the cubies," says Jess. "It looks like one Walter Mueller uses."

Heather Vogel Frederick

Mr. Mueller is the animal rehabilitator she works with back in Concord.

As we watch Artie carry the trap down the path toward Lower Camp, the buses begin to lurch out of the parking area. We bounce and rattle our way up the Hill and onto the winding back roads leading to the fair.

"This will be good practice for you for living in the Midwest," Cassidy teases me. "They're big on state fairs there, from what I hear."

"Shut up," I tell her.

"I went to hockey camp in Wisconsin one summer, and we stopped at the state fair. I've never seen so much cheese in my life."

"Shut *up*," I tell her again.

"Maybe you can be the Butter Queen," she muses. "They really have those, you know."

"Cassidy!"

"Becca Chadwick, Minnesota's Butter Queen," she crows in a fake radio announcer voice, and this time I have to laugh. "It has a nice ring to it, don't you think?"

Actually, I love state fairs. Not that I've been to that many, but my grandparents used to take me and Stewart to the one in Minnesota when we were little. I still have happy memories of seeing all the animals and going on the rides and eating fried dough and stuff.

It takes us nearly an hour to get to the fairgrounds, and we're all thoroughly sick of sitting on the hot buses by the time we arrive.

"Remember to stay with your counselors!" Sergeant Marge bellows as we spill out onto the parking lot. "And remember we're meeting for lunch at high noon in the picnic area!"

"What do you girls want to do first?" Megan asks our campers.

"See the quilts," says Amy, and the other girls all groan.

"No way—roller coaster!" cries Grace.

"Bumper cars!" adds Mia, jumping up and down.

"Ball toss!" says Kate. "I want to win a stuffed animal."

In the end, we agree to split up. Megan will take Grace, Mia, and Kate on a couple of rides while Amy and Harper and I check out the quilts.

"Meet us by the Thunderchicken in an hour," Megan tells us. "We can do the ball toss together before lunch."

We counselors have been given our cell phones back, just in case somebody gets lost or there's an emergency and we have to reach Marge or Gwen. The camera on mine is working overtime as I try to capture all the gorgeous quilt designs. The exhibit is pretty phenomenal.

I'm snapping away when I feel a tug on the hem of my T-shirt. It's Harper.

"What's up?"

"Can Amy and I go on the Ferris wheel?" she asks.

I look over at Amy, surprised. "Really? You want to go for a ride?"

She hesitates, glancing over at Harper, then nods.

Broadening horizons for over a hundred years! The camp motto comes floating into mind and I smile at my campers. "Well, okay then, let's go."

Heather Vogel Frederick

The cars are just two-seaters, so I put Amy and Harper together into one of them, making sure the seat belts are secure and the safety bar fastened. "I'll be on the one right behind you," I assure them, but my phone rings just as they're whisked away. It's my mother.

"Hey, Mom!" I say, deciding to answer it. I motion to the next person in line to take my spot. "What's up?"

"Wow, you actually answered! I was just going to leave you a voice mail. You know, something about how much I miss my favorite daughter, that sort of thing."

I laugh. "I'm your only daughter, Mom. And I'm kind of busy right now." I glance up at the wheel, which is revolving slowly. Another car is approaching—I should get on.

Amy and Harper wave at me in excitement. I wave back. There's really no need for me to go on the ride, I decide. I'll be able to keep an eye on them from down here.

"I guess I can talk for a couple of minutes, though," I tell my mother, stepping out of line.

She fills me in on life back in Concord, and then I tell her about the quilts, and about my latest letter from Theo.

"His *snake* went missing?" she squeals with an audible shudder. "His poor mother!"

Eventually, we get around to college.

"Your course catalog arrived today," my mother says. "I had a poke through it. Wow—there's so much to choose from! I don't know how you're ever going to decide what classes to take, or what to major in."

My heart sinks at this. She knows I've been struggling, trying to figure out what I might want to focus on. "Not helpful, Mom."

She laughs. "Oh honey, it's a good problem to have! So many avenues are open to you right now. You have a rich four years ahead!"

"You think so?"

"I know so."

I wave to Amy and Harper again. The cars are all full now, and the Ferris wheel is starting to pick up speed.

"Are you enjoying being a counselor?" my mother asks, changing the subject.

"Yeah."

"You sound surprised."

"I guess I am," I tell her. "I didn't think I'd like it this much."

"Maybe you should think about taking some education classes."

I'm silent for a moment. "Education? You mean teaching?"

"You've heard of it, then?" She laughs again. "It's a fine profession."

I've never, ever, not once in my life thought about being a teacher. It's not even on my radar screen.

"Um, maybe," I reply cautiously. "We'll see." Which is borrowed mom-code for "not a chance."

Amy and Harper swoop by, both of them clutching the safety bar and shrieking—with delight, I think. Looking again, I'm not so sure.

"Gotta go, Mom," I tell her.

"Love you!"

"Love you, too."

The Ferris wheel whips around again, so fast it makes me slightly dizzy. Harper's red braids are flying behind her, and she and Amy are clutching each other. Uh-oh. Not a good sign. Suddenly, just as my campers' car reaches the very top, the wheel jerks to a stop. I stare up at the two girls, aghast, as their car swings wildly back and forth. They stare back down at me, equally aghast. Then they both burst into tears.

"Oh no," I say aloud to no one in particular. Of all the girls for this to happen to, why on earth did it have to happen to these two?

I text Megan: COME QUICK! FERRIS WHEEL!

She texts back: CAN'T! JUST GOT ON THUNDERCHICKEN!

I'm on my own.

Think, Becca, think! Maybe I can distract them? What if I pretend this is fun? I wave my arms over my head, grinning madly. This gets their attention. I give them two big thumbs-up, like this is the coolest thing ever, then start blowing kisses at them. They exchange a glance. Cautiously, Harper pries one hand loose from the safety bar and blows me a kiss back.

Amy's face is still white, though, and she's still sobbing. No way is she letting go of that bar.

Throwing caution to the wind, I do a little dance, right there in the middle of the fairgrounds. I shimmy and shake for all I'm worth to the tune on the nearby merry-go-round, wagging my bottom at my campers and grinning up at them.

Both of Harper's hands are free now, and she throws them up in the air, laughing as she uses her upper body to dance along with me.

One down, one to go.

"What on earth are you doing?" booms a voice behind me.

I turn around. It's Sergeant Marge.

"Um," I reply, and point wordlessly upward.

Spotting the girls, she nods grimly. She doesn't hesitate, and in an instant the two of us are dancing. As we proceed to make complete fools of ourselves, the gathered crowd begins to clap, urging us on.

I glance up. Is that a glimmer of a smile on Amy's face? I wave, and she briefly lets go of the safety bar and manages a quick wave back.

By now the crowd has figured out what we're trying to do, and a few others join in the dance. We have quite a flash mob going by the time the Ferris wheel finally begins to move again. One by one, the cars descend and the passengers get off. When it's Amy and Harper's turn, both girls come flying over and fling their arms around me.

"You two were incredibly brave," I tell them. "Wait until the rest of Balsam hears about this."

"And you were incredibly creative. Good work, sport." Sergeant Marge gives me a pat on the back and walks off before I can reply.

The rest of the day passes uneventfully, which is fine with me. I've had about all the excitement I can handle. I nap most of the way back to camp on the bus.

As we're climbing off the buses, dinner is announced by a mournful toot on Felicia's sackbut.

"What's the deal with that?" asks Megan as we lead our campers to the Dining Hall. "Aren't we using the bell anymore?"

Heather Vogel Frederick

I shrug. "No idea."

Gwen and Sergeant Marge are standing on the porch, deep in conversation.

"Our bell has gone missing," I hear the head counselor say as we walk past. "It must have been Pinewood. They took it while we were at the fair. I'm going to call and give them a piece of my mind."

"Leave it for tonight, Marge," Gwen tells her. "It's been a long day, and you don't want to say something you'll regret. It's just a prank."

After dinner, we all head into Lower Lodge to watch a movie. Half of Lower Camp falls asleep as soon as it starts, thanks to too much Thunderchicken, too much Ferris wheel, and too much other excitement in the fairgrounds' hot sun.

"Did you hear about what happened to the bell?" Cassidy leans over a snoring Freddie.

"Yeah," Megan and I both reply. Jess and Emma nod too.

"Enough is enough," Cassidy mutters, shaking her head. "Pinewood's not going to know what hit them."

"What are you planning to do?" Jess asks.

But all Cassidy will say is, "It's going to be epic."

A couple of hours later, I wake up needing to visit the Biffy. Pulling my hoodie on over my pajamas, I slip out the door of Balsam, shutting the screen door quietly behind me.

"Chadwick!" someone whispers as I start down the path. I nearly jump out of my skin.

"Who's there?" I shine my flashlight toward Primporium.

Cassidy is standing there, holding something in her arms.

"Could you give me a hand?"

"With what?" I ask suspiciously.

"The trap."

I leap back about three feet. "The *skunk* trap?"

"Shut up! It's sleeping! Do you want to wake it?"

I should be sleeping too, not standing here having to go to the bathroom and instead being asked to lend a hand with a skunk trap.

"I know just the place where he'll feel right at home," Cassidy whispers, and I can hear the glee in her voice.

My heart sinks. "Pinewood?"

"Where else?"

I was afraid she was going to say this. "How are you planning to get him over there? Without waking him up, I mean?"

"It's easy. I looked it up on the Internet in the Counselors' Cabin." Cassidy sounds pleased with herself. "You just throw a blanket over the trap—I already did that—and make sure the latch on the gate is secure. Which it is. So go ahead and grab your end."

"I don't think this is a good idea," I tell her, but I take one end of the trap anyway. Cassidy has that effect on people.

"And now we'll carry it very gently to the canoe—"

"The *canoe*?" My whisper goes up an octave.

"*Shhhhhh!*"

"I am not getting in a canoe with a skunk!" I whisper furiously.

Heather Vogel Frederick

"Where's your spirit of adventure?" Cassidy retorts. "They stole our *bell*, Becca. Doesn't that mean something to you?"

"Only that maybe we'll finally get some peace and quiet around here!"

Cassidy is quiet for a moment; then her shoulders droop in resignation. "How about you just help me take it to the minivan, then. I'll find a wheelbarrow or something when I get to Pinewood."

"Oh, fine," I snap. "We'll take the canoe. Just tell me what you want me to do."

Gingerly—very gingerly—we carry the blanketed trap toward the boathouse path. The skunk must be asleep, because he doesn't make a peep. Or chirp, or bark, or whatever it is that skunks do.

I start to giggle. "This really will be an epic prank."

Cassidy brightens. "I know, right?!"

"Where are you going to let him loose?"

She shakes her head. "I don't know yet. Their shower house, maybe? I'll figure that part out when we get to Pinewood. Wherever I can get the most bang for my buck."

"The most stink for your skunk, you mean?"

Now we both dissolve in giggles.

"Shhhhh!" Cassidy shushes me as we approach Cabbage.

And then it happens.

"Hey, you guys!" someone calls out behind us in a loud whisper.

Startled, I whirl around. It's Jess. Before I can answer her, one of my hands starts to slip. I clutch frantically at the trap. Cassidy angles her knee underneath, trying to keep it upright.

Too late.

The trap slips to the ground with a loud crash, leaving me holding the blanket. Cassidy and I both stare at the gate. It's been jolted ajar, and the cage's furry occupant is trying to wriggle through. Jess lunges forward to try to help the panicked creature.

Behind us, the door to Cabbage flies open with a bang. "What is going on out here?" demands Sergeant Marge, just as the skunk decides to do what skunks do when they're startled or scared.

Jess shrieks. Sergeant Marge flips on her cabin's outside light and the skunk scuttles off into the darkness.

Jess is standing rooted to the ground, a horrified look on her face. That's not all that's on her face, unfortunately. Thick yellow goo drips from her forehead to her chin—and onto her braid.

I don't need to ask what it is.

I know by the smell.

Things have gone terribly, horribly wrong.

Cassidy's epic prank just backfired—literally.

Heather Vogel Frederick

AUGUST

"What would Cousin Ann do if she were here? She would think of something."
—*Understood Betsy*

❦ Jess ❦

"That was herself she was looking at! How changed she was! How very, very different she looked from the last time she had seen herself in a big mirror."
—*Understood Betsy*

I am so mad at Cassidy and Becca, I could just spit!

I still can't believe they would do such a boneheaded thing. That poor skunk! The thing is, if they'd only thought to ask me first, I might have been able to help. I know a lot about transporting trapped animals, from my volunteer work.

And forget about the skunk—poor me!

My hair looks awful and smells worse.

In the end, there was no saving it. Not even after Artie doused me with his special "plum guaranteed to de-stink the stink" potion, as he put it. Maybe it works on dogs, but I could still smell skunk even after I shampooed three times. There was nothing to be done for it: my hair had to come off.

Megan did the honors. She has some experience, thanks to a prank that was played on us once during a sleepover at Colonial Academy, when Cassidy got homemade taffy stuck in her hair. Megan managed to salvage things then, and I was hopeful that she might be able to repair the damage this time, too. Whether it was the fact that I woke her up in the middle of the night or the quality of the scissors that she used on me down at the Art Studio, the end result is that I'll be going off to college in a few weeks looking like a little boy.

And it's all Cassidy and Becca's fault.

It's been two days, and I'm still not speaking to either one of them. Sergeant Marge is beside herself over the whole thing, and ready to string Cassidy up by her thumbs, which would be fine by me. Cabbage stinks to high heaven. Someone stuck a sign on the cabin door that said SKUNK CABBAGE, but the head counselor didn't find that funny at all, and the sign quickly disappeared.

I gaze at myself morosely in my teeny cubie mirror. There's no way my hair is going to grow back before I go to Juilliard. And I still haven't figured out how I'm going to tell Darcy. He loved my braid.

There's a loud bleat from the Grove, and the cubie house starts to empty out. Ever since the camp bell disappeared, Felicia and her sackbut have been doing their part to keep us on schedule. Making one last face at myself, I turn the mirror to the wall. There's no point torturing myself any longer.

Of course this would have to happen just in time for the stupid allcamp photograph. I'm about to be immortalized forever looking like one of my little brothers. For the next zillion years, every time I visit camp I'll have to see the picture on the wall of the Dining Hall and be

Heather Vogel Frederick

reminded of the time two of my closest friends ruined my life.

I slouch outside, wondering if the photographer will let me wear a hat.

"Jess!" Emma trots over to join me. "I've been thinking about our book club meeting tonight."

"What about it?" My voice sounds cranky, even to my ears.

She frowns. "What are you so grumpy about?"

I point at my head. "Look at me, Ems! I don't have time to think about book club—I have to go get my picture taken looking like *this*! I'm practically bald!"

She laughs. "First of all, you're not bald," she says, linking her arm through mine. "And second of all, it's been two days. Get over yourself already. I told you, I actually like your hair better this way. You look adorable."

"I don't want to look adorable!" I burst out. "I want to look like me! Besides, I've always worn it long. It feels like I'm missing a limb or something."

"I get it, I understand, really I do," she replies. "The braid was your security blanket. But maybe you don't need it anymore. You're grown-up Jess now, sophisticated Jess, about-to-move-to-New-York-City-and-go-to-Juilliard Jess! Plus, Darcy's going to love the new look, I promise."

Emma keeps telling me this, but I'm not convinced. I finger Darcy's necklace, which I haven't taken off since I opened the box it was in. "You go ahead," I grumble, trying to untangle my arm. "I need to get something from my cabin."

Emma grips me more firmly, steering me away from Twin Pines. "You are not going to run off and hide, Jessica Joy Delaney, you are going to hold your chin up and march over to where your campers are waiting. Then you are going to line up alongside Cassidy and Becca, who may be idiots but who still love you to pieces and who would never do anything deliberately to hurt you, and you're going to smile for the camera."

I hate it when Emma gets bossy like this. The thing is, though, she's right, and I know it. I just don't want to admit it yet.

"Fine," I mutter, and grudgingly allow myself to be towed down the path to the steps of Lower Lodge, where the photographer is waiting.

"Don't forget to smile," Emma whispers, shoving me in line between Freddie and Nica.

After the group picture, it's time for cabin pictures. Cassidy lobbied for the Gazebo, and we head on down the Point to pose. We're just finishing up when a loud *Blaaaaaaaaaaat!*—much louder than Felicia's sackbut, almost like an air horn—brings everyone scurrying to the Dining Hall to find out the source of the commotion.

A pair of Hawaiian shirts are waiting on the porch. One of them contains Cassidy's friend Jake, from Pinewood. His buddy Chase is wearing the other one, blowing on a conch shell.

Blaaaaaaaaaaaat!

"Aloha!" Jake calls out when the sound dies away.

"Aloha!" a bunch of campers and counselors call back.

"Triton's trumpet summons the *wahinis* of Camp Lovejoy to join the Pinewood *brahs* for the annual luau across the waters!" Jake ceremoniously unfurls the scroll he's carrying to reveal the image of a giant tiki head.

Beside me, Cassidy scowls. "Pinewood better give us our bell back, or I'm going to stick Triton's trumpet in someone's ear."

We shush her.

"Camp Lovejoy gratefully accepts your kind invitation," says Gwen, striding up the steps and taking the scroll from Jake.

He bows, and Chase blows on the conch again. Then the two boys turn to leave.

"We want our bell back," Cassidy tells them as they pass by.

"I don't know what you're talking about," Jake replies smugly. He saunters off across the lawn toward the parking lot, then looks back over his shoulder at us, grinning.

"Just don't, okay?" I tell Cassidy, grabbing her arm to keep her from following him. "Whatever it is you're planning—don't."

"Even if I promise it won't involve skunks?"

I manage a smile.

She gives me a hopeful look. "So are we good again?"

"Yeah, we're good." And it's true. Maybe it's the talking-to that Emma gave me earlier, but suddenly I'm not mad at her anymore.

My day continues to improve too, because I have two letters and a postcard waiting for me at mail call.

"Savannah *and* Frankie *and* Madison?" Cassidy reads the return addresses over my shoulder. "Lucky you." She sighs. "All I got is another bridal magazine from my mother."

Cassidy's mom is in high gear with preparations for Courtney's Thanksgiving wedding. She's been sending Cassidy clippings from magazines, fabric samples, reception menu ideas, and other updates all summer long. I know it will be a fabulous event—and perfect in every detail, since Mrs. Sloane-Kinkaid is in charge—but wedding planning is not exactly Cassidy's cup of tea.

I open Savannah Sinclair's letter first, which is postmarked Washington, DC. Savannah is the daughter of a U.S. senator, and a former roommate of mine from Colonial Academy. We got off to a rocky start in the beginning, but she was my closest friend at school by the time we graduated. She's working for one of the Supreme Court justices this summer, and I can't wait to hear how it's going. I quickly scan her greeting and dive into the meat of the letter:

> I'm just a gopher—even my father couldn't pull enough strings to get me an internship, so I'll have to wait until after college to try for one of those. I'm doing mostly boring stuff like making photocopies, but overall, it's still really interesting, and the people I'm working with are supersmart and really funny.

She goes on to tell me that last weekend Darcy gave her a tour of the Smithsonian's National Museum of American History, where he's working this summer.

We had so much fun! He's such an awesome guy, Jess.

I feel a teeny stab of jealousy, but then I read the next paragraph:

And guess what? I brought my shiny new boyfriend
along! His name is Henry, and he's working for his
congressman this summer. His mother catered this big
party my parents were hosting, and he was helping her out
and that's how we met. You'll like him. He's a sophomore at
Georgetown, so now I REALLY can't wait until September!

Savannah's going to Georgetown too.

Smiling, I fold up her letter and put it back in its envelope, then
turn to Frankie's—Francesca Norris officially, another friend from
Colonial. She got invited to spend the summer with Adele Bixby. The
three of us roomed together again during our senior year. Adele lives
in San Francisco, and she and Frankie are working as au pairs for some
of Adele's mother's colleagues, which is kind of like being a camp counselor, I guess, except that they have to change diapers and stuff. The
two of them are going to be staying in the Bay Area for college, with
Adele at Stanford and Frankie at Mills College.

Dear Jess,
I have to keep pinching myself, knowing that I'll be

living here for the next four years! San Francisco is the most beautiful city I've ever seen. The Golden Gate Bridge is amazing, and with all the hills, there are views of the water everywhere I turn. It's cold here, though, and foggy. Adele says it's always that way in the summer. We've been exploring the neighborhoods on our days off, and in one of them she showed me this fabulous staircase all made of colorful tile. And we've been to the ballet twice, and guess what else? I just found out that I can apply to study at the San Francisco Conservatory of Dance my senior year through a special program at Mills. Isn't that cool?

I'm so glad my friends are as excited about college as I am. Madison's postcard is typically brief—my mother calls her a woman of few words—but her excitement about the future spills over in an abundance of exclamation points:

> T-MINUS ONE MONTH AND COUNTING!!!!
> SEE YOU SOON!!!!

Madison and her mother are going to stay with my family at Half Moon Farm the weekend Madison moves into her dorm. She's another of our Wyoming friends, part of a mother-daughter book club out West that we became pen pals with back in eighth grade. Madison's been accepted to the Berklee College of Music, and we're

Heather Vogel Frederick

already making plans for a big reunion in Boston at one of Cassidy's hockey games. Bailey Jacobs said she'd take the bus into the city from Mount Holyoke, and Megan and I will take the train up from New York. I can't wait to see everybody.

It's weird to think about how long ago our Wyoming summer seems. It's really only been four years, but it feels like a lifetime! I'm glad our mothers forced us all to be pen pals. The habit stuck, and we all still write to each other. I like keeping in touch with real letters or postcards now and then.

I lie back in my bunk, staring up at the ceiling. It's already August! In a little over a month from now I'll be starting college. I have this strange feeling of being on a downward slope these days, hurtling toward the future.

A future with radically different hair, I think morosely, running my fingers through my shorn mane. Oh well.

I must have drifted off after that, because my eyes fly open a few minutes later at the sound of another loud bleat from the grove—not a conch shell this time, but my cousin's sackbut, signaling the end of rest hour.

"We have *got* to get our bell back!" growls Cassidy. "That thing is even more obnoxious than the bell!"

Poor Felicia. She means well, and she's trying to help, but Cassidy is right. Her hourly sackbut blasts are pretty annoying.

"Who wants to serenade Pinewood at the luau?" I ask my third period chorale group.

By the number of hands that fly up—all of them—I'm guessing this idea's a hit.

"Great! I have just the song for us to do," I tell them. "How many of you know 'Somewhere Over the Rainbow'—the Israel Kamakawiwo'ole version?"

"Kamakawaka-who?" asks Pippa Lovejoy, her little forehead furrowing in confusion.

I laugh. "*Kamakawiwo'ole*," I repeat slowly. "He was a really famous Hawaiian musician."

Felicia raises her hand. "I know that version."

For some reason this surprises me. When it comes to songs, Felicia mostly seems interested in period folk ballads about knights in shining armor rescuing fair maidens.

"Can you sing it for us, Jess?" begs Amy.

Out of the corner of my eye, I see Felicia leaning against the wall. None of the campers are paying any attention to her; nobody's clamoring to hear her sackbut, or anything else for that matter. Sometimes you don't need to be sprayed by a skunk to feel like an outcast.

With a stab of guilt, I remember that I was going to do something to make up for her not getting invited to my mini-birthday party. "Okay," I tell the girls. "I'll sing it for you. But only if Felicia accompanies me."

My cousin looks at me, surprised.

"That's the deal," I continue firmly. "Felicia and I are a team."

Felicia's face lights up, and I feel another stab of guilt. It really

Heather Vogel Frederick

doesn't take much to make someone feel included. She grabs her sack-but and warms up with a low toot.

"Um, how about something a little less, uh, strident?" I suggest. "You know, more like Iz's ukulele?"

She nods slowly. "I might be able to do something with my lute."

Somehow, by strumming on the instrument's neck, she manages to make it sound just like a ukulele. Which doesn't surprise me. The thing is, everybody already knows how smart Felicia is—mostly because she's always so eager to tell them—but they don't necessarily know how creative and talented and fun she can be too. I keep thinking maybe there's a way I can help her be a little more, well, normal.

I sing the song through once for the girls, and then we practice it a couple more times all together.

"That was awesome!" I tell them when we're done. I wait until my cousin darts out of the lodge with her sackbut to trumpet the end of third period, then turn back to the campers. "Let's try it one more time, really quick—with a little twist," I say in a conspiratorial whisper. "But we're going to keep it a surprise, okay?"

Later that afternoon, I'm at the boathouse finishing up with my Junior Naturalists—we canoed over to Cherry Island to check on the bald eagle family—when a tremendous racket breaks out all over camp. A herd of CITs flashes past us, banging on pots and pans and shouting "UTENSIL NIGHT!"

The girls who have been to camp before all start to shriek with delight. Utensil Night is one of everybody's favorite traditions, and like the all-camp birthday party, nobody knows when it will be held, which makes it doubly fun. I remember it vividly from when I was a camper here myself.

"This should be interesting," says Cassidy a few minutes later, as we line up by cabins outside the Dining Hall. Artie is standing at the top of the porch steps. When we file past him, each camper reaches into the big garbage bag he's holding and blindly grabs a utensil.

"No way!" says Cassidy when it's her turn. "I seriously have to eat with these?" She holds up a pair of extra-long barbecue tongs.

"Yup!" Grinning, I wave the garlic press that I snagged.

Of course, Ethel and Thelma always make sure to cook the messiest possible meal on utensil night. Even Carter, who usually never has a hair out of place, manages to smear spaghetti sauce all over her face trying to take bites off a spatula, and watching Freddie trying to eat with a giant whisk—she's our messy camper anyway, so this was a disastrous choice—sends our table into gales of laughter. Cassidy laughs so hard she actually cries.

"I love camp!" she gasps.

I smile at her. Of all of us, I think Cassidy is having the most fun this summer. I envy her sometimes. She has such a gift for throwing herself wholeheartedly into things.

"I'm going to starve to death," complains Brooklyn, daintily spearing a single strand of pasta with a lobster pick.

Heather Vogel Frederick

I pat her shoulder. "I doubt it. Don't forget, we have book club tonight. At least there'll be snacks."

She brightens at this.

And in fact, there are snacks—good ones, too. It's Balsam's turn to host, and they serve applesauce, since in one of this week's chapters Betsy makes applesauce from scratch. We also have cookies in honor of Emma, who's been running around for days spouting one of her favorite quotes from the book: "It's against my principles to let a child leave the pantry without having a cookie."

"That's kind of a perfect life motto, isn't it?" she muses, taking another one from the plate. They're chocolate chip, her favorite. "We should get it put on T-shirts or something. We'd make a fortune."

"We wanted to make maple syrup on snow, the way Cousin Ann taught Betsy to do in the book," Becca tells us. "But it's August, so that was out."

"Fine with me." Cassidy grabs a handful of cookies as the platter comes around. "I like cookies better than maple syrup, anyway."

"So," says Felicia, who's livelier than usual tonight. I'm wondering if it has something to do with me making a point of including her earlier today. "What plot points did you discern that advanced the theme of transformation?"

Emma looks over at me and crosses her eyes. "How about we keep it simple?" she says, turning to the campers as I smother a giggle. "What are some of your favorite things that happened in the chapters we read this week?"

Meri waves her hand in the air. "Betsy isn't scared of dogs any-more—at least not Shep."

"We have a dog," Pippa volunteers. "Her name ith Mith Marple, and nobody'th thcared of her."

"That's great, Pippa," says Emma. "Anybody else have a favorite part in the book?"

"I like it that Betsy's figuring out how to do things on her own," says Harper.

"Me too!" Becca agrees. "She's starting to develop a little backbone."

Tara pulls her thumb out of her mouth. "I didn't like it when Betsy and Molly got lost in the woods," she whispers.

"Me neither," I tell her. "But what did Betsy learn from that?"

Tara's forehead puckers.

Grace's hand flies up. "Maybe that she can find a way to rescue her-self. She's figuring out how to do things on her own, like Harper said."

We all nod.

"I don't like it when everybody makes fun of Elias Brewster because he's raggedy and dirty and he never combs his hair," says Kate.

For the second time today, my eyes slide over to Felicia. Her hair is tidy and her clothes aren't raggedy, and she's hardly Elias Brewster, but still, she's been the butt of a lot of jokes around here this summer, and I'm betting it stings.

"Who's got the Fun Facts?" Emma asks, and Megan holds up a sheaf of papers. Amy rushes forward to pass them out.

Heather Vogel Frederick

FUN FACTS ABOUT DOROTHY

1) Dorothy was the first woman appointed to the Vermont Board of Education, working to improve conditions in rural schools.

2) She counted the famous poet Robert Frost and the writer Willa Cather among her friends.

3) Dorothy was nominated for the Nobel Prize in Literature, but she didn't win.

4) Eleanor Roosevelt once named her one of the ten most influential women in the United States.

5) During World War I, Dorothy and her husband and family moved to France to help with war relief work.

6) An educational reformer, bestselling author, and social activist, Dorothy was a champion of women's rights, racial equality, and lifelong education.

7) She died in 1958 in her adopted hometown of Arlington, Vermont, after having lived a rich and fulfilling life.

"Finally!" says Cassidy. "It's about time one of the writers we read didn't die tragically or too young."

"She was an accomplished woman," says Felicia, scanning the list.

"That means she did a lot of stuff," Emma translates for her campers.

"One more question for you all," says Becca. "What do you think of Betsy's plot to help Elias?"

I'm surprised to see Monica's hand go up. She so rarely says anything.

"Yes, Nica?" says Becca.

"I like it that she wants to do something nice for him, and help sew him some new clothes," Freddie's twin says softly.

I look ruefully at Felicia again. I should want to do something nice for my cousin, shouldn't I? Helping her with her clothes would be a good place to start.

Two nights later, I get the opportunity.

We're waiting for the buses to Pinewood's luau. Everybody's dressed for the occasion, with fake grass skirts that camp provided and big fake flowers in our hair.

"I can't believe you talked me into this," mutters Felicia, who's standing beside me, hugging her lute to her chest. "It's so embarrassing."

No more embarrassing than those dumb medieval capes you insist on wearing half the time, I'm tempted to tell her, but instead I just say, "You look great. And besides, we're all wearing the same thing."

My cousin looks down at her top. "I'm going to freeze to death. I really think I should bring a cape."

Heather Vogel Frederick

I sigh, wishing she could at least *try* to be normal.

In the end, I'd enlisted Emma's help in the Felicia Project, as we're calling it. We cornered my cousin in her cubie, where she was getting ready for the luau, Felicia-style. Which meant grass skirt, baggy T-shirt over it, plus a cape. Over her protests, Emma and I managed to whisk the cape away, then find something nicer for her to wear than an old T-shirt.

"How about this?" I'd asked, holding up a bright turquoise yoga top.

"That's an *exercise* top," Felicia had responded indignantly. "I am not wearing that in public!"

"Yeah, but it doesn't look like an exercise top," I'd told her. "It looks more like a pretty bathing suit. Plus, turquoise is a great color on you. This is supposed to be a party, remember?"

It took some doing, but we managed to wrestle her out of the ratty T-shirt and into the yoga top, and we fixed her hair, too. Hers is long-ish, like mine—or like mine used to be, pre–skunk fiasco—and when we unbraided it, it fell in ripples down her back. Since the no-makeup rule was relaxed for tonight's dance, as a final touch we brought in Megan and Becca. They're way better at all that stuff. While they were busy glamming Felicia up, Emma and I gave her some pointers in the social graces department.

"Who's that?" asks Cassidy as we finally board the bus.

"You're joking, right?" I reply. "It's Felicia."

Cassidy whips around to take a second look. "Whoa!"

"You seriously didn't recognize her?"

She shakes her head, and I settle into my seat, feeling proud of my efforts on my cousin's behalf. Now if I can just get a boy or two to take a second look at her.

Our bus chugs up the big hill, then continues on around the lake to the far side, where Pinewood is located. I guess back in the early days, Camp Lovejoy used to canoe across for the luau, but there are a lot more campers now, and it's easier to take the buses.

The WELCOME TO CAMP PINEWOOD sign has been draped with paper flower leis, and flanking it are two counselors holding big tiki torches. They start waving them when they spot our buses, pointing the way to the parking lot.

Pinewood is laid out completely differently from Camp Lovejoy. It's up at the top of a hill, for one thing, instead of at the lake's edge. There are a lot more sports fields, for another, and the cabins are clustered around one big central lodge, the porch of which is alight with more tiki torches. Hawaiian music blares from hidden speakers, and a greeting party of counselors, including Jake and Chase, drape paper flower leis around our necks as we get off the bus.

"Nice skirt," Cassidy says to Chase, who is sporting a grass one identical to ours over his shorts. "Did you borrow it from your sister?"

Before he can think up a snappy comeback, Felicia steps off the bus.

"Uhhhh," he mumbles.

"This is my cousin Felicia," I tell him.

"Uhhhh," he says again.

"Whatever," snaps Felicia, and starts to walk off. I grab her by the arm and quickly steer her back to Chase.

Heather Vogel Frederick

"What are you doing?" she mutters under her breath.

"Making sure you get asked to dance," I mutter back. Smiling broadly at Chase, I gesture at the lodge and the lawn in front of it. "The decorations look great! Right, Felicia?"

My cousin doesn't say anything. I nudge her with my hip.

She grunts. "Unh-huh."

Seriously, if there's a picture next to "clueless" in the dictionary, Felicia's face is on it.

"We pull out all the stops for the luau," Chase tells us proudly. Well, tells *Felicia*, to be more accurate. He hasn't taken his eyes off my cousin since she got off the bus.

The pillars on the lodge porch have been wrapped in white paper and painted to look like tiki totem poles, and in front of them long tables have been set up. Each one is topped with a bright tropical table-cloth and loaded with food, and each is flanked by two inflatable palm trees that sway gently in the breeze.

"This looks great! I'm starving!" says Cassidy, surveying the food.

"We used to roast a whole pig," Jake tells us, "but I guess it grossed out some of the girls, so now we just have barbecued chicken."

We load up our plates, then head for a big sign that says TIKI SMOOTHIE BAR.

"How adorable is this?" says Becca, twirling the little pink umbrella in her pineapple-mango smoothie. "Wouldn't this be fun to add to the Pies & Prejudice menu? A tiki bar, I mean."

My mother says Becca could totally be an event planner someday.

She's really good at both the creative and the organizational side of things.

After dinner, there are games. First up is the hula hoop contest, which is a riot to watch, especially with the little kids. The hoops are nearly as big as they are.

"And now, it's time to do the limbo!" announces Pinewood's camp director as a few of the counselors start setting up the pole that contestants will shimmy under.

"The limbo isn't Hawaiian," scoffs Felicia. "It originated in the West Indies. In Trinidad, to be exact. It was—"

Sensing that she's winding up for one of her long, pompous lectures, I sidle closer and elbow her sharply in the ribs. "Knock it off," I whisper.

She looks over at me, frowning. "Knock what off?"

"The know-it-all stuff," I murmur. "Remember how we talked about that back in your cubie?"

She flushes.

That was a difficult conversation to have, but someone had to do it.

"Felicia, nobody—I'm talking guys *and* girls—likes a know-it-all," I'd told her as Megan was applying her mascara.

"What's wrong with being smart?" my cousin had grumbled.

"Nothing," I'd replied. "I'm smart, you're smart, a lot of us here at camp are smart. The thing is, you don't need to rub everybody's noses in exactly how much you know all the time."

She'd reddened at that, and I worried that maybe I was being too mean. "Look, you're my cousin and I love you. You know that, right?"

Felicia had shrugged.

Heather Vogel Frederick

"I'm just trying to help. That's what cousins—and friends—are for. Right, guys?" I looked at my book club friends for support.

Megan stood back, surveying her handiwork, then leaned in again with the mascara wand. "Absolutely," she told Felicia. "You should have been there back in sixth grade, when I almost got kicked out of our book club for some mean stuff I did. The moms actually made me sign rules of conduct before they allowed me to stay. It was mortifying, but it made me a better person."

Becca laughed. "Megan almost got kicked out, but I wasn't even allowed in!"

"You were such a pill," Emma told her, smiling broadly.

"Shut up," Becca replied, but she was smiling too. "Megan's right, Felicia. If I hadn't had to face my flaws, I'd probably still have them."

"It's kind of like when you've got spinach in your teeth, or toilet paper stuck to your shoe or something, you know?" Emma added. "It's embarrassing, but you're glad somebody said something."

Felicia didn't look convinced. "But what if I think I'm fine just the way I am?"

My friends and I exchanged a glance.

"It's not that you aren't fine, Felicia," I told her. "But you know what they say: The biggest room in the house is the room for improvement."

My cousin looked down at her yoga top with a sigh. "I guess."

The limbo music starts and Chase grabs Felicia by the hand. "Come on, let's limbo!"

She snatches it away. "I don't limbo," she says huffily.

I shake my head in disbelief. This is a lost cause.

Jake grabs Cassidy, who wins, of course, contorting herself until she's nearly flat on her back as she snakes her way under the bar each time it's lowered.

After the limbo, I lean over to Felicia. "Time to get your lute," I tell her. She nods and trots off toward the bus. I approach Pinewood's head counselor, meanwhile, and tell him my plan for the serenade.

"What a great idea!" He leads me up onto the front porch. "I'll introduce you when you're ready."

I watch as everyone mills around, waiting for the dance to start. After Felicia returns, I give Pinewood's head counselor a thumbs-up, and he nods.

"And now, directly from Camp Lovejoy, it's the Camp Chorale!" There's a polite spattering of applause, but people aren't really paying attention. As the head counselor passes me the microphone, I signal to Felicia, who strums the opening chords. This is the signal for our chorale group to step forward. The audience finally quiets down as I begin to sing. The first part is a solo, but as the campers come up on the porch one by one to join me, the song gradually shifts into an ensemble piece. Before long the words and the melody work their magic. People are swaying in time to the beat, and everyone is smiling. "Over the Rainbow" is that kind of a song.

When it's time for the final verse, I motion to the chorale, and as we rehearsed earlier this afternoon in secret, our voices all drop to a quiet hum. Suddenly, the spotlight is on Felicia. Her eyes are closed,

Heather Vogel Frederick

she's really into the music, and at first she doesn't notice that she's the center of attention. Then she opens her eyes, and they widen in alarm. I give her an encouraging smile and nod.

She finishes to wild applause.

"You're a rock star!" I whisper to her.

Sergeant Marge and Pinewood's head counselor lead the younger campers into the lodge for games, and the DJ fires up the dance music. This time Chase won't take no for an answer. Felicia's face flushes with embarrassment as he takes her hand and sweeps her out into the middle of the crowd. The music starts and she begins to dance, stiffly at first, but if there's one thing Felicia loves, it's music, and eventually she relaxes.

I lean over to Emma. "Our work is done," I tell her. "I think we can safely say she's launched."

Emma laughs. "Just wait until she starts lecturing him on the history of the hula," she says, then adds, "Hey, do you have a minute?"

I nod, and she leads me away from the party, past the lodge and on toward the parking lot.

"Where are we going?"

"You'll see."

We stop in front of Artie's truck. Emma reaches under the tarp in the back and fishes out a couple of screwdrivers. She hands one to me.

I look at it, mystified. "What's this for?"

"Cassidy's not the only one who knows how to play a prank," she says smugly. "It's Pinewood's fault that my best friend had to cut off her braid, and it's time they paid for it."

I gape at her.

"Am I right, or am I right?" Emma continues. "If these guys didn't steal our bell, Cassidy never would have tried to move that skunk."

Actually, knowing Cassidy, she probably would have. A potential weapon of mass stinkification would have been way too tempting for her to resist.

"So what is it you have in mind?"

Before Emma can explain, the gravel crunches behind us and we turn to see Cassidy and Becca and Megan crossing the parking lot.

"What are you two up to?" asks Cassidy.

"Payback," Emma tells her. "We're going to steal Pinewood's toilet seats. Every last one of them."

We're all quiet for a minute, staring at her. This is so not like Emma.

"That's pretty brilliant," I say finally.

She smiles. "I know, right?"

"Except for one thing," Becca notes.

Emma looks over at her. "What's that?"

"Boys don't use toilet seats."

"Sure they do—some of the time, at least." Cassidy grins. "Jess is right, it's a brilliant plan. What do you want us to do with the seats once we remove them?"

Emma points to Artie's truck. "Stash them in the back, under the tarp. We only have two screwdrivers, so we'll have to work in teams. Jess and I will take the cabins and buildings on the lake side of the lodge; you guys take the rest. We've gotta work quickly, or they'll notice we're gone."

Heather Vogel Frederick

Fifteen minutes later, it's done. Every single toilet seat at Pinewood is now stashed in the back of Artie's pickup truck.

"That's that," Emma says with satisfaction, pulling the tarp over them.

"That's what?"

We all freeze.

Sergeant Marge is standing behind us. And worse, Gwen is with her.

"Um," Emma says weakly.

The two women step forward and peer under the tarp, then turn and look at us, their mouths twin O's of astonishment.

"They took our bell," says Emma, by way of explanation.

Gwen nods slowly. "Indeed they did." She glances over at Marge. "I'm thinking this might qualify as a memory-maker. How about you? Stretch the rules this once?"

The head counselor purses her lips, considering. "I'm thinking maybe we should take all their toilet paper, too."

Now it's our turn to stare at them in astonishment.

Gwen grins broadly. "I know where the supply shed is," she says. "And where they hide the key."

"What are we waiting for?" says Marge.

As the two of them trot off across the parking lot, I look over at my friends.

A slow smile spreads across Emma's face. "I think we're going to get our bell back."

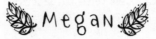

Megan

"It was great fun, sewing all together
and chatting as they sewed."
—*Understood Betsy*

We get our bell back.

Pinewood totally caves first thing the following morning.

"Well, look who's here!" crows Cassidy as Jake and Chase walk in during breakfast. They're carrying our bell, and looking sheepish.

Gwen and Marge play it for all it's worth.

"You're missing *what*?" Gwen asks loudly, as Jake mumbles something to her. "Toilet seats? And *toilet paper*?"

As her questions register with the campers, most of whom haven't heard about the prank, laughter begins to ripple through the Dining Hall.

"How many toilet seats are missing, exactly?" Marge's brow furrows as she pretends to be puzzled. Jake mumbles something else, and the head counselor cups her hand to her ear. "What's that? *All* of them?" By now everyone is howling. The head counselor winks at Gwen. "Good heavens—who would do such a thing?"

Eventually, after all but making Jake and Chase get down on their knees and beg, Gwen and Sergeant Marge finally relent.

"I think these boys have learned their lesson, Marge, don't you?" says Gwen.

Marge crosses her arms over her chest and regards Jake and Chase skeptically. "Have you learned your lesson, boys?"

They nod vigorously.

"Good. In that case, I suppose we can let you off the hook," says the head counselor.

Gwen turns to her husband. "Artie, sweetheart, would you mind driving these gentlemen back to Pinewood? Now that our bell is safely home again, I think you'll find what they're looking for in the back of your truck."

Jake and Chase follow Artie out of the Dining Hall, accompanied by loud catcalls and the drumming of many feet.

Cassidy can't resist a parting shot. "That's what you get for messing with Camp Lovejoy!"

"Tell us again how you did it," pleads Freddie a while later, when fourth period rolls around.

"Seriously?" My friends and I have spent the day retelling the story of the prank. We have all rocketed to superstar status here at camp, thanks to our part in it.

"Please, Megan?" Nica begs. "We really want to hear it again."

The other girls all nod too.

"Okay, then," I say, handing them each a length of purple fabric.

We're in the Art Studio, working on accessories for Queen for a Day, yet another in the seemingly bottomless pile of Camp Lovejoy traditions. Tomorrow at breakfast, each cabin will draw a name from a hat, and the camper chosen will dress up as royalty and rule her fellow cabinmates for the day. It sounds kind of childish and silly to me, but everybody who's been here before says it's really fun.

"Especially at the end," Brianna told me at our staff meeting, "when the queens get dunked in the lake."

Freddie and Nica are helping several other girls and me sew purple capes for the queens-to-be, while out at the tables on the deck, Becca is supervising the crew crafting crowns and scepters out of cardboard and paper towel tubes. There are lots of plastic jewels and sequins and glitter involved, along with barely suppressed excitement. The younger campers love anything involving glitter.

"So, it was all Emma Hawthorne's idea," I begin, and the girls hang on my every word as I relate in elaborate detail how we fanned out around Pinewood, hunting down every last toilet and removing every last toilet seat. I don't tell them about Gwen and Marge's involvement. I figure maybe that piece of information should remain confidential.

"What would have happened if you had gotten caught?" asks Pippa Lovejoy's older sister Lauren, her eyes wide.

"Something dreadful, I'm sure," I tell her, with a dramatic shiver. "We were lucky that everyone was having such a great time at the luau."

During free period, my fashionistas and I set our own projects aside—quick and easy miniskirts glammed up by my most sumptuous

Heather Vogel Frederick

leftover fabrics—and put the finishing touches on the royal robes and other adornments. When the bell rings, signaling the end of the period, my campers help me transport everything down to Cabbage for safekeeping. Sergeant Marge will distribute them at tomorrow's crowning ceremony.

Afterward, I stop by my cubie to change and grab a few things. Tonight is my night off, and I can't wait. Cassidy said I could borrow her car, but I don't really feel like going anywhere. Simon and I are planning to videoconference, so I'll do that first at the Counselors' Cabin; then I'm thinking maybe I'll spend some time by myself in the Art Studio. I haven't had much time this summer to do any sewing on my own, and I'm itching to get back to it.

There's a new issue of the *Birch Bark* waiting for me on my dressing table, along with a note from Emma: "Handing these out at dinner tonight—knew you'd want one hot off the press." She signed it with a smiley face. I stuff it in my shoulder bag to read later.

Even though I'm staying here at camp, I decide to change into my civvies. I dig through my trunk, ending up with yoga pants and a T-shirt—a pretty tangerine-colored one, since Simon will see that part of me—plus a fleece for later, since it's been getting colder at night. Becca pokes her head in as I'm changing and starts to laugh.

"Yoga pants? You're turning into your mother, Megs!"

"Hey, it's camp!" I protest. "Nobody's going to see me."

"So what are you going to do tonight?"

I shrug. "Talk to Simon and then just hang out."

"Sounds perfect. Wish I could join you."

"Yeah, me too." Co-counselors don't get days or nights off together though, unfortunately. "What's the plan for you guys?"

She wrinkles her nose. "Evening activity is square dancing."

I grin. "Wow, sorry I'm going to miss that."

She grins back. "Yeah, I'll bet." The dinner bell rings and she waggles her fingers at me. "Gotta go round up the troops. See you later!"

Peering into my teeny mirror, I see Mirror Megan peering back at me. The shade of tangerine she's wearing gives her face a nice glow, and she looks happy.

"You should be happy," I tell her. "Only ten more minutes until Simon!"

I'm way too old to be talking to Mirror Megan. I made her up when I was younger and desperate for a sister. But once in a while I still can't help myself.

I put on mascara and a swipe of lip gloss, brush my hair one more time, then grab my shoulder bag and head out. I'm hoping that if I'm quick about it, I'll have the Counselors' Cabin to myself—at least for a while. There isn't much privacy around here, and it would be nice to be able to talk to Simon without having a bunch of other people listening in. Earlier today I heard some of the other counselors talking about going to the movies, so maybe I'll be in luck.

I am in luck—the cabin is deserted. Flipping on the lights and crossing to the desk, I boot up the computer and wait.

Heather Vogel Frederick

"There you are!" I hear Simon say a few minutes later.

"Hang on a sec," I tell him. "I can't see you." I tap a few keys and his face appears on-screen.

"Hi," I murmur, feeing suddenly shy. His eyes are so brown and warm! Like velvet.

"Hi," he replies.

We smile at each other, and neither of us says anything for a long moment. Then we both start talking at once. We stop, laughing.

"Ladies first," he says.

"Okay. How are you?"

"Wonderful! Amazing! Fantastic!" Simon has been interning with a video production company this summer.

"So you don't like it at all," I reply somberly, teasing him. "That's too bad."

He grins. "How about you?"

"Things are going well." I catch him up on all the news, including last night's prank and Jess's run-in with the skunk.

"Epic prank!" he says when I'm finished. "Well done! But I do pity poor Jess."

"I know! It was awful. I had to cut her hair, and I practically had to hold my nose as I did. It looks cute short, though."

"Jessica Delaney would look cute even if she had no hair at all," Simon remarks, and I feel a pang of jealousy until he adds, "Not as cute as you, though."

Pleased, I feel my face go pink. Simon is such a good boyfriend.

"How's Amy doing?" he continues. "She's the one who's been so terribly homesick, right?"

I nod. "Better. She seems to have settled in, for the most part at least."

"And you'll be heading to New York in just a few weeks! Excited?"

I nod again. "Definitely. How about you? Oxford doesn't start until later in the fall, right?"

"That's right. Michaelmas Term begins mid-October. I'll probably go up a week early to get settled."

We continue to make small talk for a while, and then there's a long pause while Simon just looks at me with that open, cheerful expression of his. "I miss you," he says finally.

"I miss you, too!"

Before either of us can say anything else, the door behind me opens. I glance over my shoulder and see Felicia walk in.

"Oh hey, Felicia, I'm videoconferencing with my boyfriend," I tell her.

"That's okay," she says, flopping onto the sofa and opening a book. "You won't bother me."

My mouth drops open. Can she seriously be this clueless? "Um, maybe you could give me a couple of minutes here?"

Flapping her hand at me, she says, "Really, I don't mind."

Furious, I turn back to Simon, who's smiling broadly.

"We're no longer alone, I take it," he whispers.

I shake my head.

"It's all right; we'll have plenty of chances to chat again before you head to New York."

Heather Vogel Frederick

I'm so mad right now I could cry. There was so much more I wanted to say, and so much I wanted to hear him say. He blows me a kiss, and I blow him one back. Then the screen goes black.

Spinning around in my chair, I leap to my feet. "What is *wrong* with you?" I yell at Felicia. "Couldn't you see I was on a private call?"

Startled, she looks up from her book. Her face flushes. "This is the Counselors' Cabin," she replies stiffly. "That's 'counselors' *plural*, not 'counselor' *singular*. I have every right to be here."

"You are just so, so—maddening!" With a strangled noise, I stomp out.

At the Art Studio, I pull an energy bar and an apple from my shoulder bag and slam the latest issue of the *Birch Bark* onto the table. Maybe reading it will take my mind off Felicia.

Fat chance.

There she is, front and center, smiling proudly for the camera with her stupid sackbut in front of the stupid flagpole.

"Nest Counselor Saves the Day!" blares the headline, and underneath there's a brief account of how she stepped in to help out after the bell was kidnapped.

I know Emma did this to be nice, because Jess is trying to spruce up her cousin's image and make sure she doesn't feel left out, but right now it just feels like my nose is getting rubbed in stupid Felicia. I grab a marker from the supply bin and vent my spite by drawing a big mustache on her picture. Then I add a dunce cap. Feeling a little better, I continue to read.

"PEANUT WEEK!" trumpets another headline. "Are you ready, campers? Camp Lovejoy's most beloved end-of-camp event is just around the corner!"

Gwen has already told us about Peanut Week. It sounds like fun—campers and counselors alike pick a name, and the person you pick is your "peanut." The one who picks you is your "shell." It's a bit like Secret Santas, in that you leave little surprise gifts for your peanut in her cubie or her cabin throughout the week, but you also do nice things for her like make her bed while she's at breakfast, serenade her at night, or have someone deliver your dessert to her table, that kind of thing. Everything's a complete secret, of course, until the big reveal on Banquet Night.

Suddenly, I have a dismal thought. What if I pick Felicia for my peanut? Or she picks me? I flash back to Christmas a few years ago, when our book club went through the horrible Secret Santa mix-up. Peanut Week could go wrong in so many ways.

Shoving the *Birch Bark* back into my bag, I get up and cross the studio to the shelves where I've stashed my sewing supplies. Pacing back and forth, I run my fingers across the bolts of fabric, letting the crisp cottons and kitten-soft velvets and buttery smooth satins soothe me. On the spur of the moment, I decide to make something for my peanut, who will definitely *not* be Felicia if I have anything to say about it. If I choose her name, I'll have to find a way to put it back, or swap with someone.

Envisioning a small, elegant evening bag—if I get a peanut from one of the youngest cabins, she can always use it to play dress-up—I select a cherry red velvet with matching silk cord for the shoulder strap. I add red-and-white striped satin to line it, swiftly measure and snip, then settle into place in front of the sewing machine. A few minutes later, lulled by the familiar whirr of the sewing machine and the rhythm of the needle as it stitches through the fabric, I'm finally starting to calm down.

Everything's going to be fine, I assure myself. Life will go on. There will be other conversations with Simon.

I smile. Who needs Mirror Megan? I'm perfectly capable of talking to myself without her.

Later, as I walk back toward my cabin, my eyes are drawn to the reflection of the full moon on the water. Picking my way carefully down the rocky path to the dance platform, I pause for a few minutes to lean on the rail and drink in the view. Camp is silent; everyone's asleep. No loons, no motorboats, nothing but a sound like rustling silk as a whisper of breeze stirs the leaves overhead. The lake is perfectly still, the moon floating in the sky barely distinguishable from its watery twin.

Maybe Simon's looking out his window in England right now, I think. *Maybe he's looking at the same moon as I am.*

I start to hum, then softly sing the words to my favorite song I've learned so far this summer:

I see the moon and the moon sees me
Down through the leaves of the old oak tree.
Please let the light that shines on me
Shine on the one I love.

The next morning, I'm awakened to the sound of a whispered argument.

"If you get picked again, it's not fair!" Grace is saying to Mia.

"Yeah!" Kate agrees, frowning down on her. Kate towers over Mia. "You were queen last year, when we were in Nest."

"So?" says Mia. "There's no rule against it."

"You should make them leave your name out," Grace tells her.

"Why should I?"

"Because it's selfish!" Kate whispers.

"I'm not selfish!" Mia protests furiously.

"Are too," mutters Grace.

"Am not!"

"*Girls!*" I shush them. "People are trying to sleep!"

Not me anymore, unfortunately. I'm wide awake now, thanks to that little outburst. I lie in bed for the next few minutes before reveille, wondering if I should be worried. I thought everybody said Queen for a Day was supposed to be fun?

I mention it to Sergeant Marge as I'm helping her carry the royal accessories to the Dining Hall.

"Not to worry," she assures me. "It's all in fun, and the girls will

Heather Vogel Frederick

adjust quickly, no matter who gets picked."

She's wrong, though. When it's our cabin's turn, Becca pulls a slip of paper from the jar marked BALSAM glances at it, and shoots me a worried look. "Mia Jackson," she reads aloud.

Mia gives a gleeful little shriek and jumps up and down with excitement as the head counselor hands her one of the purple capes. Harper and Amy applaud and cheer, as do Becca and I, but Kate and Grace look positively mutinous.

"It's not fair," I hear Grace whisper, and Kate nods.

"Let us proceed to Lower Lodge for the crowning ceremony," Gwen announces when all the cabins have picked a queen.

"There was a split second there after I picked Mia that I thought about reading someone else's name," Becca tells me as we head out of the dining room behind our campers.

"Maybe you should have," I reply, watching our girls. Mia is prancing regally down the path with Amy and Harper close behind, holding up the train of her purple cape. Kate and Grace, meanwhile, are keeping their distance, arms linked and heads together as they whisper their discontent.

"You are our royal court today," Gwen tells the queens as they line up beside her in front of the lodge's big stone fireplace. "You reign supreme; your word is law. There are a few rules, however: No mean-spirited decrees, and nothing dangerous or demeaning. You will be allowed one decree at each mealtime, one during rest hour, one for each of the four periods today, and then we will gather on the beach during free period for the royal finale."

She motions to the counselors, and we all step forward to join our queens. "These are your royal advisors," the camp director tells the queens. "They will help you reign wisely. Are you ready to make your first decree?"

An excited buzz ripples through the room as the queens nod.

"Then let us begin with Nest."

Tara Lindgren, thumb firmly in mouth, steps forward, flanked by Emma and Felicia.

Gwen places a crown on her head and a paper tube scepter in her hand. Then Felicia leans down and whispers something in Tara's ear. Tara makes a face, but a second later out pops the thumb. "My subjects will all wear their uniforms backward today," she decrees, holding up her scepter.

"Yeth, your majethty," says Pippa, and she and Meri both drop a curtsy, which gets a laugh.

It's our turn next. Gwen places a crown on Mia's short curls. Sergeant Marge had given us all a bunch of things for us to suggest to our queens, but before we can even step forward to join Mia, she holds up her scepter, looks directly at Grace and Kate, and says, "My subjects will volunteer for Lower Camp Biffy duty."

Amy and Harper's faces fall. Grace and Kate look like they're going to explode. My eyes slide over to Becca. "I thought this was supposed to be fun," I mutter.

Even Sergeant Marge looks taken aback. "That's very, uh, civic-minded of you, Queen Mia."

Heather Vogel Frederick

Mia may only be eight, but she sure knows how to act. Putting on a pious expression, she inclines her head and gives her scepter a regal wave in response.

Our morning goes downhill from there. First period finds us all in the Biffy, up to our elbows in rubber gloves and toilet scrub. For second period, Mia decrees that her subjects will do twenty cartwheels and then stand on their heads, which ends up giving Kate a nosebleed.

"Mia did it on purpose!" Kate sobs as I'm cleaning her up. "She knows this happens when I do headstands!"

I'm about ready to pull the plug at this point, but Becca takes Mia aside first and orders her to lighten up. "This is Queen Becca speaking, and trust me, you don't want to cross Queen Becca."

Mia meekly promises to behave, but she turns right around and breaks that promise at lunch, clearly still bent on punishing Grace and Kate. We have a full-blown mutiny on our hands when she orders her subjects to hand over their Congo bars.

Harper's eyes widen. "But we only get them once a week!"

Congo bars are Camp Lovejoy's most popular dessert. They're kind of a cross between a brownie and an extra-rich, extra-gooey chocolate chip cookie.

"You have to do what your queen orders," Mia tells her sharply.

"They're my favorite," says Amy, her dark eyes starting to fill with tears. She clutches her dessert protectively to her chest.

"It's the rule!" Mia's voice rises along with her paper towel–tube scepter, and for a moment I fear she's going to bop someone over the head with it.

"Knock it off," I warn her.

Grace glares defiantly at Mia from under her Yankees cap. She holds up her congo bar and takes a big bite, then tosses it across the table.

Becca stands up. "That's it. No congo bars for anyone! We're going back to Balsam."

By the time we get to our cabin, Amy's tears have spilled over and Harper is on the verge of revolt.

"I don't want to do what Mia says anymore!" she states flatly.

"Me neither!" sniffles Amy.

"You have to," Mia insists, her face nearly the same shade of purple as her royal cape. "It's the rule!"

I glance helplessly at Becca. "How did our mothers do it? Raising kids without going crazy, I mean?"

"I have no idea," Becca replies wearily.

I turn back to our campers. "Girls, Queen for a Day is supposed to be a *game*," I remind them. "A fun game. Come on now, Mia, think up something fun for your rest hour decree."

Grudgingly, she obeys, decreeing that we all play cards. A truce is established over a game of gin rummy, and we manage to limp through the rest of the afternoon.

"How'd it go?" I ask Jess as we gather at the H dock for the big finale.

"Great!" she enthuses. "Brooklyn thought up some really funny stuff for us to do. We just spent fourth period pretending to be chickens, and could only talk in squawks. Cassidy really got into it."

"Lucky you."

She looks at me sharply. "Why? What happened with Balsam?"

"You don't want to know."

A loud fanfare sounds behind us, and we all turn to see Felicia blowing her sackbut for all she's worth. She's dressed in full medieval regalia—long velvet dress complete with one of those crisscrossed lace-up bodices, and on her head a hat that looks like an honest-to-goodness dunce cap with a scarf flowing from the end. Recalling my doodle on the *Birch Bark* last night, I stifle a laugh.

"What?" says Jess.

I shake my head. "Nothing."

"Time for the royal review," Felicia announces, then raises the sackbut to her lips again for another fanfare as Gwen and Artie emerge from the Director's Cottage. Like Felicia, they're in full regal garb, but with crowns instead of dunce caps. They proceed to parade past the assembled cabins, pausing to invite each of the queens to join their procession.

"Hey, Artie looks good!" Becca says as they draw closer. "I've never seen him in anything but overalls."

"That's King Arthur to you," Felicia tells her, coming over to join Emma and the girls from Nest.

"Wait, his real name is Arthur?" I exclaim. "Gwen is Guinevere, right? So that makes them King Arthur and—no way!"

"Duh," says Felicia. She looks at me with an expression that clearly says, *You are dumb as toast*, then sweeps off onto the H dock to trumpet the procession's arrival.

"So much for 'room for improvement,'" I mutter to Becca. "I have had just about enough of Miss Know-it-all Felicia Grunewald."

"She sure knows how to be a pain sometimes," Becca agrees.

"By the way, speaking of King Arthur—did Theo ever get his snake back?"

Becca nods. "He was hiding in Theo's brother Sam's closet. Sam found him when he was looking for his running shoes. He about hit the ceiling."

I have to smile at that. "I can imagine."

Queen for a Day ends with hilarity, as Artie/King Arthur decrees a royal dunking. While the rest of us stand on the beach and clap and cheer, each of the queens hands in her scepter, robe, and crown, then climbs up the ladder, turns and waves to her subjects, and slides into the lake. Sergeant Marge is waiting in the water at the bottom to catch the youngest ones and give them a boost back onto the dock. Emma and Becca quickly wrap Tara and Mia in towels.

"Go dry off and get changed, and we'll meet you at the Dining Hall, okay?" Becca tells Mia, who nods and runs off. Kate and Grace go with her, their earlier falling-out forgotten in the excitement of the finale's big splash.

Halfway through dinner, I get up from the table to refill my glass. Felicia's ahead of me in line at the drink machine. I'm still stinging from

Heather Vogel Frederick

her earlier remark, and suddenly, all the anger from last night comes flooding back.

As she turns to go back to her table, I decide we need to talk.

"Felicia," I begin, tapping her on the arm, but before I can say anything else she leaps back, startled. Milk sloshes out of her glass and down the front of her polo shirt. She glares at me, sputtering.

"What is your problem?" she snaps.

"*My* problem? What is *your* problem?" I snap back. "All I did was say your name!"

"And grab my arm!"

"I barely touched it!"

"Is there something going on over here that I need to know about?" the head counselor asks, coming over to investigate.

"Uh, no," I reply. "Just a misunderstanding."

Sergeant Marge raises an eyebrow at Felicia, who shoots me a look.

"Yeah, just a misunderstanding," she says after a long pause.

"Let's be sure and keep it that way," Sergeant Marge tells us.

I wait until she's well out of earshot. "Look, Felicia, all I wanted to do was talk to you about last night."

"You were upset. I get it." She mops the front of her polo shirt with a napkin.

"With good reason! And then, a few minutes ago, when I finally figured out the whole King Arthur/Queen Guinevere thing—"

"What about it?"

"You didn't have to say 'duh.'"

She looks at me blankly.

I heave a sigh. "The thing is, you could maybe think about other people's feelings once in a while, that's all."

"You and your friends don't need to point out every single thing I do wrong," Felicia says stiffly.

So that's what this is all about, I realize. She's still chafing about the Felicia Project. "We don't point out *everything.*"

"Close enough."

I pause for a moment, trying to put myself in her shoes. Yes, she's annoying, and yes, she's a little O-D-D, but maybe we have been a little hard on her this summer. "Fine. I'll try to be better about that, okay?"

She lifts a shoulder.

"And I'll talk to Emma and Jess and the others. Are we good, then?"

She nods, and I head back to my table.

Later, for evening activity, everyone gathers in Lower Lodge for a movie—some animated thing about a girl who's searching for Excalibur, King Arthur's sword. I yawn all the way through it.

"What a day!" I groan, flopping onto my bed afterward. Our campers are in the cubie house changing into their pajamas. "I thought it would never end."

"What do you say we try to salvage something from it?" Becca replies. "Maybe now's a good time to bust out our memory-maker."

"Right now I could use a memory eraser," I grumble.

Heather Vogel Frederick

Becca swats me with her pillow. "Come on," she orders. "I'll round up our campers; you go tell Gwen."

"We're raiding the kitchen for ice cream sundaes, right?"

"Yep."

I slip out of our cabin and start down the path to the Director's Cottage.

"Hey, Megan, wait up!"

It's Cassidy.

"Where are you going?"

"To ask Gwen permission for a memory-maker," I tell her. "Today was a bust." I tell her about Balsam's big fight over Queen for a Day, and my run-in with Felicia.

"Sorry to hear it," she says. "We had a great time. I'm on my way to see Gwen, too. Jess and I just want to keep the fun rolling tonight."

"What are you planning to do?"

"We're taking the girls over to Hairbrush Island for s'mores. How about you?"

"We were going to raid the kitchen for ice cream."

"Nah, that's lame!" Cassidy says. "You should join us. A campfire on the beach is much more fun."

"I should check with Becca first," I tell her as we knock on the Director's Cottage door.

"Come on in, girls," says Gwen.

Cassidy tells her our plan, and she nods. "Good choice. Just try to keep the noise down. Nest looked completely worn out tonight and I don't want you waking them." She shoos us out and closes the door.

"Meet us on the beach in ten minutes," Cassidy tells me when we reach Balsam. I nod, then head inside to inform Becca about the change of plan.

"Sounds like a blast!" she tells me. "I haven't been over to Hairbrush yet this summer."

A few minutes later we're all gathered at the Gazebo with our campers, who are barely able to contain their excited giggles.

"We're going to wade over single-file," Cassidy explains. "I'll be in front, Jess will bring up the rear, and Becca and Megan will be in the middle. Everybody hold hands, and be super quiet because people are sleeping."

We set off across the sandbar. The night air is cool and the water feels warm by comparison.

"I might have to accidentally fall in," Becca whispers to me.

"I know, right?" I reply.

The lake is perfectly still, and the reflection of the moon is as beautiful as it was last night. I start humming "I See the Moon" again to myself. Becca was right; this was exactly what I needed. I can feel the grudges and disappointments of the day washing away.

Once on Hairbrush Island, Cassidy quickly builds a fire on the beach. We sit around it with our girls, eating s'mores and telling stories. Cassidy tells our campers about the time she put stinky cheese in Savannah Sinclair's suitcase to get even for Savannah putting taffy in her hair. Then Emma tells how she and Jess put a live chicken in a box and gave it to Emma's mother as a joke Christmas present. We're having so much fun that Becca has to keep shushing everybody.

Kate Kwan scoots over next to me. "What if Pinewood sees our campfire and comes over in their canoes?" she whispers.

"Then we'll get caught!" I whisper back, and she lets out a little squeal and scurries away to share this exciting news with her friends.

Becca and I exchange a glance and smile. Gwen is right; memory-makers are best when spiced with the prospect of getting caught.

Suddenly, a voice calls over to us from the Point.

"Cassidy? Cassidy Sloane?" It's Sergeant Marge.

"What did I do now?" mutters Cassidy. "We got permission from Gwen!" she calls back.

"Your mother's on the phone, sport!"

Becca and I exchange a glance. This can't be good. Late-night phone calls usually mean something important. Or something awful.

"I hope everything's okay," Becca whispers to me as Cassidy splashes back across the sandbar.

"Yeah, me too."

We hang out with Jess and all of our campers for a little while longer, then decide to call it a night. Worrying about Cassidy has kind of taken the shine off our memory-maker.

We're all in the Gazebo drying off when Cassidy returns. At first

I think it's just the reflection of the full moon that's making her look paler than usual.

"Are you all right?" Jess asks, and she shakes her head.

Even in the dark, I can see that she's been crying. She swipes angrily at her eyes, and it takes some effort for her to get the words out:

"My sister eloped."

Becca

"It was fun to teach, lots of fun!"
—*Understood Betsy*

"Shhhhh! I'm under here!"

Megan lifts up a corner of the sail and pokes her head underneath. Spotting me crouched in the bottom of the boat, she squeezes in beside me and we lie there like a pair of silent sardines.

It's Counselor Hunt Night, an elaborate form of hide-and-seek that has the entire camp swarming the grounds, looking for hidden counselors. When the girls find us, we become the property of whichever team they belong to—Emerald, Ruby, Sapphire or Amethyst—and then the real fun begins as the teams choose captured counselors to compete in a series of challenges.

Too bad Cassidy isn't here, I think. *She'd totally love this.*

As we lie there listening to the excited shrieks from the girls running past the boathouse, I feel Megan start to shake. She's trying not to laugh.

"Shhhh!" I scold her again. "They're right outside!"

The boathouse door creaks open and we freeze.

"Check the war canoe!" says a familiar voice. It's Jennie Norris, one of the CITs. "Somebody always hides in the war canoe!"

At the sound of footsteps scurrying toward the far end of the boathouse, Megan starts shaking again. I elbow her sharply.

"I can't help it," she whispers in protest.

"Hey, wait—did you guys hear something?" The footsteps come pounding back, and suddenly the sail that covers us is ripped away. "Found you!" cries Jennie in triumph.

We're dragged laughing from our hiding spot and marched to Lower Lodge, where a handful of other captured counselors are gathered. Sergeant Marge writes our names on her clipboard under the Sapphire column. Megan and I join Jess, who's sitting outside on the steps, as our captors go running off to rejoin the hunt.

"Too bad Cassidy isn't here for this," she says.

"I was just thinking the same thing," I tell her.

It's Cassidy's night off. Her mother drove up from Concord to see her, and the two of them are probably commiserating over dinner in Pumpkin Falls right now. Poor Cassidy's been beside herself ever since she got the news about Courtney. Personally, I think running away to get married is totally romantic, but Cassidy is mad as heck about it.

"I thought you didn't like weddings and poufy dresses and all that stuff," Megan had said as we were walking back to our cabins after our outing to Hairbrush Island.

"I don't!" Cassidy had replied. "It's just that Courtney is my sister

Heather Vogel Frederick

and I was supposed to be there for her on her big day, and now, well, now that she's eloped, all I get to do is go to some lame reception at Thanksgiving."

There was some confusion in Nest about what had happened to Courtney, apparently. Emma couldn't wait to tell us about the conversation she'd overheard.

"Why is Cassidy sad about her sister and the cantaloupe?" Meri had asked her cabinmates, mystified.

Tara was quick to correct her. "Not cantaloupe, silly!" she'd scoffed. "*Antelope.*"

Emma's desperate to put this exchange in her "Overheard" column in the final issue of the *Birch Bark*, of course.

Half an hour later, all the counselors' hiding spots have been discovered, and it's time for the challenges. I don't get picked for the first round, which is yodeling (Felicia wins that one handily, which is no big surprise—of course she knows how to yodel). And I don't get picked for the balancing-a-spoon-on-the-nose challenge or the hands-free banana cream pie eating challenge. Instead, I get picked for the final round, which is the balance-a-full-glass-of-water-on-your-head challenge.

"I can already tell how this one is going to end," I remark to Megan when my name is called.

Predictably, I end up drenched and sputtering, just like everybody else. Somehow I manage to pick up another point for our team, though, as I balance my glass a split second longer than the other counselors.

"Sapphires win!" Gwen announces when the points are tallied.

"But there's a prize for everybody—ice cream sandwiches on the beach in ten minutes!"

I dash back to my cubie to change out of my wet clothes. While I'm toweling my hair, I hear whispering out in the hallway.

"What if she hates it and gets mad at us? You know how she can be sometimes."

I frown. Something's up. Something that sounds suspiciously like mean-girl stuff. I stick my head out into the hallway to find out, but all I see are the backs of several campers in navy blue hoodies heading out the door.

"Hey!" I call, but either they don't hear me or they don't want to hear me, because nobody turns around.

Now I'm worried. Which "she" were they talking about? Somebody's plotting something, that's for sure. I finish getting changed and head back down to the water ski beach to loop Megan in.

It's growing dark, and everybody's either sprawled on the sand or milling around the fire pit with their ice cream sandwiches. It takes me a while to find her.

"Hey, Megs," I begin, but what I have to tell her will have to wait, as the CITs are already starting the singalong.

> *The Cannibal King with a big nose ring*
> *Fell in love with a sweet young maid*
> *And every night by the pale moonlight*
> *Over the lake he came . . .*

Heather Vogel Frederick

Megan gives me a quizzical look as I plop down on the sand between Amy and Harper. *Later,* I mouth, slinging my arms around my campers. They look up at me and smile. As we reach the tempo change, the three of us sway along to the music, laughing.

We'll build a bungalow big enough for two
Big enough for two, my darling, big enough for two
And when we're married, happy we'll be
Under the bamboo, under the bamboo tree!

Feeling fiercely protective all of a sudden, I give both girls a squeeze. If anybody's plotting something involving either of them, they're going to have to deal with me first.

Later, on the way back to Balsam, I tell Megan what I overhead in Cubbyhole.

"Uh-oh, sounds like we'd better keep our radar on," she says when I'm done. "Especially after the fiasco with Queen for a Day."

"Exactly what I'm thinking."

My radar goes off again a few minutes later, when I hear whispering from the two top bunks at the back of our cabin. When I go over to investigate, I find Grace and Mia staring back at me innocently.

"What's going on?" I ask them. Besides a whole new repertoire of songs, the other thing I'm taking away with me to college from camp is a suspicious mind. Especially where girls and whispering are concerned.

"Nothing," says Grace sweetly.

A little too sweetly, perhaps? I regard her thoughtfully. "Just make sure it stays nothing," I tell her before heading back to my own bed. I pause for a moment by Megan's. "Seriously, how did our mothers do it?"

She smiles at me. "Don't worry so much. They're probably just keyed up about Peanut Week."

Maybe she's right. Peanut Week has been a hot topic at camp ever since Gwen announced that we'd be choosing our peanuts at the next Council Fire.

"This would be a good time to get busy with those crafts, girls," she'd said. "Nothing makes a better gift than something homemade."

Gwen and Mrs. Wong sound like kindred spirits. Megan's mom loathes commercialism and is always trying to get the book club to make homemade gifts.

The following afternoon, I'm at the Art Studio as usual with my quilters during free period when Grace comes in.

"Hey, Grace, what's up?"

"I need a glue gun," she replies.

My eyebrows shoot up. Grace is more of a tennis and rock-climbing and whatever-else-she-can-throw-herself-into-physically kind of girl. In fact, this is the first time I've seen her at the Art Studio all summer.

"Making something for your peanut?"

She fidgets. "Um, it's kind of a surprise."

I've been hearing this all week. "Come on in and I'll get you set up."

Mia is with her, and so, surprisingly, is Brooklyn Alvarez, who is

Heather Vogel Frederick

carrying a canvas bag filled with pinecones. I make space for them at one of the tables and dig out a glue gun.

"Need anything else?"

The girls look at each other. "Maybe some paint?" says Brooklyn.

"No problem." I fish out the additional supplies, then turn my attention back to my quilters.

Amy's wall hanging is almost finished, and I'm sure she'll have it done by the time she heads home. I'm not so sure whether I'll finish my own project in time. I've tackled a quilt for Theo, for his dorm-room bed. It's maroon and gold, the University of Minnesota colors, and it has a picture of Goldy Gopher in the middle, and a motif of snakes around the border. Gold snakes, of course.

It's a little unconventional, but I think he'll like it. He'd better—it's taken me all summer to make it.

"This is my favorite part of camp," Amy pipes up suddenly.

I smile back at her. "I'm so glad to hear it!"

"I wish summer didn't have to end."

My eyebrows shoot up again. This is something, coming from the little camper that Megan and I despaired of ever recovering from the homesickness plague. Gwen was right, though, I guess—the girls always recover, it's just finding the right cure. Which for Amy was quilting. With maybe a little book club thrown in.

I can't wait to tell Megan.

I bend my head to my quilt again, feeling so pleased I could burst. Is this the way Cassidy feels about coaching?

My thoughts drift back to the conversation I had earlier in the summer with my mother. Maybe she's right, maybe I should sign up for some education classes. I don't know, though; wrangling a classroom full of students is probably a lot different than dealing with a handful of campers. But I could at least explore the option, couldn't I, whether or not I decide that teaching's for me?

What was it my mother said? That I have a rich four years ahead of me. That's probably a better way to look at it than being worried all the time. Maybe I don't need to know right now what I'm going to be—an architect, a businesswoman, a teacher, or something else entirely.

I'm still pondering this when the bell rings, signaling the end of free period. Megan wanders over as I'm putting away the quilting supplies.

"The weirdest thing happened a few minutes ago," she tells me.

"What?"

"You know Brooklyn, from Twin Pines?"

"Duh! Of course."

Megan smiles. "She asked me for a bunch of fabric. Brooklyn! Who's never sewn a stitch in her life!"

"That is kind of weird," I agree.

"Something's up."

"It's probably just Peanut Week stuff, remember?"

By Sunday night, Peanut Week anticipation has reached fever pitch. The campers can barely contain their excitement through the

Heather Vogel Frederick

first part of Council Fire, and by the time beads are being given out, they're literally bouncing on the benches.

"Ready for our closing song?" says Gwen, teasing them.

There's a collective groan. "Gwen!"

"What?!" she says, grinning. "Oh, that's right. I seem to have forgotten something." She beckons to Marge, who emerges from the shadows carrying a large papier-mâché peanut. Megan and I labored over what's inside—dozens and dozens of real peanuts, each with the contents removed, a name on a slip of paper tucked inside, and the shell glued back together again and spray-painted gold. "Let's start with Nest, shall we? Come on up, girls."

Tara, Meri, and Pippa file obediently over, flushed with the importance of being first. One by one, they reach in and select their peanuts. Emma and Felicia each pick one too.

"Don't look inside until you get back to your cubies," Gwen tells the girls, who obediently grip their peanuts tightly in their fists. "And remember, it's a secret!" She holds her finger to her lips.

We're next, then Twin Pines, and on through all the cabins until every peanut has been accounted for. It's nearly impossible to maintain silence on the walk back down the trail to camp. Excited giggles keep escaping from the girls, like popcorn bursting from a bunch of kernels.

"I can't wait to see who I have!" whispers Harper.

"Shhhhhh!" Megan whispers back.

To be honest, I can't wait either. I've been hoarding things all summer to give to my peanut. Silly things, mostly—a tiny snow globe I got at the General Store with the covered bridge from Pumpkin Falls inside; a rock I painted to look like a ladybug; some candy, that sort of stuff. If the person whose name is inside the peanut in my pocket is an older staffer, I have a really pretty quilted shoulder bag that I made, and if she's into fashion, I have all sorts of beauty products. It's going to be fun.

The minute we emerge from the woods, campers explode in all directions, racing for their cubies to crack open their peanuts and get the party started. Megan and I quicken our pace a little too.

"I just hope I didn't pick Felicia," Megan says glumly. Jess's cousin still gets under her skin sometimes.

"Tell you what," I say. "If you do, we can swap, okay?"

She brightens. "Really?"

"Sure, why not?" I smile at her. "What are best friends for?"

"Even if I wouldn't do the same for you?"

We both laugh.

Fortunately, Megan doesn't get Felicia, and neither do I. She chooses someone she only identifies as "a staffer," and I have one of the campers from the Hill.

By the time I brush my teeth and change into my pajamas, my "shell" has already struck.

"Hey, what's this?" I say, surprised to find a mint on my pillow, along with a postcard of a loon. On the back is written, "Sweet dreams! Love, Your Shell." I look around at my campers, who are already in their bunks. "You guys know who it is, don't you?"

"We'll never tell!" says Amy, her dark eyes shining with excitement.

Heather Vogel Frederick

I can see why Peanut Week is one of the highlights of the summer.

The tradition has its downside, though, as I quickly discover. Two days later, Kate Kwan comes slumping into my cubie.

"What's up?" I ask her.

"Nothing," she replies.

Judging by the expression on her face, this is a big fat lie. "Define 'nothing.'"

"My shell hasn't given me anything," she says, and bursts into tears.

Gwen warned us that this might happen.

"Every year, there are a few girls who for whatever reason don't get into the spirit of Peanut Week, or who get off to a slow start," she told us. "Since there's no way of keeping track of who the peanuts and shells are, the simplest solution is just to bridge the gap yourself."

Which is exactly what I do. Within the hour, there's candy on the dressing table in Kate's cubie, and Megan and I keep it up for a couple of days, until her shell finally gets her act together.

"I still can't believe this is the last week of camp!" Megan says as we're lounging on the Art Studio deck between our afternoon crafts workshops.

"Me neither."

She peers over her sunglasses at me. "So, are you ready for college?"

I shrug. Megan knows I've been feeling a little worried. "As ready as I'll ever be, I guess."

"Yeah, me too."

We're quiet for a moment.

"It's going to be weird, being so far apart," I finally say. Megan and I have been best friends since elementary school. "You'd better promise to call me a lot."

She nods. "Call, text, e-mail, videoconference. You'll be thoroughly sick of me."

"Never." I smile at her. Then I sit bolt upright. "Oh hey, I just remembered—I left the package from Summer Williams with the batting I need to finish Amy's wall hanging in the cabin. Back in a flash."

Megan waggles her fingers at me as I jog off down the path.

Opening the door to Balsam a minute later, I walk into the middle of something. What exactly, I'm not sure at first. Grace, Mia, and Brooklyn are pulling a bag out from under Amy's bed. They look up with a guilty start.

"What's going on, girls?" I ask, my radar switching into high alert. It suddenly occurs to me that I'm probably looking at the trio whose suspicious discussion I overheard from my cubie house the other night.

"Nothing," says Grace quickly. "Just some, uh, peanut stuff."

The other two exchange a glance, and my radar ratchets up another notch.

"Okay, guys, seriously, what's going on?"

Brooklyn blushes a deep crimson. Mia looks at her feet. Grace doesn't say a word.

"Look, I know 'nothing' when I see it, and this is not nothing," I tell them, starting to feel a little angry. Especially since they're clearly plotting something against Amy.

Heather Vogel Frederick

Grace slumps. She looks over at Mia and Brooklyn. "I guess we have to show her, huh?"

They nod. Grace holds out the bag. I look inside, puzzled at first, and then—

"Wait a minute, *this* is what all the whispering was about?"

The three of them nod again. Brooklyn points to Grace. "It was her idea," she says, sounding a little nervous. Like maybe I'll get mad or something.

Grace shakes her head vigorously. "I got the idea from the book," she tells me. "*Understood Betsy*, I mean. You know, the part where they make all that stuff for Elias?"

I frown, still not quite connecting the dots.

"And I got the idea from you, too," she finishes, her gaze dropping to the floor.

"Me?"

"Back on that first night, when you got mad at me, remember? When I said Amy was a crybaby. You told me to be a leader."

I look at her, shocked. Those words I'd said in haste and anger had sunk in? She'd actually remembered them? I look back in the bag again. "So does everyone in the book club know about this?"

"We didn't tell Nest yet, because we didn't think they could keep it a secret," says Brooklyn. "But Freddie and Nica and Carter all know."

"And everybody from Balsam," Mia adds.

"Do you think she'll like it?" asks Grace, looking worried.

"Like it?" I smile. "She'll *love* it. It's perfect."

"You won't tell her?"

"I wouldn't dream of it."

Grace flings her arms around my waist and gives me a big hug. I hug her back.

When I get to Minneapolis next month, I'm definitely signing up for an education class.

Heather Vogel Frederick

CASSIDY

"The girls took turns in carrying the big paper-wrapped bundle, and stole along in the shadow of the trees, full of excitement, looking over their shoulders at nothing and pressing their hands over their mouths to keep back the giggles."
—*Understood Betsy*

I lean my head back, trying to peek underneath the blindfold. Nothing. Nada. Zip. Total darkness.

"Where are you taking me?" I ask. The only response is excited giggles. "C'mon, you guys!"

From the moment my campers ambushed me outside the Biffy, I could tell they had something up their sleeves. I'm willing to go along for the ride, but I just hope it doesn't involve total humiliation. Or a skunk.

I stumble on a root or a rock or something and nearly do a face plant, but instantly I feel many little hands grabbing me and setting me upright again.

"Almost there," says someone—Grace, I think. From the sounds of it, whatever is going on is a joint operation between Twin Pines, Balsam, and Nest.

Finally, after another big helping of whispers and giggles, we come to a stop. The blindfold is whisked away, and I look around, blinking, at—nothing. It's still pitch-black.

"On the count of three," says a voice to my left, Carter's this time. "One, two, THREE!"

A whole bunch of flashlights switch on, illuminating the last thing I ever expected to see.

My mouth drops open.

Directly in front of me, on the dance platform overlooking the lake, are a pint-size bride and groom.

I peer at them. "Freddie? Nica? What are you guys *doing*?"

More giggles.

As I stand there, something is draped around my shoulders, something soft, like a quilt. I glance down. It is a quilt. Another something is thrust into my hands. Jess, who is standing beside me, shines her flashlight on it. It's a bouquet made of pinecones. They've been spray-painted sky blue and sprinkled heavily with glitter, and the whole thing is ornamented with sprigs of pine and yards of white ribbon.

"Um," I say, not exactly sure what other comment to offer. "I don't know what to say."

"How about 'thank you,'" whispers Jess, elbowing me in the ribs.

Tara smiles up at me. "It's because of the antelope."

"Cantaloupe," whispers Meri, frowning at her.

Heather Vogel Frederick

"*Elopement*," Pippa corrects them both firmly.

"We know you're sad that you didn't get to be in your sister's wedding—" Grace starts to explain.

"—and we wanted to do something to make you happy," Brooklyn finishes.

I'm finally starting to get the picture. Touched, but at the same time afraid I might laugh out loud, I carefully avoid looking at my friends. "Wow," I tell the girls. "Really? This is amazing."

"You like it? You're not mad?" Grace asks anxiously.

My friends are shooting me evil-witch-mother-eyes-of-death from all directions. The kind that say, *Don't blow this*.

I don't.

"Why would I be mad?" I reply. "I love it!" I look down at the bouquet I'm holding, feeling a lump rise in my throat. "And I love you all for planning it."

I called home on my day off earlier this week—I'd really wanted to talk to Courtney, but she's still on her honeymoon, so I figured I'd talk to my mother instead. My stepfather answered, and told me that Mom was at her Mommy & Me yoga class with Chloe.

"Guess you're stuck with me, kid," he joked.

The two of us ended up having a great talk. Stanley explained to me that Courtney had been feeling a lot of pressure about having a perfect wedding, especially because of my mother's TV show. I guess Mom had been filming some of the preparations, and she even floated the idea of filming the wedding itself.

Courtney was worried that if she said no, it would come as a huge disappointment, so she'd asked Stanley for his advice.

Our stepfather is a rock star in the advice department.

It turns out he was the one who suggested the elopement! When I saw my mother recently, she didn't know this, because Courtney and Stanley figured it was best to keep his involvement a secret. But my mother found out because Grant let it slip to his mom, and well, moms talk.

"So how come you told her to elope?" I asked, puzzled. It's not like Stanley to go behind my mother's back.

"First of all, I didn't tell her to elope, I merely offered a suggestion," he pointed out. "And second of all, it was the right thing to do. If Courtney eloped, it would be a done deal. Sure, your mother would be disappointed. But she'd get over it, and eventually she'd understand. There'd be no question of her trying to talk your sister into something she didn't want to do, and Courtney could just have a big blow-out wedding reception afterward, which your mother could organize to her heart's content. All of the fun for Clemmie, and none of the pressure for your sister. Does that make sense?"

I had to admit that it did. In fact, I probably would have done the same thing if I were in Courtney's shoes.

"Your mother was furious with me when she found out, though," Stanley admitted.

I laughed. "Yeah," I replied. "I can imagine."

Heather Vogel Frederick

"She's happy as a clam now, though, planning the party," he assured me. "You know your mother."

I certainly do. She's already redesigning my bridesmaid dress into something more suitable for a reception instead of a wedding.

Now, standing here, I glance down at the "bridesmaid" outfit my campers have given me to wear, and at the lumpy, homemade, absolutely perfect pinecone bouquet. Then I look across the flashlight-lit dance platform at the shining faces of Nica and Freddie—whose face really is shining, despite the splotch of chocolate on her chin. They obviously can't wait to play bride and groom.

I smile. "Let's have a wedding!"

And we do.

Our campers are still talking about it the next evening, when it's Nest's turn for a sleepover on *Dreamboat*.

"Finally!" says Emma as we load her and Felicia and their girls into the war canoe. I thought it would be fun to ferry them out in style.

"Great idea, sport," said Sergeant Marge, which was high praise, considering I still don't think she likes me very much. The skunk episode didn't exactly do me any favors, although I may have redeemed myself a bit with my part in the Great Toilet Seat Heist, as we're calling it. That whole thing certainly raised the head counselor a notch or two in my eyes. Who would have guessed that Marge the Barge had such a wild streak?

The ironic thing is that Sergeant Marge is my peanut.

Talk about someone who's hard to figure out gifts for! I've never once seen her in civvies all summer, so I have no idea what kind of a person she is in real life. I've mostly given her candy so far, but I found something at Lovejoy's Books on my day off that I think she'll really like—a book of historic postcards showing Lake Lovejoy through the decades—and for my grand finale present, I enlarged one of the pictures I took of the Gazebo at sunset and had it framed. I figure I can't go wrong with a couple of mementos from camp.

Twin Pines and Balsam pile into the canoe behind the girls from Nest, and Artie and Sergeant Marge shove us off from the beach.

"*Here comes the bride*," sings Tara, and the rest of us pick up the refrain as we start to paddle. I glance over my shoulder to see the head counselor and handyman watching us with puzzled expressions on their faces. Last night's escapade on the dance platform is still our little secret.

I did manage to get a picture of all of us, though. Jess was smart enough to bring along my camera, and I set it on the railing and used the timer. It turned out really well. My family will get a huge kick out of it.

"See you guys in the morning!" I tell Emma and Felicia and their girls after we unload them onto *Dreamboat*. "Camp Lovejoy's Chauffeur Service will be here at seven a.m. sharp to pick you up."

The five of them line up behind the floating cabin's white picket fence and wave to us.

"Let's serenade them," whispers Jess, so we paddle on around the

Heather Vogel Frederick

Point, out of sight, and wait for a while, practicing in whispers until we figure they're settled. Then we paddle back and quietly glide up beside *Dreamboat*, launching into a Nest-friendly version of "Good Night, Irene":

> *Nesties, good night, Nesties, good night!*
> *Good night, dear Nest—Good night, dear Nest*
> *We'll see you in our dreams. . . .*

Tara, Meri, and Pippa press their faces to the screen windows of the floating cabin, smiling broadly at us as they listen to our song. Watching them, I feel that lump rise in my throat again.

I'm going to miss this place.

I've had a *great* summer. If I'm lucky—and if Sergeant Marge doesn't torpedo my application—maybe I'll get to come work here again next year.

Back in my cubie, I find a present waiting for me from my shell: a roundish stone painted black to look like a hockey puck, with the initials "BU" painted on top in red.

Like I said, I'm going to miss this place.

Next morning, I'm up at the crack of dawn as per usual. I'm so not in the mood for a run it's not funny, but the thing about sports is, it's a mental discipline. It's about you telling your body what to do, and not the other way around. So I force myself to stumble over to my cubie, where I pull on shorts and a T-shirt, then sit down to lace up my running shoes. I'm thinking I'll do the Pumpkin Falls loop again today, the same route I ran during Four on the Fourth.

Eva Bergson's silver whistle catches my eye as I'm heading out the door, and I reach for it impulsively, looping the lanyard over my head. I could use a talisman this morning, a tangible reminder of someone else who knew the importance of discipline.

I use the hill as a warm-up, climbing briskly. Once I reach the main road, I turn toward town and break into a jog. I'm just approaching the covered bridge when I see another runner coming toward me. To my surprise, I recognize Jake.

"Hey!" I call in greeting.

"Hey!" he calls back. Slowing, he turns to run beside me. "Mind if I join you?"

I shake my head. "Not at all. The more the merrier."

He matches his pace to mine, and we trot along in silence for a bit.

"So I guess we're even now, right?" he asks finally.

I grin at him. "Even enough."

We turn up Hill Street and are soon both panting. "So," he says, "I've been meaning to ask you . . . when you get to BU—"

"Yeah?"

"—would you maybe, um, want to go out sometime?"

I nearly stop in my tracks. Is he saying what I think he's saying?

"I'm just across the river," he pants. "At MIT. We could go to a movie or something."

Seriously? He's asking me out? At 5:30 in the morning, with me dripping sweat and smelling like last week's dirty gym socks? I give him a sidelong glance. I will never in a million years understand the male species.

"Uh, maybe," I tell him cautiously.

"I'd love to come to one of your hockey games, too."

I shrug. "Sure. It's a free country."

The thing is, romance complicates things. Not in a bad way, just in a, well, complicated way. Tristan Berkeley will be in Boston this fall too, for an international ice dancing competition, and even though we're not exactly boyfriend-girlfriend, we've had a few "romantic interludes," as Emma calls them, and I'm looking forward to seeing him again. *Really* looking forward to seeing him again. Do I want to add Jake to the mix as well?

Boys. Can't live with 'em, can't live without 'em.

"So I can call you?" Jake's voice is normal again. We've crested the hill and are on the long downhill stretch back toward the covered bridge.

"Why not?" I say, throwing caution to the wind, and I promise to give him my cell number before the end of camp.

Looking pleased, he sketches a wave and peels off on the road toward Pinewood. The wind starts picking up as I loop around the village green a few minutes later. The sky, which was overcast when I got up this morning, has turned a dark slate color. We're clearly in for some rain, and I decide it's time to head back.

It starts coming down just as I turn off the main road. I sprint past the office and into the forest, grateful for the cover of the trees overhead. I jog on down the hill, and when I emerge from under the canopy of trees, I stop in my tracks.

Down the lake, just past Cherry Island, is the scariest thing I've ever seen in my life. A dark cloud is churning through the water, heading straight for camp. I look around wildly for help, but no one is in sight. It's too early—everyone is still sleeping.

I grab Eva's whistle and start blowing like crazy, the SOS Morse code distress signal that my father taught me years ago when we used to go sailing.

The door to Cabbage flies open and the head counselor tumbles out, looking wildly around for the source of the alarm. She spots me pelting toward her and I point frantically at the cloud, which is flattening trees on Cherry Island like matchsticks. Sergeant Marge turns to look and her mouth drops open.

Poor bald eagles, I think, hoping they managed to fly away in time.

Back at the beginning of the summer, Gwen told us that Sergeant Marge is the kind of person you can count on in a crisis. It turns out she was right.

"Ring the bell!" she hollers to me. "NOW! Get everybody into the Dining Hall and make them take cover under the tables!"

I nod.

"Give me your whistle!"

I don't even hesitate.

"I'll do a sweep to make sure we don't miss anyone," she says,

Heather Vogel Frederick

and takes off at a run, desperately blowing my whistle to rouse camp's sleeping inhabitants.

I grab the bell and start ringing it like fury. As I'm whipping the rope back and forth, I glance past Lower Camp's cabins to the cove and see something even scarier than the black cloud.

Dreamboat *is gone!*

Completely gone, as in disappeared, vanished, vamoosed. The buoy is all that's left, tethered to a big fat nothing and spinning in the wind.

Final score: I don't know and I don't care. My friends are missing.

 Emma

"*Not a thing had happened the way she planned, no, not a single thing! But it seemed to her she had never been so happy in her life.*"
—*Understood Betsy*

I'm dreaming.

Dreaming on *Dreamboat*. The words float on the surface of consciousness, far above where I'm submerged in languid half-sleep.

Stretching lazily, I smile. In my dream, I'm at the skating rink in Concord, doing a layback spin. Unlike in real life, where I've never quite been able to master it, my dream spin is precise, flawless, a perfect 10.

"Perfection on ice!" Eva Bergson calls to me from where she's standing rinkside.

Something must be wrong, though, because all of a sudden I hear her whistle. High and shrill, it pierces my slumber as she blows it again and again.

Frowning, I crack open an eye. A split second later I'm bolt upright, scrambling for my glasses.

What I see when I look out the window terrifies me.

It's not a dream—I really *am* spinning. And not just me, but all of *Dreamboat*.

"Felicia!" I call in a panic.

She doesn't hear me. Raindrops—or is it hail?—detonate on the metal roof overhead, nearly drowning out the howl of the wind.

How could anyone possibly sleep through this? Screaming my co-counselor's name, I extricate myself from my sleeping bag and lurch to my feet. Grabbing at the metal frames of the bunk beds to steady myself, I make my way over to her.

"Felicia!" I grab her shoulder and shake her roughly awake.

She opens her eyes with difficulty and looks at me in annoyance.

"The anchor must have come loose in the wind!" I have to holler to be heard. "We're being blown down the lake!"

Suddenly fully alert, she sits up and stares outside. Our campers are awake now and looking at us in confusion.

"Get their life vests on!" Felicia shouts, and I nod. She rips open her sleeping bag and in a flash the two of us are stumbling across the roller coaster that is our floating cabin's floor. Somehow we manage to grab the vests, pull our pale, stricken campers from their bunks, and wrestle them into their flotation devices.

"Put yours on too!" I yell to Felicia, buckling mine over my pajamas.

We gather our campers into the middle of the floor, huddling in a tight circle with our arms around them. *Dreamboat* is completely out of control, pitching and tossing as it's blown this way and that by the wind. I'm hoping it's my imagination, but I think it's starting to list to one side.

Our girls are sobbing, and I feel like sobbing too. This is far, far more frightening than the time we got lost on a mother-daughter book club camping trip, or the time some of our friends got caught in a flash flood in Wyoming. At least in Wyoming, I was safe and sound inside the ranch's lodge.

Which was anchored securely to the ground.

This time, I'm spinning down a lake in an antique boathouse with three very small, very scared little girls in my care.

I hear it again then, above the roar of wind—a series of shrill blasts from a whistle. There's something familiar about the pattern the sound is making, and all of a sudden I realize that it's Morse code.

"Hear that?" I shout. "SOS—it's a distress signal! I think they know we're in trouble."

Felicia cocks her head a moment, then nods. "They might not be able to get to us while the weather's like this."

We look at each other grimly.

"Should we close the shutters?"

Felicia shakes her head and points to the floor, which by now is clearly tilting to one side. She presses her lips directly against my ear. "If worse comes to worst, we might have to swim for it. We'll need to be able to get out."

I feel the blood drain from my face.

"I want to go home!" wails Tara.

Me too, I desperately want to say, but I don't. Instead, a passage from *Understood Betsy* flashes into thought: *"What would Cousin*

Heather Vogel Frederick

Ann do if she were here? She wouldn't cry. She would think of something."

This is hardly the time for literary allusions, but it spurs me into action.

"Let's sing!" I shout, remembering the book club camping trip. Singing helped bolster everybody's spirits back then.

Unfortunately, it doesn't work this time. We can't even hear ourselves above the wind, for one thing. After a feeble attempt to boost the girls' spirits with "Blue Socks," we give up and just sit there, holding on to one another for dear life as the cabin bucks and swirls.

I really, really hope that whoever built this thing knew what they were doing.

And then, just as suddenly as it started, it's over. The wind drops from a roar to a rush to a rustle, the rain ceases, and *Dreamboat* slowly stops spinning. Its list is more pronounced now, though, and water is seeping in rapidly through the rear left corner.

I look over to Felicia. "I think maybe it's going down."

"We'd better get out of here."

Taking our campers by the hand, we scramble up the tilting floor and through the door onto the front porch.

"Wow," I say, looking around. The white picket fence has vanished, ripped away by the wind. Ditto the window boxes. Plus, I have absolutely no idea where we are. Camp is nowhere in sight, and the shoreline seems very far away. Farther than the Cherry Island swim, that's for sure.

"How big is Lake Lovejoy again?" I ask.

"Thirty-four kilometers long and fourteen point five kilometers at its widest point," Felicia says crisply.

"In English, please."

Felicia rolls her eyes, but I detect a glimmer of a smile. "About twenty miles long and nine miles wide, at its widest point."

"We could be anywhere, then."

She nods.

I sigh. I'd suggest raising a flag—we could use a pillowcase—but there's nobody around to notice. The wind saw to that.

Peering over the edge of the porch, which is now just a precarious deck, I spot the rope used to tie up the canoes. It's still there, drifting in the water. "I might be able to tow us to shore," I tell Felicia, frowning. "Or we could just swim, if we have to."

Tara, who had stopped crying once we got outside, looks like she's on the brink again when she hears this.

"Sweetie, look at me," I tell her, crouching down. "You guys, too," I say to Meri and Pippa, drawing them close. "I'm your swim teacher, right?"

Three little heads nod in unison.

"So I know better than anybody what good swimmers you are, right?"

Again the trio of heads bob up and down.

"Plus, you may have noticed that we're all wearing life vests. Nobody's going to sink. We can make it to shore, I promise. Felicia and I will be with you every inch of the way."

They don't look convinced.

Heather Vogel Frederick

"I'll tell you what," I continue. "I'll make you a deal. If we end up having to swim, once we get back to camp I'm going to pass all of you straight to Sharks. No more Guppies, no more Minnows or Dolphins. Straight to Sharks. How does that sound?"

This gets their attention.

"Some of your friends in Twin Pines didn't even make it to Sharks this summer, and they're two whole years older," I remind them.

That clinches the deal.

"Okay," says Pippa, and the other two nod in agreement.

We drift for a while, watching for boats or signs of life from the distant shore. The lake is so peaceful, if it weren't for the litter of branches and shore debris floating by, you'd never know there had been a storm. And then I hear two things: rumbling tummies—it must be getting close to breakfast time—and *Dreamboat*, which is starting to make ominous creaking noises.

I turn to Felicia. "This is it," I tell her. "I'm going to hop in and see if this thing is even towable first. If not, I want you to hand the girls down to me one at a time. No point hanging around on a sinking ship."

I walk to the edge of the deck, and just as I'm preparing to jump into the water, I hear it.

A whistle!

Turning around, I spot boats—a whole flotilla of them—rounding a point of land in the distance. It's a rescue party! We all start jumping up and down, waving and screaming at the top of our lungs. The rescue party spots us and surges forward, with Camp Lovejoy's water ski boat leading the way. Sergeant Marge is behind the wheel and Cassidy is beside her, blowing her whistle like mad. I've never been so happy to see anybody before in my life.

Close behind them I spot Lake Lovejoy's game warden and an assortment of motorboats and jet skis.

"Hey, it's Jake and Chase!" I tell Felicia as the boats pull up beside us. She tries to look disinterested, but I catch her waggling her fingers at Chase. He grins broadly and gives her a big thumbs-up. I remind myself to tell my friends about this development—maybe the Felicia Project isn't a lost cause after all.

A few minutes later, we've been plucked from the foundering *Dreamboat* and are safely aboard *The Lady of the Lake*, being swaddled in towels as everyone talks at once.

The story comes out in a tumble, starting with how Cassidy first spotted the cloud—a microburst, the game warden calls it, explaining that it's sort of the opposite of a cyclone, pushing air down instead of sucking it up.

"They can be just as dangerous as twisters," he says, eyeing our floating cabin, which by now is tilting at an alarming angle. "You ladies are mighty lucky."

"Your whistle woke me up," I tell Cassidy.

"It woke everybody up," says Sergeant Marge. "Cassidy is a hero."

Cassidy, who almost never blushes, turns pink. "I just happened to be in the right place at the right time," she says modestly.

"Nonsense," Marge replies, nodding at Eva Bergson's whistle. "You had the right equipment and knew exactly what to do with it. You're a credit to camp, sport."

I don't think Cassidy minds that nickname anymore.

Jake and Chase, who had been checking on *Dreamboat*, zoom back over to join us.

"I think we can stabilize it with one of our jet skis," Jake tells Marge. "With any luck and a little help from these volunteers, we should be able to tow it back to camp for you."

They head off with the other boats to put their plan into action, and we say good-bye to the game warden, thanking him for his help.

"You wouldn't believe how brave these three were," I boast, nodding at my campers as we speed across the water toward camp.

"Absolutely amazing," Felicia chimes in.

"Doesn't surprise me in the least," says Sergeant Marge. "They're Camp Lovejoy girls."

Meri and Pippa and Tara lap up the praise.

"Can we still be Sharks?" Meri wants to know.

I wink at Felicia. "We'll talk it over back at camp, okay?"

Rounding Hairbrush Island a few minutes later, we all fall silent, gazing soberly at the wreckage from the storm. Recalling the romantic reunion with Stewart that I had pictured for us in the Gazebo, I can't help feeling sad when I see that it's completely gone.

The wind has flattened all the trees on the Point, snapping them off at the roots like matchsticks. Half of the roof on the Director's Cottage is missing, the H dock is in tatters, kayaks are scattered helter-skelter along the shore and in the shallows, and all the windows on Lower Lodge that face the water ski beach have been shattered.

"It doesn't look like it, but we were extremely fortunate," says Marge. "As it hit land, the microburst sheared off down the Point. If it had continued in its original path, there'd likely be nothing left of Lower Camp."

"We can rebuild," says Gwen, addressing us all a little while later as we gather for breakfast. The power is still out, so Ethel and Thelma are busy making pancakes on the gas grill out on the Dining Hall deck. "Things are replaceable; people are not. The main thing is, thanks to Cassidy Sloane's presence of mind and our head counselor's quick action, everyone is safe."

"What about our banquet?" asks one of the CITs, sounding worried. The CITs are in charge of the decorations for the end-of-camp party tonight, and they've been slaving over them in secret all week.

"What about it?" says Gwen. "We're not going to let a little thing like a storm stop us from celebrating, are we?"

"NO!" we all shout.

The camp director smiles. "That's the Camp Lovejoy spirit! We have a lot to celebrate tonight—and a lot to be grateful for."

The morning passes in a flurry of activity as everyone pitches in to help put camp back together again in a SCUM-style cleanup. Artie has called in a team of workers from Pumpkin Falls to begin the repairs, and our efforts are accompanied by the sound of chainsaws and hammers.

After lunch, Artie and his team take a siesta while we're given an extended rest hour. I sleep straight through the entire stretch. All

Heather Vogel Frederick

of us in Nest do, exhausted from our eventful morning.

Refreshed by our naps, Felicia and I turn to the task of helping our campers start to pack. Their parents will finish the job tomorrow, but Gwen says it helps to give them a head start.

"Hey!" I exclaim as I pop into my cubie to grab a broom and discover another gift from my shell waiting on my dressing table. It's a spiral-bound notebook with a picture of an old-fashioned typewriter on the cover. Beneath it is written: "We write our own stories."

My shell has given me the best stuff this week. Cool pens, two books of poetry, a T-shirt that I know came from Lovejoy's Books that says SO MANY BOOKS, SO LITTLE TIME. I even got a bag of chocolate chips! She seems to know exactly what kinds of things I like. So much so, in fact, that I suspect she's one of my book club friends. I'm guessing Megan, maybe, or even Jess.

Which would be ironic, since Jess is my peanut.

I steal a few minutes to slip up to the Art Studio, where I have something special up my sleeve for my campers, and then I head back to my cubie to put the finishing touches on my final present for Jess. It's a pretty notebook filled with my favorite quotes from all the authors whose books we've read in our book club these past seven years, starting with "I'm not afraid of storms, for I'm learning how to sail my ship," by Louisa May Alcott. It's my favorite, and it's especially timely, considering our experience this morning.

The authors are represented in the order we read them. In addition to Louisa, there's Lucy Maud Montgomery, Jean Webster, Jane

Austen, Maud Hart Lovelace, and Charlotte Brontë. I add a final one from Dorothy Canfield Fisher, to make it complete. It's from a Fun Fact sheet I gave out earlier this summer: "A mother is not a person to lean on, but a person to make leaning unnecessary."

Somehow it seems appropriate, what with our work here this summer as counselors.

I blow on the ink to dry it, admiring my handiwork. Now that I'm finished, I love the booklet so much I'm actually tempted to keep it, but I know Jess will love it too. I'm going to give it to her tonight during the Big Reveal.

"Calling all Nesties!" It's Felicia. She tromps through Cubbyhole, knocking on cubie doors. "Report back to our cabin in five minutes for skit practice!"

I hide Jess's booklet in my trunk and follow Felicia out the door. Ours is probably going to be the shortest skit in camp history, but it's funny, and that's what counts. Felicia and I coached Meri and Tara and Pippa in a medley of the best bits from my "Overheard" column this summer, including the cantaloupe-antelope-elopement mix-up. I think it's pretty clever, if I say so myself.

By the time the bell rings for dinner, we're ready. I tuck Jess's present in the pocket of my hoodie and head over with Felicia and our girls.

"Wow," says Pippa, gazing around in awe as we walk into the Dining Hall.

The interior has been transformed. There are candles on every

Heather Vogel Frederick

possible surface, and white tablecloths with snowmen for centerpieces. A fire crackles in the fireplace. Hanging from the ceiling is a blizzard of paper snowflakes, and the windowpanes are lined with cotton wool. A large paper banner strung with bright mittens is stretched across the mantel, proclaiming the banquet's theme: WINTER WONDERLAND. It certainly looks and feels wintry. So much so that I'm suddenly in the mood for hot chocolate.

Which is in the process of being served up. The kitchen is functional again, thanks to an emergency generator that Artie brought in, and in addition to cocoa we're soon feasting on prime rib with Yorkshire pudding and all the trimmings.

After dessert ("snowballs," which are actually cupcakes with coconut frosting), it's time for the skits. Ours goes over as well as I'd hoped, and our trio of campers basks in the laughter and applause.

Next up is the poetry slam. When it's Nica's turn, she flicks me a glance and smiles as she reads a free-form acrostic she wrote as a surprise for Freddie:

Funny and faithful, my favorite friend.
Ready for laughter that never ends.
Inner secrets sharing—
Ever kind and caring—
Nearest on whom I depend.
Dearest companion for days and days—
Sisters are friends for always!

"Thanks for your help with some of the words, Emma," Nica whispers as she bounds over to my side.

"I am so proud of you," I tell her, giving her a big hug. She heads back to her seat, beaming at her twin—whose face is clean for once.

It's Balsam, though, that is the hit of the evening, with a hilarious fashion show of camp uniforms through the decades. Megan and Becca talked Gwen into lending them some outfits from camp's historical archive for it.

"You couldn't make this stuff up," Megan tells me, snapping pictures as Kate Kwan sashays across the stage in bloomers and a midi blouse from the 1930s. "This is going straight onto *Fashionista Jane* the minute I get home."

Home! It's hard to believe we'll be heading back to Concord tomorrow night. And after that, it's on to college.

Thinking about college brings all my fears crashing in again. British Columbia? What was I thinking!

I can't worry about that now, though. Now it's time for the Big Reveal. I push thoughts of big scary Canada aside as I mill around the Dining Hall with my fellow campers and counselors, all of us searching out our peanuts and meeting our shells.

"You were my shell? No way!" says Jess when I tell her.

"You didn't guess?"

She shakes her head.

I pass her the booklet that I made for her and she flips through it slowly, reading each quote. When she looks up again, her blue eyes are bright with tears.

"I'm going to miss you, Emma," she says, giving me a fierce hug.

Hugging her back, I can't bring myself to speak. And we're not the only ones getting choked up. It's an emotional night.

One that's about to get more emotional.

"Thanks to the windstorm earlier today, the path to the Council Fire is too much of a mess for us to risk using," Gwen tells us, "so we're going to break with tradition and meet by the fire pit on the beach instead. Five minutes, please."

After we're all assembled on the shore, she makes a brief speech.

"It's been a long day, girls, and I know you're all eager to get to the special awards and then enjoy your final night with your cabin. So I'll simply say that this has been the best summer yet here at Camp Lovejoy, for me at least. Watching you all stretch yourselves and grow, both individually and collectively, was a true delight, and I hope to see as many of you as possible back here again next year."

The distribution of beads proceeds briskly until it's my turn. I have a little surprise for my campers, and I plan to play it up.

"Would Meriwether Milligan, Tara Lindgren, and Pippa Lovejoy please come and join me?"

I keep my expression solemn as they dutifully troop forward, then make them turn around and face the group. Pippa's pink sparkly glasses shimmer in the reflected light from the fire pit.

"As you all know, these three girls displayed exceptional bravery this morning, in the face of what could have been serious danger. And so, with the permission of the camp director and the head counselor, and with all the authority vested in me"—from her spot on the sand I see Cassidy roll her eyes at this, and I grin at her—"I'm awarding Meri, Tara, and Pippa the Most Distinguished Order of the Lionheart bead for courage."

Meri looks crestfallen. "You didn't make us Sharks?" she whispers.

"We didn't end up swimming to shore, remember? This is way better than Sharks, anyway," I whisper back, pressing a bead into her hand. It's white, with a tiny red heart on one side and, thanks to Megan's skill with a paintbrush, a lion's head on the other. "Plus, nobody else in the whole camp has a bead like this one."

Meri looks down at the bead, and her face brightens. "Cool!"

"You bet it is—and so are you."

As I'm taking my seat again, I suddenly realize that I never found out who my shell was. Odd.

Camp nicknames are next. Gwen has us gather by cabins as we hand out the round wooden nameplates. Thanks to all the inside jokes, there's a great deal of hilarity as the campers turn them over and learn the secret nicknames we counselors have bestowed on them. My trio was pretty easy—Pippa is Sunshine, since she's always so happy, and Tara and Meri are Antelope and Cantaloupe, respectively, thanks to the mix-up about Cassidy's sister.

Finally, it's time for the Firelighter awards. Sergeant Marge stands

Heather Vogel Frederick

to announce the winners, which she does in her own no-nonsense fashion, calling Jennie Norris, one of the CITs, and a well-liked girl from Shady Grove to come receive their awards. Then she pauses, pressing her lips together for a moment. *Wait,* I think, *is she getting choked up, too?*

"We're breaking with tradition in this category this year as well," the head counselor says. "In the past, there have only been two Firelighters, one from Lower Camp and one from the Hill, but this year we're adding three more: Cassidy Sloane, Emma Hawthorne, and Felicia Grunewald, would you please come up here? Your actions this morning made you a credit to camp, girls."

Cassidy and I look at each other, surprised. Felicia springs to her feet, beaming from ear to ear, and we follow her as she steps forward to where Sergeant Marge is standing. The head counselor pins the award—a small gold flame—onto each of our T-shirts.

"Well done," she says to me when it's my turn, shaking my hand. "And thank you."

She's definitely choked up! I note with surprise. Sergeant Marge clearly has unplumbed depths.

As Cassidy and Felicia and I move to the water's edge to join the other Firelighters, Gwen stands up to speak again.

"Before we begin the ceremony," she says, "I'd like to take a moment to recognize the counselors from Nest, Balsam, and Twin Pines, for starting what I intend to make a new Camp Lovejoy tradition: a camper-counselor book club!" Gwen leads the applause, the campers from our cabins cheering the loudest. "We'll be expanding it to the rest of the cabins next summer," she continues, smiling at my friends and me. "And we'll be tapping you ladies for advice on books."

The sun has fallen below the horizon by now, and as dusk settles over Lake Lovejoy everyone files past Artie, who's handing out paper lanterns from his wheelbarrow. Each one is mounted on a flat piece of wood and contains a votive candle inside.

"A favorite memory, and a wish for the coming year," Jennie Norris instructs softly as Gwen holds her lantern out.

Jennie lights her candle for her, and Gwen places the lantern on the water and gives it a nudge. We watch as it floats gently away from shore.

One by one, each camper and counselor steps forward to one of us Firelighters until the water before us is ablaze with glowing lanterns.

Finally, it's the Firelighters' turn, and the five of us light one another's candles. I pause for a moment before placing my lantern on the water. My favorite memory? All of them. Well, except for Parents' Weekend, when Stewart didn't come.

As for my wish for the coming year, when it comes right down to it, it's simple, really: I just want to be happy.

"Emma, I have something for you," says Gwen as I'm heading back to Nest with my campers a few minutes later. She passes me an envelope.

"Thanks." She walks away and I open it. Inside is a piece of paper. I

Heather Vogel Frederick

read it aloud: "The camper-counselor book club is invited to report to Upper Meadow immediately."

"How come?" asks Pippa.

"I don't know, honey," I reply. "I guess we'll find out."

When I go to round up my friends, though, Cassidy balks.

"Seriously? I'm wiped out," she says. "I don't think I can take one more activity."

"I know, I feel the same way. But I think Gwen has something special planned for us, and I don't want to disappoint her."

It's not Gwen who's waiting for us at the top of the hill, though.

It's our mothers.

"Surprise!" they chorus, waving madly. They're all here, even Mrs. Delaney and her sister Bridget, Felicia's mom. Only Gigi is missing—she and Edouard and Sophie left a few days ago for France.

"Hey, that's our trailer!" Megan exclaims, spotting the silver burrito behind them.

"Yep," says Mrs. Wong. "We moms are camping here tonight."

"Have party, will travel," adds Mrs. Chadwick, busting out a dance move.

Mrs. Delaney gives Jess a big hug. "I've missed you so much!" she tells her. Holding her by the shoulders, she cocks her head and regards her for a moment. "Your hair is adorable, honey! From all the fuss you made, I was prepared for something a lot worse."

"It smells a lot better than it did a few weeks ago, at least," Jess replies, smiling.

"Shall we get this party started?" Mrs. Wong beckons us inside.

Somehow, we all manage to cram into the trailer. It's ridiculously crowded, of course, with campers and counselors piled on the bed, the sofas, and around the small table, but that's part of the fun.

"I like the twinkle lights, Mom," says Megan, admiring the strands strung up over the kitchen-sink window and the dining table. "Nice touch."

"It was your grandmother's idea," Mrs. Wong replies.

Of course it was. Gigi loves any excuse to decorate. Especially if there's a party involved.

"I can't believe they're off to college in a few weeks, can you?" Mrs. Chadwick says to the other mothers as she gazes at my friends and me.

"Don't start, Calliope," Mrs. Sloane-Kinkaid warns. "I'll be a big weepy mess if we go down that road."

My mother leaps in to change the subject. "So, what did you girls all think of *Understood Betsy*?"

I knew she wouldn't be able to resist asking. She can't help herself. She's a librarian.

Little hands shoot up all around the trailer. My mother points to Brooklyn Alvarez.

"I loved it," Brooklyn says. "I didn't think I would at first, but now it's one of my favorite books."

"Funny how that happens," my mother replies, winking at Cassidy, who smiles sheepishly. Cassidy started out not liking any of the books we read in our book club at home.

Heather Vogel Frederick

My mother points to Carter next.

"I liked how the narrator talked to us," she says. "It made me feel like I was right there in the book with the characters."

"That's a literary device called 'direct address,'" Felicia offers.

"We'll all make a note of that," Becca says drily.

Meri's hand is waving frantically, and my mother points to her.

"I wish I could live with Betsy at Putney Farm," my camper says with a sigh.

"I think that's the highest compliment an author can receive," my mother tells her. "It means he or she has created a world so real that readers want to crawl inside the book and live there. I feel that way about Jane Austen's novels."

She looks over at me and smiles. I smile back. Of course my mother would have to drop an Austen reference.

"The biggest thing I learned from the book is not to judge someone too quickly," Cassidy says. "You know, the way Cousin Ann seems like a bit of a tyrant at first, and Betsy is scared of her, but in the end she proves an ally. Kind of like Sergeant Marge."

I stare at her. "Cassidy Ann Sloane! Listen to you drawing a comparison between literature and life!"

She grins. "I am about to go off to college, in case you hadn't noticed. I'm allowed to do that."

"The overarching theme of transformation was the key point for me," Felicia chimes in. "Along with Fisher's portrayal of everyday life in a rural community of a bygone century."

Jess and I both shoot her a look, and a little of the starch goes out of her shirt.

"Hey, I liked the book!" she says defensively.

Camp has been good for Felicia, too. Even her horizons have been broadened.

She turns to her mother. "How come you never read it to me when I was a kid?"

Jess's aunt Bridget shrugs. "I never heard of it," she replies. "And I wasn't lucky enough to find women who wanted to start a book club and introduce me to some of these gems, I guess."

Mrs. Wong hops up from her seat. "Who wants ice cream?"

"Am I dreaming?" Megan pretends to be shocked. "Did my mother, the mayor of Concord, the politician who successfully lobbied to take sugar off the menu in the schools, just offer us dessert?"

Mrs. Wong waves the ice cream scoop at her. "It's a party. Parties are exceptions to the rules."

"Since when?"

Ignoring her, Mrs. Wong pulls a bunch of containers from the trailer's freezer. "We figured since you girls can't come to Kimball's Farm, Kimball's Farm would just have to come to you."

Jess's mother joins her at the counter and starts taking orders while Mrs. Wong scoops.

"Um, no thanks," says Felicia primly when Mrs. Delaney asks her what she'd like. "It's not really the right time of day for ice cream."

Heather Vogel Frederick

"It's never not the right time of day for ice cream!" Cassidy scoffs. "Lighten up already, Felicia."

"Oh fine," Felicia relents. "I'll take butter pecan."

Without even asking, Mrs. Delaney dishes me up a scoop of strawberry and hands it to me with a smile. She knows it's my favorite.

"Feel like taking a walk?" my mother asks.

"Sure."

Grabbing a sweatshirt, she steps outside. I start to follow, but as I pass Felicia, I pause. "Would you mind keeping an eye on our girls for a few minutes?" I ask. "I'm going for a walk with my mother."

"Okay." She stands there awkwardly for a moment. Which for Felicia is kind of her natural state. "Um, I got distracted at the Dining Hall earlier," she says. "I just wanted to let you know that I was your shell."

I blink. "Really?"

She nods.

"I had no idea."

She shrugs.

"The presents were brilliant," I tell her, wishing now that I'd been a little nicer this summer. "Really."

She smiles. "Glad you liked them."

I think about the notebook she gave me. The one with "We write our own story" on the cover. I need to write a happy ending for this one.

"So I was thinking—maybe you could come visit me sometime? At UBC, I mean."

Felicia's face lights up. "I'd love that! I've always wanted to go to Vancouver."

"Great. I'll look forward to it." And the funny thing is, it's true.

Outside, I find my mother waiting for me at the picnic table.

"Let's skip the walk," she says. "We can sit right here and chat." She pats the seat beside her.

I sit down and rest my head on her shoulder for a minute.

"How's my girl?" she says. "Better?"

I sit up and look at her. "Better than what?"

"Than when you were pining away back during Parents' Weekend."

I sigh. "That obvious, huh?"

She smiles at me. "You're an open book, remember?"

"How could I forget?" I'm quiet for a minute; then, "Yeah, I'm better. But I still miss him, Mom, and I'm beginning to worry that I always will. I just want to be happy, you know?"

"Your happiness doesn't depend on a boy, sweetheart. Any boy, not just Stewart."

"What does it depend on, then?"

She takes a bite of ice cream, considering. "Happiness is about doing some good in this world," she says finally. "It comes from finding what you were meant to do, and doing it."

I mull this over. "But Dad makes you happy, doesn't he?"

She laughs. "Of course! I love being married to your father. But I bring my happiness to our marriage, I don't depend on our marriage to provide it for me."

Heather Vogel Frederick

I turn this thought over in my mind.

Happiness without Stewart? Was it possible? Drawing a shaky breath, I tell her, "I'll try."

She pats my knee. "Of course you will. I have no doubt about it, because I raised a strong young woman." She leans over and kisses the top of my head. Then she gives me a sly look. "Besides, there's always Rupert."

"Mom!"

She laughs. "I'm kidding! Well, mostly. You never know what surprises lie ahead. But for now, go forth and be happy, Emma! You have something unique to contribute—something you, and you alone, were meant to give. The world is waiting for you, sweetheart."

Why is it that talking to my mother always makes me feel so much better?

Back inside, I squeeze onto the sofa between Pippa, whose eyes are drooping shut behind her pink sparkly glasses, and Meri, whose eyes already are shut and who's snoring lightly.

Jess and I exchange a smile. "It's been a long day," she whispers.

I sit back, letting the conversation wash over me. Gazing around the trailer at my friends, I start thinking about what lies ahead for all of us. There's my beloved Jess, who is like a sister to me already, and with any luck will be a real one someday, if she marries my brother. Which she probably will. He's already given her a diamond, after all. Maybe it's not a ring, but it still counts, right?

As for Cassidy, I have absolutely no doubt that she'll be a rock star on the ice for the Boston University Terriers, and will probably end up leading the U.S. Olympic hockey team to victory eventually. We'll all be there to cheer her on. And I suspect Tristan Berkeley will be there too, cheering the loudest.

Megan is bound for glory as well. She's already halfway there, a blazingly talented fashion designer who will soon have all of New York at her feet, and whose creations will no doubt grace the covers of every fashion magazine in the world someday. When that happens, we'll all be claiming our bragging rights to Wong originals.

Becca is my most unexpected friend. Back when she was the queen bee of middle school and had me in her sights, I never could have imagined we'd develop as close a relationship as the one we have. Now she has Minneapolis in her sights. Becca is as strong-minded as any of us, and she'll carve out her own path, and be successful at whatever she chooses to do—and happy, too, with or without her Mr. Rochester and his snakes.

I think about Camp Lovejoy's motto: "Broadening Horizons for over a Century." It's no idle boast. Our horizons have all been broadened this summer, and so have those of our campers. Tara Lindgren isn't such a 'fraidy cat any longer, something she proved today on *Dreamboat*. Amy Osborne has gained new confidence too—and a tan, thanks to six weeks of swim lessons. Nica Simpson has found her own voice and is speaking up for herself through her poetry. And not just these three, but all of our girls have grown this summer.

We've done some good here, I realize. That's something for my

Heather Vogel Frederick

friends and me to be proud of. I think about the wish I made for the coming year, down by the lake earlier this evening. For happiness. I may as well be happy about my college choice instead of worrying about it, or worse, regretting it. Why shouldn't college be an adventure?

We write our own stories, after all. Why not write happiness into mine?

And maybe someday, in the far-off years when my friends and I are grown and married and have families of our own, I'll put pen to paper and write our story—the story of an unlikely group of girls who joined a mother-daughter book club once upon a time and became friends for life.

But meanwhile, I have plenty to keep me busy. Because my mother is right.

The world is waiting.

"That room was full to the brim of something beautiful, and Betsy knew what it was. Its name was Happiness."
—*Understood Betsy*

Never say never again, right?

After I finished writing *Wish You Were Eyre*, the sixth Mother-Daughter Book Club story, I was sure I was done—although not in a "never again" way, but simply in an "I don't have any more ideas worth writing" way.

And then, unexpectedly, many months later, I got another idea.

Writing often works that way.

And now here we are with *Mother-Daughter Book Camp*, the seventh and (really truly) final installment in the series. This one was a sheer joy to write on so many levels. First and foremost, it allowed me to introduce you to yet another of my favorite classic novels, Dorothy Canfield Fisher's *Understood Betsy*. I still remember stumbling upon this book as a young reader and being drawn in from the very first line, when I felt a shiver of delight at being addressed directly by the author.

Writing *Mother-Daughter Book Camp* also gave me the bittersweet pleasure of spending many months again with "my" girls—and I hope I've given Emma, Jess, Cassidy, Megan, and Becca the send-off they deserve.

And finally, writing this book transported me both emotionally and physically back to my own summer camp experiences on the shores of Long Lake in Maine.

I was twelve the first time I went to sleep-away camp. Homesick doesn't begin to describe my initial misery. I was definitely a "trembling leaf," as Sergeant Marge so colorfully puts it! Like Emma, my favorite part of camp was rest hour, as that was the only time during the day when I could retreat into the familiar comfort and safety of a book.

The plague of homesickness had a silver lining, as it turned out: it launched my career as a writer. Because in addition to reading during rest hour to console myself, I also started writing. By the end of that summer, I had a complete handwritten manuscript that clocked in at over a hundred pages. More important though, writing the story had been enormously fun. (In fact, camp itself ended up being enormously fun.) From that time on I knew I wanted to be an author. So thank you, Camp Newfound—and specifically the upper bunk along the back wall of Twin Pines—for nurturing a writer!

I have a bouquet of thanks to offer—to my husband, Steve, always and forever; to Kristin Ostby, my brilliant and delightful editor at Simon & Schuster, who humored me when I turned up on her doorstep with this idea and helped shepherd it to completion; to Jonatha Wey and Bonnie Bower and Anne Wold for generously sharing their memories of camp with me; to Marjorie Kehe, my partner in crime on our adventure in Maine; to Cyn Keith, the Thelma to my Ethel one summer long ago; and to camp friends old and new, especially Susan Newbold and Michele Parsons, who gave me the gift of an artist-in-residence writing retreat.

Here's a funny story for you from that autumn retreat. I was staying in one of the cabins at the neighboring boys' camp, which is located on a hill above the lake. Like many of the other guests, I decided to keep my swimsuit and towel in one of the cubies (they really exist!) down at Camp Newfound, so I'd be ready if I wanted to swim. I randomly stashed my stuff and didn't think any more of it until a few days later, when we finally had an afternoon warm enough to venture into the water. I went into the cubie house (Primporium, in case you're wondering) to change, and was absently reading the names of generations of girls written on the walls when I spotted it: *Heather Vogel was here*. I couldn't believe it—I'd accidentally chosen my old cubie!

Or maybe not accidentally. Call it muscle memory, call it serendipity, call it the ties that bind—the past is always just around the corner, waiting for us to step back into it.

Finally, my deepest and most heartfelt thanks to you, dear reader, for being my traveling companion as we've journeyed together through this series of books. We've had fun, haven't we? One thing is for sure—I couldn't have done it without you!